# HEATWAVE

## WOMEN IN LOVE AND LUST
## LESBIAN SHORT FICTION

Edited by Lucy Jane Bledsoe

Copyright © 1995 by Lucy Jane Bledsoe.
Individual authors retain copyright of their work.
Cover photograph by Mark Davison/Tony Stone Images.
Cover design by Christopher Harrity.

Typeset and printed in the United States of America.

This is a trade paperback original from Alyson Publications, Inc.,
P.O. Box 4371, Los Angeles, California 90078.

First edition, first printing: December 1995

5  4  3  2  1

ISBN 1-55583-318-7

Acknowledgments

"Me and My Appetite" copyright © 1994 by Lesléa Newman from *Every Woman's Dream* by Lesléa Newman (New Victoria Publishers, 1994). Reprinted with permission of the author and publisher.

"Tattoo" copyright © 1994 by Nisa Donnelly from *The Love Songs of Phoenix Bay* by Nisa Donnelly (St. Martin's Press, Inc., New York, N.Y.). Reprinted with permission of the author and publisher.

For Patricia

# Contents

# Introduction

When Alyson Publications asked me to edit a book of lesbian erotica, the voyeur in me perked right up. I looked forward to finding out, through the sheer volume of information I expected to receive, what lesbians *really* do in bed, just how exciting our sex lives *really* are. Secretly, don't we all wonder if everyone else is having a wilder time than we are?

As the manuscripts flooded in, sometimes a dozen a day, I plowed through the fictional sex lives of hundreds of women. I also talked to lots of prospective contributors at readings and over the phone. "What do you want?" women asked me. "What are your limits? Do you want hard core? Hard *hard* core?" I'd blush, stammer, say, "Uh," try to grasp the question. I finally learned to blurt the truth: I want great stories, period.

And that's what I got. These twenty-nine fabulous stories run the gamut from somber and ardent lovemaking to raucous and earthy sex, from a tender first kiss next to a stream on womyn's land to knife-edge sexual tension in East Berlin. Witness the arrival of a new and mysterious woman to Portland's dyke scene in Diana Thompson's "Illegal Alien." Get a behind-the-scenes look at a foot fetishist in Katya Andreevna's "The Perfect Fit." Experience the hot, lustful warm-ups of Cuba's *rockera* star in Maria Santiago's "Las Rockeras Warm Up — Con Swing." Enjoy the sweet expression of longtime love in Wendy Caster's "Renaissance."

I looked for stories that were not only hot but said something about sex, stories that revealed the ancient practice for everything that it is. Opinions about lesbian sex, what it is and what kind is hot, are as varied as opinions about what constitutes good writing. These stories are about getting beyond the hairsplitting debates of sexual politics and, I hope, opening readers up to the *bigness* of lesbian eroticism. By turns funny, painful, sweet, embarrassing, taunting, punishing, arousing, provoking, and satisfying, this anthology shows, through the power of storytelling, lesbian sex to be so much more than what we do in bed.

I owe a tremendous thanks to Karen Barber for her patience in answering my sometimes daily questions, her trust in (though not necessarily agreement with) my decisions, and her guidance in getting *Heatwave* from idea to book. Much thanks also to Helen Eisenbach, who came on this project midstream offering her enthusiasm and insight. Kiki Zeldes is copy editor and proofreader extraordinaire: thank you! A big thanks also goes to Patricia, Garcia, Laura, Vivian, Ari, and Reyna for hilarious evenings thinking up names for the book. While I didn't adopt many of our more inspired titles — *Green Legs and Hams, Hand Sandwich on Thigh, Vulvacano, Lava or Leave Her, Bawdy Talk, Sheruption, Hades Ladies, Cuntflagration, Flambe Babe* — these brainstorming sessions were helpful and definitely some of my most fun times in putting this book together. Most of all, I want to thank all the contributors. Not only did each one make working on this book a great pleasure, each taught me much about my subject.

So what conclusions did I draw after immersing myself in fictional lesbian sex for a year? Read the book and draw your own.

Lucy Jane Bledsoe
Fall 1995

# The Secret Life of Mitzi Walters
## (with apologies to James Thurber)

### by Teresa Palomar

*"*A*s this chart clearly shows, sales of Vagilube are up over eight hundred and fifty percent from this time last year. I think we all know who to thank for that." Every eye in the boardroom turned admiringly toward Mitzi Walters. Since she had been elected to chair the board six months earlier, Mitzi had been responsible for the most dramatic turnaround of any corporation in history. Their stock had split three times in the last month alone.*

*Mitzi smiled beatifically at the other women sitting around the table and said, "Thank you, but I certainly can't take all of the credit. Everyone on this board has had a hand in the direction this organization has taken, and I will see that each of you finds a five-thousand-dollar bonus in your pay envelope next week. Now, if there is no further business, I think we can adjourn."*

*Christine DeSalvo fiddled with the reports in front of her as the board members filed out. Mitzi locked the doors behind the last of them, then spoke. "Well, Ms. DeSalvo, it seems we are alone." Mitzi walked over to her executive secretary, who put her arms around Mitzi's neck and kissed her hard. Mitzi's tongue probed deeply into Christine's oh-so-familiar mouth as she felt her hair being held firmly. After what seemed an eternity, they broke free, gasping for air. Christine, her deep brown eyes glazed with desire, looked at Mitzi and panted, "How long can we keep this up? How long can we hide what we feel from the others?"*

"How long will it take you to finish that filing, Ms. Walters?"

A little dazed, Mitzi looked up from her desk. "I'm sorry, Ms. DeSalvo. What did you say?"

Standing at the entrance to Mitzi's tiny cubicle, Christine shook her head slowly. "Off in your own little world again, I see? I asked how long you were planning to stay this evening. It's already a quarter after five and just about everyone has already left the building."

"I'm almost finished now. I should be leaving in another minute or so."

"Fine, Mitzi. Enjoy your weekend."

Mitzi filed the remaining few documents, then gathered her sweater and purse and left the office. Sharon, Mitzi's lover, had asked her to stop at the store on her way home to get some cat food and something else. Now, what was it? Cat food and ... Sharon would remember it the minute Mitzi stepped through the door. "Did you get the what-do-you-call-it?" Mitzi knew she should have written it down.

At the end of the hall, Mitzi called for the elevator. When it arrived, she stepped into the empty car and pushed the first-floor button. The speakers in the ceiling allowed a silky orchestral arrangement of the Beatles' "Why Don't We Do It in the Road?" to fill the elevator. On the fifth floor the doors opened again, and a blond woman got on.

*As soon as the doors closed, the woman set her attaché case on the floor of the elevator and put her left hand inside her blouse. Mitzi watched as the woman began fondling her breasts, playing with her now-protruding nipples. Mitzi could feel herself growing warm and wet. The stranger, ignoring Mitzi completely, slid her other hand down her side, caressed the inside of her thigh, then reached up and unfastened the clasp at the side of her skirt. Slowly, slowly, as she continued stroking her breasts, she unzipped her skirt and let it fall to the floor of the elevator. Mitzi was reaching a level of arousal that would soon demand her own attention. She continued to watch as the strange woman lifted her slip and slid her hand into her red silk panties.*

"Miss." Mitzi turned and looked out of the open elevator doors at the security guard sitting at his desk in the lobby. "Are you all right, miss?" Mitzi stood alone in the stopped car.

"Y-yes," Mitzi stammered. She quickly walked to the door and left the building.

The grocery store was only a block from her office. As she entered, Mitzi again wondered what else she was supposed to buy. She found the one brand of cat food that Sharon's cat would deign to eat and headed for the checkout counter. As she stood in line, Mitzi could see the array of tabloids lying in wait for all of the impulse buyers. Although Mitzi rarely bought a tabloid, she did enjoy reading the headlines. Now one in particular caught her eye: Lesbian Sex Scandal Rocks Tennis!

*On center court, the award ceremony was nearing a close. The crowds sat in hushed reverence as the queen mother made the official announcement. "It has been an honor for all of us to have witnessed the historic display of athletic skill that this young woman has given us," she intoned. "Never before in the history of the Wimbledon tournament has anyone, man or woman, demonstrated the caliber of play that Miss Walters has displayed. In all of her matches during the past fortnight, Miss Walters lost not one game. In fact, none of her opponents were able to score so much as a single point against her!" Then the queen mother handed Mitzi the trophy for the champion to hold aloft, and the crowd cheered uncontrollably for more than twenty minutes.*

*When order was restored, Mitzi stepped to the microphone and said, "I'd really like to thank all of you for your support, especially my doubles partner and current lover, Sharon 'Fishnets' Leatherwoman." The crowd gasped in astonishment as Fishnets leaped from her seat, ran to Mitzi's side, and kissed her long and hard. Flashbulbs exploded from every angle. Press photographers knew they would make the front page with any shot of this event they could manage.*

"I said that'll be a dollar eighty-nine, hon." The checkout clerk was glaring at her from beneath the cruelest set of bangs Mitzi had ever seen. Mitzi fished in her purse for her wallet and paid for the cat food. "Your change is eleven cents. Thank-you-for-shopping-at-Food-World-have-a-nice-day."

Mitzi walked back to the parking lot next to her office, got into her car, and headed home. The expressway wasn't too crowded for a Friday afternoon. Maybe staying a few minutes later had allowed her to miss the heaviest part of rush hour. She switched on the radio.

*"We interrupt our regular programming to bring you this news bulletin. There are reports from all over the city of sightings of an enormous unidentified flying KZZSSTK-SKZ..." Mitzi fiddled with the tuner, but could find only static. When she turned off the radio, though, she heard a loud humming noise. It seemed to be coming from all directions at once. Just then everything outside turned shades of gray, and she could feel her car being lifted off the ground. It rose into what appeared to be a loading bay in the bottom of some sort of immense hovering craft. After her car settled into a space that appeared custom-made for it, Mitzi stepped out and walked to the only door she could see that led out from the bay. Upon stepping through the door, Mitzi found herself in a tastefully furnished lounge. Around the room were several soft chairs and cushions as well as a low table and, to one side, a vast water bed. Mitzi noticed that a blue glow, apparently emanating from the walls themselves, put her mind immediately at ease.*

*An opening appeared in one of the walls, and a woman with dark blue skin and extremely long black hair entered the room. She wore no clothing, but carried a very thin cigarette, from which she took a long draw. Her single breast, centered on her torso, began to glow a deep red. The woman set the cigarette down on the table and approached Mitzi. Mitzi suddenly realized that she too was wearing no clothing at all. How this had been accomplished, she didn't know, but she was grateful for it. The alien woman put a hand on each of Mitzi's breasts and smiled. "It's so nice visiting this planet," she said, then leaned forward and nibbled on Mitzi's ear. Mitzi found herself becoming aroused very quickly. She reached up and began fondling the glowing red breast. Its radiant nipple reacted immediately to her touch, growing larger, firmer, and brighter. The woman put a hand on Mitzi's cheek and kissed her. As she did, she blew a little of the cigarette smoke into Mitzi's mouth. Mitzi's brain exploded with colors and smells she had never before encountered. The woman surprised Mitzi by wrapping her tongue completely around Mitzi's and tugging gently. As they kissed, the ringing of a small bell came from within one of the walls. The blue woman looked annoyed. "Damn that hyperdrive," she said. "We're already in your driveway." She grinned devilishly, said, "I'll just have to come back for another visit when you have a longer trip to make," then turned and left the room.*

Mitzi looked around and saw that she was indeed sitting in her car in her driveway. Noticing somewhat thankfully that she was once again fully clothed, she grabbed the cat food and headed for the house. The front door, she discovered, was unlocked.

Upon stepping inside, Mitzi found Sharon waiting for her. She wore a black leather bustier, red silk panties, stiletto-heeled pumps, and a black garter belt attached to fishnet stockings. She held a riding crop in her hand. "You forgot to buy the Vagilube, didn't you?" she asked. "You will atone for that sin." Mitzi closed the door behind her.

# Voice of Temptation

## by Delane Daugherty

The phone rings. A deep, sultry voice slithers into my ear: "It's me."
Miles and years slip away; you come crashing into my cozy world.
That voice, that breathy voice that made my head spin, my knees
weaken, my panties wet. So long have I fought the lingering memory of
that voice, your voice, and now it's here, in my hand, at my ear.

"Can we talk?" you ask, as if it were a natural thing to do. There's no
apprehension in your voice, no sign of the five years that have passed. I
hear you light a cigarette and immediately imagine that you're French
inhaling, the way I taught you when we were young and thought it
looked cool.

"Sure," I say, trying to sound as casual as you. I sit down on the edge of
my bed and wait, fingers tightening around the phone, palms beginning
to sweat.

"How's your life?"

I bite my lip and try not to laugh. How should it be? You broke my
heart, said you didn't love me. Couldn't, wouldn't.

"Fine. How's yours?" I ask, an evil, juvenile part of me hoping that
you're miserable without me. I light a cigarette and exhale, waiting for a
response, waiting for that voice.

You start talking about your world: your new job, new house, new
lover. Sounds as though you've never been happier. But the reason for
the call eludes me. Do you know how long it's taken me to remove your
pictures from the wall? How hard it's been to stop rereading those old
letters? To stop referring to me as "we"? Now your words force me to
try and picture you with someone else ... fighting over the bathroom
mirror for morning make-ups, hurried conversation over coffee and
toast, cuddling up to a good book before you go to sleep. Is she really

what you want? Shrouded in a fog of domesticity, can you really be happy?

"I've never been happier," you purr into the phone.

And I smile. Who knows better than I that you can't be tamed? There's a wild side in you. I can hear it thick in your voice, bubbling inside like a tea kettle about to whistle.

"But, I still think of you sometimes," you say. Again, no hesitation.

And I am at a loss for words. You think of me sometimes? Baby, you're a daily interference. I listen to our music, the songs that were played just for us. I hear a joke and know you'd smile, devilishly at first, and then you'd laugh in great, hearty waves. And at night, when I lie in my bed, our bed, I spread my legs wide, imagine your fingers, your tongue, inside me. I can almost smell you, feel your thighs around my ears, delight in licking you as you lick me, tasting you ... Yes, I think of you sometimes, too.

"Her name is Rhonda," you tell me, which is more than I really want to know.

I ask questions politely: What does she look like? Where did you meet? What does she do? But my mind screams the questions I'd really like to ask, the questions I already know the answers to: Can she make you quiver with lusty anticipation as you're being teased and tempted, like I could? Does she bring you to sweet orgasm as slowly, deliciously as I did? Will she try anything, go to wild extremes as I did, just to see the look of ravenous ecstasy in your eyes?

"This is her first time with a woman," you inform me.

"Just as I was your first."

Silence. Did you hear the sarcasm in my voice, mistake it for nostalgia?

"It seems like so long ago."

"Five years," I say. Five years, four months, twenty-some days. I shake my head and exhale a stream of smoke into the dark room.

"I'd like to maybe get together," you say with no implications.

"Why?" My heart threatens mutiny.

"There are things we need to talk about."

Emotions swirl. Why didn't we talk about these things before you left? Why now, when your life is supposedly perfect? Could it be that good ol' Rhonda isn't all she's made out to be?

"Susan?" you ask, sounding worried that I might have hung up. You never could read me very well.

"I'm here."

"Could we get together? Have lunch or something?"

My hand tightens around the phone, imagining the appetizing possibilities. "No, I don't think so."

"Why not? Come on, please?" Your voice adopts a deep, pouty affect, the same tone you used to use when you wanted to eat me.

Suddenly my senses begin to throb. Lunch with you would be intriguing, to say the least. Watching your every move; seeing your tongue lick your upper lip like it does when you're nervous about something; watching you brush your hair out of your face and over your soft shoulders; hearing your words and laughter, the hot voice that still commands my dreams; feeling your presence, your closeness, the magnetic pull of our bodies, and being able to do nothing about it.

"Come on, it's just lunch."

"That's the problem," I whisper, aware of the electric currents surging through me.

"What?"

"I just don't think it would be a good idea."

"Why?" you ask, your voice breathing sex into my ear.

I moan audibly. I never could resist you. "Because I'll see the outline of your leg beneath your pants. I'll imagine the beauty mark on your hip. I'll want to put my hands in your hair, my mouth on your neck. I'll watch your hands attempting to accompany your civilized conversation and I'll want them on me..."

I hear you sigh, or is it a gasp?

"Lynne?" I say cautiously. "I'm sorry. I just—"

"No," you whisper. "That's all right."

Confidence showers me as I recognize your quiet surrender. "Saying it is all right or wanting those things is all right?"

"Both," you groan.

I hear you light up another cigarette and palpable memories invade my mind. I used to love it when you smoked. I always loved the way you tasted, inside and out. "Why did you call me?" I ask. I smile at your brief hesitation.

"She's not you," you say finally.

My heart beats faster, my breathing deepens, my skin burns. Sensations, precious sensations, swirl around between my legs. I uncross them, let it flow.

You lower your voice. "She's just not you."

I imagine you spread out on your bed, phone in one hand, the other hand in turmoil, lingering over your body, wishing I were there. "You shouldn't have called," I warn, moving my skirt higher up on my thighs.

"I know," you breathe helplessly.

I can hear desire drip from your words. Five years and I know you like yesterday. I close my eyes, see your hand begin to unbutton your blouse, your fingers scorching a path along your smooth skin.

"Where are you now?" A loaded question from the past, from our afternoons of sexy phone calls from your office to mine.

"I'm on the bed."

"Me too."

"Is *she* there?" I ask.

"No."

"Has she been there today?"

"No."

I rest my hand lightly on my thigh. My fingers ease my skirt back farther.

"Do you remember the last time we made love?" you ask, seduction hanging on the air.

Mind stops, rewinds, plays a rainy December night. Fireplace, Christmas tree, colored lights. Champagne bubbling in our glasses, over your breasts. "Yes, I remember."

"Mmm," you hum into the phone.

Your voice reaches my ear, sends tingles down my spine. I fall back onto the bed and stretch out, loving what you can do to me. I remember our love that night, earthy, lusty. Your head rearing from side to side, your hands pushing my face harder against you. Everything I had wanted to be inside you ... fingers, tongue, face. Wild, cathartic cries in the night.

"It's too bad it was our last time," I sigh.

"Maybe it doesn't have to be," you hint provocatively.

Instant tingling, tightening. One finger reaches farther, touches drenched black lace. I let it linger, trail along the wet material. I breathe deeply.

"Are you touching yourself?" you ask in a hushed, raspy voice that I recognize to the core.

"Are you?"

"Yes."

"Ah, yes." I push harder now, push the fabric into my labia, rest the heal of my hand on my pounding clitoris.

Your breathing changes suddenly and I imagine you unzipping your pants, sliding a hand in, touching your full lips, grinding against your own fingers.

"Imagine me licking you," you command. "Feel me on top of you. Open to me..."

I can feel you on top of me. I open my legs wider, push the underwear to the side.

"Do it."

My fingers plunge deep within me, slide out slowly, and thrust back in. Precious memories move me: your beautiful fingers claiming me, fucking me. My other hand rests on my clit, caressing it at first, then rubbing harder, harder. I can feel your tongue encircling it, flicking it, loving it.

I hear you cry out and I know you're feeling me beneath you, sixty-nining it in your new house, on your new bed, with your new lover only miles away. God, to lick you again. To trail my tongue over your breasts, around your nipples, over your quivering stomach. To bury my face in your cunt, drawing you out, breathing you in.

As you cry out again, I imagine your whole body shaking, writhing under my touch, your mouth still on me. You breathe hard, shutter, lick me through your own beautiful spasms.

My hands work fast now, feeling the waves of your body, your heavy breathing in my ear, at my lips. My fingers slide in and out, creating their own fervent rhythm. I rub the side of my clit, teasing the pounding sensations to the edge and back again.

You begin to moan my name, sensuous, arduous, then faster, harder. It becomes an urgent cry, fulfilling you, saving you. If only I could taste you spilling forth, lap up your honey-sweet juices, savor them once again.

I feel myself riding your wave, as I've done so many times before. Your imaginary tongue licks me with abandon, shows me no mercy. It teases my clit then thrusts into me, over and over again. I feel the muscles tightening, pulling together, grasping your tongue. I thrust my fingers in, my back arching, feel the orgasm tighten and release, tighten and release. It encircles my fingers, believing them yours.

I let it wash over me, let your body, your memory, wash over me. I listen to your strained breathing slice through the phone, the miles, the years. Our passion, so intense, so consuming, ultimately our downfall. I try to picture you and your new love doing the laundry, washing the dishes, arguing over a burnt meal — things that have robbed you of your passion. Things that probably would have robbed us.

"You're right," you gasp, still coming down from your exhilaration. "Maybe we shouldn't do lunch."

I smile, moving my fingers gently in my wetness. "No. I think we definitely should."

"I don't think it would be wise," you say, attempting to grasp at your senses.

"It's too late for wise," I answer, knowing that we'll meet, that I can provide you with the intensity that has been stolen by domesticity, by your lover's first-time hesitancy.

"What are you suggesting?" you ask with mock surprise, probably talking yourself out of believing the real reason you called.

"I suggest," I say in a low voice, "that you take a mistress." I smile at your gasp and hang up the phone. I stretch my arms over my head, feeling wonderfully exposed with my skirt up around my hips. I close my eyes and let out a satiated sigh.

The phone rings.

# Galaxy Lust

## by Etelka Lehoczky

"I wonder if she likes leather?" I thought, tugging at the edge of my tight miniskirt as I tottered into the hotel lobby. A bearded, paunchy guy in a Star Trek t-shirt gave me a slow, up-and-down leer as he tried to catch my eye. I ignored him, pausing by a wall covered in pink mirror to check the effect for myself.

She had to want me. She wouldn't be able to help it — I was too perfect. The skirt was black cowhide, with front lacings that tied into a pretty little bow right underneath my burnt-red leather bustier. Then there were the high-heeled boots and the perfectly battered bomber jacket I'd found at a thrift store. Sure, my slicked-back hair was brown instead of maroon, but otherwise I was the spitting image of her own character, Molly M.

I bent my knees and held up my hands in a karate pose, just like Molly on the cover of *Galaxy Run*. A little gaggle of teenaged boys passed, snickering and eyeing me. "Nice ass, babe," one of them chirped. I whirled fiercely, arms akimbo.

"Muzzle it, you moon-faced little stargoat," I snarled, curling my lip Molly-style.

They stared, then began laughing too loudly and jostling one another as they backed away. "She's Molly Malone, dude!" I heard one of them say. Damn right I was.

I headed over to convention registration to find out when the authors' party would be held. The plushy pink and black carpeting of the hallway was even more treacherous under my heels than the granite tile of the foyer had been, but eventually I made it to the big purple banner reading "OtherWorlds '94 Science Fiction/Fantasy Convention." Even without the banner I would have known in a minute that the two scrawny crater-faces sitting at the folding table were convention officials. Why sci-fi attracts such a passel of gross, squirrelly little guys is beyond me. It really offends my aesthetic. Fortunately sci-fi women are dazzling — there's nothing like a woman in Klingon armor, brandishing a three-foot-long plastic phaser rifle, to sweep a girl off her four-inch heels.

I gave the geeks my name, grabbed a registration packet, and edged over to the corner of the table. I was trying to keep walking to a minimum. Scanning the convention schedule, I finally found it.

*Jude Michaels is our featured guest at the authors' party. She'll be signing copies of Galaxy Crash, the last in the Molly Malone series, and can probably be persuaded to sign any of the other Galaxy novels for all you fans. Other guests include...*

The last in the Molly series. I felt a familiar twinge. I can still remember, like it was yesterday, that night six months ago when I got to the final pages of *Galaxy Crash*. It was three a.m. on a work night, but I couldn't stop reading as Molly, cursing around the damp end of her trademark cigar, struggled to pull her hopped-up interstellar runabout off a collision course with Aldebaran. She'd been hurled toward the star by the black-market boss whose latinum shipment she'd stolen. Her viewscreen glowed mottled orange, and the control capsule heated up. My hands wouldn't stop shaking as I turned the pages. And then it happened: Molly's ship exploded in a brilliant white flash.

Jude killed her! I couldn't believe it. I lay there and watched the red LED on my bedside clock change from 3:33 to 3:34. She killed Molly Malone, the woman I loved, the woman I admired. Not to mention the only decent female character I'd ever run across in sci-fi.

Then I flipped past the last page to the photo inside the back cover.

It was Jude. I'd never seen her before. I hadn't even been able to imagine her, really. She didn't look that much older than me. Thick, dark hair framed her face; clunky horn-rims shielded a cool, wise stare. Her eyes were lighter than mine, gray or blue — I couldn't tell which from the black-and-white photo. I scrutinized it for long minutes before turning off the light.

The book got pretty battered in the next few weeks. I carried it with me everywhere, pulling it out in the grocery line or on the bus and just staring at the photo, learning her face. I don't remember exactly when I started wanting her.

Lost in memories, I was still standing by the registration table when I heard the geeks both talking at once.

"Ms. Michaels! Uh, you don't have to register. Shut up, Paul. Ms. Michaels, your appearance is tomorrow at three. Of course you can go to any of the other events, anything you want. Man, I really loved *Galaxy Heat*..."

And the woman standing three feet from me — god, what a profile — was Jude. She had such a cute little nose. I stood and stared as she stuck her glasses in her shoulder bag and turned away from the registration table, ignoring the nerds. She was so cool, so perfect. Pale beige blazer and pants, black shoes. Narrow shoulders under the blazer, widening to a sweet round butt that was moving away...

Moving away. Right. Got to catch her while she's alone, don't miss this chance, move your ass over to where she's waiting by the elevators. These damn heels ... now she's getting on the elevator...

"*Wait!!*" I screamed. Pressing an arm across my chest to keep my boobs from jouncing out of the bustier, I ran, cursing the heels and the tight skirt with every mincing step. I reached the elevator just as the doors were sliding together — and then a tiny white hand shot into the gap and the doors rebounded.

"Thanks!" I said, still a little too loud, breathing hard as the doors closed us in. She didn't respond, just smiled. A very small smile.

I leaned against the wall, trying to catch my breath. Frankly, I was at a loss. The plan had been that I'd sidle up to her in a crowded room and murmur something husky in her ear. Now here she was, reflected in every surface of this tiny mirrored box, and she wasn't taking any notice of me whatsoever. She just fingered the strap of her shoulder bag and watched the numbers light up above the door. They were rising fast.

"Uh, Ms. Michaels?"

Her eyes slid toward me. They were gray, not blue, and were shadowed by the beginnings of dark circles. Her face seemed naked without the glasses. I tried to remember some of the sexy things I'd thought about saying to her, but all that came out was garbage.

"Um, I just wanted to tell you, uh, I really love your work. Especially *Galaxy Run.*"

"Well, that's very nice of you," she answered tonelessly. "It means so much to me to know that people like my books." She smiled again, an even smaller smile than before, and looked back at the numbers above the door.

I stared helplessly at this remote, weary person sagging against the elevator wall and waiting for those numbers to climb. I tried to imagine what Molly would do. Nothing came to mind.

"You're really beautiful, you know that?" I blurted. Her eyes swung back to me, startled. I talked fast. "No, I mean it, really! I have a huge crush on you."

She actually blushed a little, but her eyes were still cold. "You don't even know me."

"I'd like to." I folded my arms and tried out a bold stare. She stared back silently, and I fumbled. "Anyway, I feel like I know you, just from reading your books."

"From reading my books. Right." She smiled ruefully. Just then the doors chimed and opened. "Look, you may think you know me, but I don't know you. Sorry." Shrugging apologetically, she stepped out of the elevator and walked off down the hall in her sensible shoes.

"Jude, wait!" I trotted over to where she stood by her room, keys in hand. "You do know me. I'm Molly Malone!"

"Huh?"

"Can't you tell? That's why I'm dressed like this. It's for you, Jude! I want to make your dreams come true." Wait a minute, Molly would never say that. Time to get into character.

Jude looked at my jacket, bustier, skirt, and boots.

"Yeah ... I get it. You really do look like Molly. Amazing! Where'd you ever find that bustier?"

"In a thrift shop." I stuck my hands on my hips and shifted them suggestively, grinning at her. "You like?"

She blushed again. "Look, this is very weird..."

Bracing my arm against the door, I leaned toward her confidentially. "Oh, come on, Jude. This is your big chance. I know what you want to do to Molly."

"I don't know what you're talking about."

"Sure you do! What about that part in *Galaxy Chase*, where Molly's muscles bulged as she straddled the soft, moist mass of the megamoeba, grappling with its slippery pseudopod as she reached for her sonic stunner..."

She laughed. The blushing really woke her face up. "Well ... maybe a little."

"I'm tellin' you, honey, I can work it like Molly would, you dig?" I purred. Sliding a hand over my leather hip, I tried to gaze seductively into her eyes without giggling.

"Oh, I don't know, this is too strange... " Her words faded into a smothered laugh. She looked away and ran a hand through her hair. Her face was pink, her mouth quirked with a smile.

Carefully, alert for her reaction, I raised my hand to trace the path hers had taken, moving my fingers gently through the dark locks. Her eyes caught mine, and something in her face changed. Slowly she reached out to touch my hair like I'd touched hers. I knew what Molly would do. I wrapped my arms around her and kissed her as hard as I could.

Her lips were pale and thin, but they opened easily to let me into the wetness inside. Stroking my tongue along the underside of hers, I drew her tongue in and sucked away traces of stale coffee taste until nothing was left but her smooth essence.

I outlined her shoulder blade under the roughness of her jacket, felt the hot skin on the back of her neck, the bumps of her small skull as I buried my hand in her hair. A far corner of my brain whispered, "This is really it. This is really her," and I pushed a hand between us and grasped her breast, searching with my thumb for the nipple.

After a few seconds she grabbed my head with both hands and really started kissing me back. She chewed on me with her lips, gobbling me, draining me with one of those deep soul kisses that start in the pit of the stomach and just pull you in. Her tongue wrapped around mine like she wanted to swallow it, and her arms locked tight against my back and held me against her grinding hips. Her little breasts and swelling tummy seemed to nuzzle me through our clothes. My limbs tingled as all the energy I'd been using to seduce her shot straight down to my cunt. I groaned into her mouth.

Her arms loosened a little then, and she pulled back to look at me, running both hands down my back to squeeze my butt.

"Molly, Molly," she said, rolling the name around her mouth. "I always knew you'd be an easy flip." Chuckling, she bent to suck teasingly on my collarbone. "Come inside."

She backed into the room, pulling me roughly along by my butt so that I lost balance, staggered, and fell on the double bed. I worked on getting my breathing under control while she pulled off her jacket.

Smiling into my eyes, she unbuttoned the cuffs of her shirt and began slowly rolling up her sleeves. I watched her eyes move from my breasts down to where the hem of my skirt bit into my thighs, her fierce and knowing expression letting me know that she was deciding what to do to me.

Bending, she lifted my left foot, briskly unbuckling the row of fastenings on my boot. Once she had my boot off she held it up quizzically for a minute before going to work on the other.

"You always wear heels like this?" she asked, cradling my calf as she unsheathed it from the leather.

"No, but Molly does," I answered. "Don't you think they're sexy?"

"Mmm, I admit it, I do." She stroked the heel with her thumb before tossing the boot aside. "Guess that's why Molly wears them."

Cradling my foot lightly, she touched her tongue to the inside of my ankle, tracing moist circles in the wrinkles of my stocking. As she pulled the stocking off, her lips scraped against my bare skin and her fingertips trickled along my sole. I twitched a little. Then she bit sharply into my arch.

I squirmed.

"Close your eyes," she said quietly.

I did, and felt her tongue press gently against the tip of my smallest toe. I felt a little spot of wet pressure, then her tongue moved on to the next toe. I jerked involuntarily when the wetness moved under my third toe's calloused tip to the sensitive skin beneath. "Sssh," she whispered, wrapping her fingers tightly around my heel to hold my foot in place. Pushing her tongue between my toes, she took one into her mouth and sucked.

My cunt convulsed, and I could feel a dollop of juice ooze into the lake that had formed in the crotch of my underwear. I moaned and wiggled as Jude slowly pulled her mouth away from my toe. Her fingers burned hot trails up my legs and under my skirt. Impeded by the tight leather, she grabbed the edges and yanked it up to my waist, then pulled my underwear off roughly. Falling to her knees by the side of the bed, she cupped my ass and drove her tongue deep into my cunt.

I bucked against her firm hands as she thrust her tongue into me again and again. She ate me the way she had kissed me, hard and deep. Burrowing her nose into my hair, she took long licks up and over my clit. She sucked it deep into her mouth, pulled once, twice, then started a hard, circling rhythm with her tongue.

Her whole head was moving as she chewed on me, pulling a little too hard on my lips, her tongue buzzing at the center of a spiral of tension that widened and spread through my legs and belly. My muscles tightened, and with a rush of that familiar almost-panic I let the shaking begin. I closed my eyes and saw maroon. Almost too quickly, the blood flush rose and crashed.

I've been told I make some pretty strange noises when I get worked up. I must have started carrying on something fierce because she stopped, gasping, and peered at me over the tight band of my bunched skirt. "Oh my god, I'm not hurting you, am I?" she asked throatily. I could feel her hands trembling on my thighs.

Breathing hard, I looked down into her face. Her mouth was rosy and slick; her pale eyes glittered. I reached out to touch the white gleam of the part in her hair.

Sliding out from under her, I sat up and began peeling off my leather. First the jacket went over the side of the bed, then the bustier. I raised my arms above my head, glad to be free of the damp, constrictive leather. She shifted onto her side and watched as I flexed my biceps.

I pushed her gently onto her back and straddled her hips. Stretching out my arms, I jiggled my breasts at her.

"Molly may flip, but she don't stay flipped for long!" I drawled. "Now that you've got my plasma coil warmed up, I'm gonna ride you like a spacebuggy in hyperdrive."

She giggled, laughing even harder when I tried to grind against her hipbone and was prevented by my skirt. I had to climb off her and yank my skirt back down to get at the laces. She leaned over to help me loosen the knots, which had worked themselves tight.

"Okay, sugarlips," I said, sliding out of my skirt at last, "Molly's got everything under control."

"She does? Are you sure?" Jude snickered.

"Sure as a supernova," I answered, climbing on top of her again. "You just relax while I bring this baby home."

She closed her eyes and shivered as I ran the tips of my fingers down her throat, over her fragile collarbone, across the thin skin just above her top button. I drew my lips over the taut tendons in her neck, nibbling her as I did so. I was trying to tease her like she'd teased me, but I couldn't keep from hurrying as I undid the buttons and pulled her shirttail out of her pants.

Her bra was a surprise. Once standard white lace, it was now stretched out, stained, and even torn a little where the left strap met the cup. It barely held her up.

"You bad girl!" I said, snapping the strap with my finger. "This is deplorable."

She raised her head and looked at it ruefully.

"Yeah, I guess I need some new bras."

"Mmm, I'll help you shop," I murmured, nuzzling a soft curve under the frayed lace.

"Shop? Does Molly shop?" she asked, giggling again.

I didn't answer. I pushed the straps down her shoulders until her nipples peeked over the cups, brownish pink and tight with pleasure.

Wrapping my arms around her back, I rolled over, pulling her on top of me as I caught her nipple in my mouth. I stroked the tip with my tongue and pushed my thigh between her legs. Her hipbone pressed into my stomach, the rough linen of her pants agitating each nerve ending under my bare skin. Remembering her passion, I sucked on her nipple hard, biting slightly and running my tongue fast across the tip. She gasped and the atmosphere tightened around us again.

I heard two thunks as she kicked off her shoes, and our hands collided as we both reached to push her pants down. I let her take care of them while I explored the small curve of her breast with my mouth, running my hands down her back and over that gorgeous bottom. She grunted and pressed her naked vulva against my leg.

"Wait."

I reached back over my head to dig into the pockets of my jacket, which lay crumpled by the bed. In the second pocket I found what I was looking for.

I pulled her body down onto mine and kissed her as I slipped a white latex glove onto my left hand. It snapped against my wrist and she pulled away from my mouth, peering over her shoulder to see what I was doing. I grinned and showed her the bottle of lubricant I'd brought, squeezing out a hefty amount into my palm.

"Close your eyes," I told her. She smiled and obeyed. Holding her shoulder with my bare hand, I lifted her slightly to slip my gloved fingers between us. Careful as I was, I couldn't keep from bumping her stomach, and she shivered as the cold lube smeared over her navel.

My fingers slid easily through her silky hair and rested on her lips. She moaned and wiggled, but I didn't move them, just let them lie gently at the opening of her vagina while I wrapped my arm around her shoulders to pull her down against me. Her breasts flattened around the arm I held between us, and she tightened her hands in my hair. I moved my mouth near her ear.

"Jude," I breathed, pressing slightly against her opening with the tips of my fingers, "Why'd you do it?"

"Aaaah-ah-ah ... Do what?" she muttered against my neck.

"Why'd you kill me?"

She shifted, lifting her head to frown at me perplexedly.

"Come on, Jude, I'm a better pilot than that. I could have bounced my ship off a solar flare and gotten clear, but you didn't let me."

She laughed. Kissing me gently, she ran her hand down my arm to the gloved wrist.

"Well, Molly, you were just getting a little out of control, you know?" she said, taking hold of my wrist and pressing two of my fingers smoothly into her. She was surprisingly loose and soft. I closed my eyes and savored.

"I mean, come on, how many books do you want me to write about you? It had to stop somewhere..."

Her voice came husky and her grip was tight on the base of my hand as she slowly rode my fingers. She moved her hips in deliberate circles, her eyes closed tight, a little frown forming between her brows as she searched carefully for her pleasure. Sweat weighted the hair on her forehead and dampened the tattered lace of her bra.

I pressed my fingers hard against her spongy inner wall, and she arched her back and moaned.

I reached as deep as I could, stroking her slick insides, spreading my fingers slightly as I pushed them into her. Releasing my hand at last, she fell forward to brace her arms on the bed. I ran my bare hand down to the small of her back, feeling for her pace so I could match it with mine.

Her face flushed as she worked against my hand.

"Don't worry, Molly, you'll come back some day," she gasped. "Nobody knows it yet, but you teleported out at the last minute..."

"It's okay, it's okay," I answered. "I know." I pulled my fingers out almost all the way, feeling her tightness squeeze the tips for an instant before I pushed deeply in again with a twist of my wrist. She bucked her hips faster and I quickened my strokes, jerking my elbow to drag my palm rapidly across her clit.

Her arms began to quiver on either side of my head, and her thighs trembled where they pressed into mine. Her breath came in shallow, quick pants that matched her movements. She scraped against my hand faster and faster until, with a look of intense concentration on her flushed face, she gave a great rocking thrust and a tremendous "aaah!"

It took a minute or two for her breathing to even out. Opening her eyes, she smiled down at me and pushed a few damp strands of hair out of her face.

Slowly I pulled my fingers out of her and raised my arms above my head to strip off the latex glove. She rolled off me and lay on her back, breathing deeply, her bra bunched under her breasts. I unhooked it and ran my hand down her chest to rest on her belly.

"That was perfect," she sighed. Smiling, she laid her hand on mine.

"Wait, I almost forgot!" Dropping her hand, I reached over the side of the bed and began digging through my jacket pockets again.

"What now?"

"You want perfect? I've got the perfect, ideal touch. I can't believe I almost forgot..."

Finally I found them. Jude started giggling again when I showed them to her. The cellophane was cracking, but the two thick cigars were still intact, and very aromatic. Just the way Molly would like.

# The Uses of Strength

## by Joan Nestle

### 1

She stood in front of me, her sweatpants low around her hips, her nipples hard. I arose from my bed and just leaned my head against the side of her thigh, and then, as if I were climbing a ladder up out of my exhaustion, I stretched up toward her, moving my hand from the curve of her belly up to her chest, where it lay, fingers splayed out along her ribs. I rested there, until I became aware of the fluttering of her heart, and then I hurried on. Soon my cheek was against hers and though she stood, and I kneeled on the bed I had come to know too well, I was her equal in the travels of the flesh.

### 2

We had driven up the coast to Gloucester on a gray spring day. She had wanted to visit the hometown of a poet she admired, but before we reached the small New England city, we came upon a park that overlooked the ocean. We walked slowly over the soggy earth until we reached a cliff that fronted the sea. She stood in front of me, catching the full force of the wind, her gray hair dancing in the autumn air. I stood behind her, leaning against her back, my arms around her waist. The ocean rolled in, over and over, gray and complete and never still. I began to cry for all the oceans I had seen with lovers, for all the leave-takings that had left their marks around my heart.

### 3

If I take you in my arms, pull your head to my breasts, if I curve my hand over the winged blades of your back, pressing you further into me, if I spread my legs to give you better purchase, settling your bones into my flesh, if I move into you, gripping your want with my openness, if I press my mouth against your neck, my tongue softening the skin where my teeth will pull at you, if I slide down your narrow belly, my breasts dragging against your skin, if I bury my face in your cunt, spreading your lips with my tongue, if I take all of you into my mouth, sucking the folds open, if I push two fingers into you, pulling at your pleasure, if I swirl my tongue over your swollen clit when your muscles tightening around my fingers tell me you are ready to come, if I close up your lips while you are still pulsing so you can keep the sweetness longer, if I pull myself up alongside your body and rest my head on your shoulder as your breathing slows down and the sweat dries on your breasts — will you think I am weak?

### 4

I turned my cheek against the rough wall, my hands stretched out above my head trying to find a hold. I felt the coldness of the wall in my belly. "Close your eyes," she insisted quietly, pressing into me. She spread my legs with one of hers, her leathered leg pushing my slip up until my ass was bare. I pushed further into the wall, wanting to escape my own nakedness. My arms, growing heavy with expectation, slid down the wall. I could hear footsteps all around me as other women moved through the narrow passageways of the bar's back room. Her gloved hand moved over my hips, my slip fell off my shoulders, but I had to let it go. My hands could not leave the wall. No rope was needed, no scarlet tie. Years of shame pinned me to the wall, while air moved over my nakedness. I waited, and then she returned, fully. Her hand curved over my ass, leaving only to deliver sharp short spanks, and then to knead the never seen, never wanted flesh, until a heat ran down the back of my thighs, a heat that made me spread my legs even more because pure want was pouring out of me. She laughed against my ear and then entered me, pushing at my tightness until resistance became a sweetness. After she left, I turned around in the darkness, too tired to move off the wall. Pulling my slip down, I faced the passing women, my comrades, quietly and directly.

### 5

The nights are hard. Often sleep does not come. She turns to me, gazing quietly at my desperation. Her hand reaches out, and for long minutes, she strokes my breasts, my belly, my legs. I move into the crook of her arm and soon her heartbeat, slow and steady, becomes my own.

# Just a Phase

## by Lucy Jane Bledsoe

"You're so rigid," my fifteen-year-old daughter Jennifer tells me Saturday afternoon. "As far as your memory goes, life began at age thirty."

I sigh deeply and control my impulse to tell Jennifer that she is dead wrong: my life *ended* at thirty, the year Robert and I split when Jennifer was five. Not that Robert was a loss. But how could I have a life while working a bizillion hours a week and raising my daughter? These last ten years have passed in a blur. I've dated two men in all that time. A life? Hardly.

"All I'm asking," Jennifer intones with a dramatic show of patience for her ancient — forty-year-old — mother, "is to get to do what all the rest of the kids get to do. What does it matter what time I come home?"

I spend my weekdays caring for old folks in a nursing home. This week four, that's *four,* died. Jennifer's adolescent arrogance, her belief that she understands all there is to know about life, infuriates me sometimes. I would like nothing better than to demand her respect for my experience. But I do in fact remember a few things about being fifteen, including my fury at adults' belief that respect was something that could be given, not earned. I have tried to earn my daughter's respect, but that's no easy task.

Jennifer continues, "Daddy says if it were up to him, I could stay out until two. He says he totally trusts me."

This is a knife. Robert is far more liberal than me. Eloquently liberal. As an attorney for a national civil liberties organization, he knows how to spell freedom backwards and forwards. What he doesn't understand is how some freedoms could kill my daughter. His daughter.

I say, "I trust you, too, Jennifer. But I don't trust everyone else in the world. I need you home tonight at midnight."

"As if I couldn't get pregnant or AIDS or become a crack addict before midnight," she says.

It's a good argument. I remember my mother not allowing me to have
boys in my bedroom. As if, I'd argue, sex couldn't happen somewhere else.
And it did. In cars, in parks, in *his* bedroom.

This all feels like a cruel joke on me. How'd I get to be forty? How'd I
become the target of an adolescent's rebellion? I know all too well that my
anger at Jennifer's demands has a lot to do with my own feelings of depri-
vation. How long since I've been touched by anyone other than the old
folks with whom I work? I feel so barren next to Jennifer's bursting and
popping vitality.

"If I were a son," she screams on her way to her room, "you wouldn't
make me come in at midnight. You're sexist!"

Her bedroom door slams. A moment later, adolescent boy voices shout
rhythmic obscenities about sex and police. Her "music." How I hated
when my parents put quotes around my music. But knowing I'm being just
like my own mother doesn't stop me.

I tell myself how much I'll enjoy the peace and solitude when she goes
to Italy in December with her father and his new wife Melinda. I've
already decided I'm not going to turn on the TV even once. I'm going to
read a pile of books, see lots of friends, and paint my bedroom. I'll have
three weeks of silent bliss. But this thought, too, is a knife. This trip to
Italy, something I could never give Jennifer, is part of Robert's scheming
to take her from me. Now that the bed-wetting has stopped. Now that
she can get to her appointments on her own. Now that there are only a
couple years of parenting left.

I go in the other room, where Jennifer's music is just a dull throb, and
call Mom. She doesn't quite get "hello" out before I say, "I'm sorry, Mom.
I'm sorry for every time I disrespected you. For every time I shouted that
you didn't understand."

"What's she doing now?" Mom asks.

I break into tears. I tell Mom only that I'm tired, and she coos to me
over the phone. But then she has to go because she has a date with Harry,
her new boyfriend. We hang up.

I try to console myself. Loud music, demands to stay out late, wearing
too much makeup, too many boys calling the house too late. These are
not crimes. Why do they feel dangerous to a mother?

Jennifer's father loves insinuating that my rigidity (did he give her that
word?) causes her "excesses." At the same time, this master of innuendo
likes to imply that I might be bequeathing her a tendency toward loose-

ness. What a joke! It is true that when Robert and I met, just after Rachel, I was in my (short-lived) sexually liberated stage. But now the closest I come to sex is in my dreams at night. Usually my partners are fictional characters from books I'm reading, or sometimes even the author. Talk about embarrassing. Even my fantasies center on people who don't exist or whom I've never met. There's one author in particular I've been dreaming about, off and on, for months. I've read all her books twice and I never read books twice.

How, I'd like to ask Robert, can I be too rigid and too loose at the same time?

I should have forbidden the trip to Italy, but on what grounds?

I get up to tell Jennifer to turn down her music because that pumping bass is about to drive me mad. Then I force myself to sit again. I remember riding in the Dodge Dart to church twenty-some years ago when I was fifteen. My parents rode in the front seat and I rode in the back with my brother. Craig leaned forward and turned on the radio. He adjusted the volume way up "so we could hear in the backseat." Thelma Houston had just begun singing "Anyway You Like It," the song where she comes about three-quarters of the way through, replete with panting and groaning and gasping. I wore a navy blue and white dress, clutched a black patent leather purse. My brother had on the suit and tie he hated. Thelma Houston was going, "unh, unh, unh," and feeling *good*. My father's temples throbbed visibly as he struggled to keep the radio on. Craig and I sat in the backseat, listening to Thelma fill the car with her sexual ecstasy, enjoying the extreme discomfort we imposed on our parents. Finally, Dad snapped off the radio. Craig and I bitterly protested. If my father were alive, I'd call him, too. Sorry, Dad.

But it was different then. Kids didn't risk death with their sexual experimentation. Giving kids the space to blunder along and find their way was so much easier. Adolescent arrogance had a place. The price could be high, but not as high as it can be today.

Tonight Jennifer is going to a party at the house of a boy I don't know. The party, she tells me, won't even start until eleven. I've ruined her life by making her come in by midnight. I rub my head and regret my impatience with her. I love Jennifer more than anyone in the world. When I can remember that I'm the adult, I ache for her, for all the things she wants. I know I must seem so irrational to her.

To make up for my strictness, I call Godfather's and order a Hawaiian pizza, Jennifer's favorite. When the pizza arrives, I shove a note under her door announcing dinner. She emerges, her face red, white, and black with makeup. We sit down to eat and she picks all the pineapple pieces off her slice, saying, "Yuck."

"I thought this was your favorite."

"Yuck," she repeats. I don't say how much I hate ham and pineapple pizza, that this was for her, how I'd love to be eating an anchovy, black olive, and capers one instead.

I look again at her makeup and say, "I know you don't want to hear this. But promise me if you're having sex you'll use a condom."

Jennifer doesn't answer until she finishes an entire slice of pizza, minus the pineapple. Then she sighs and says, "I wonder why you're so obsessed with sex."

I want to slap her. I keep myself to an electric glare. "I'm obsessed," I say, "with keeping my daughter alive."

"Do *you* protect *yourself*," she asks, "when you have sex?"

This is more ammunition from her. She knows perfectly well there hasn't been anyone in my life for years, ever since she hit adolescence, as a matter of fact. Who could do romance *and* parent a teenager?

"Maybe," she suggests, "you should concentrate more on your own life."

I jump to my feet and throw a dish to the floor. It bounces instead of breaks, making me feel all the more impotent. I burst into tears again, run to my room, and slam the door, acting every bit the adolescent she is and I'm not. It doesn't take me too long to realize my smart daughter is right. Bull's-eye. My own life. I consider going out tonight, too. But with whom? Where would I go? What if Jennifer got into some kind of trouble and called?

An hour later, a piece of paper slides under my door. "I'm sorry, Mom," it reads. "I love you."

Jennifer comes home Sunday morning at half past one. I don't say anything to her about it because I don't know what to say. In fact, I refrain from asking my daughter any personal questions for two weeks. I'm delighted when, inexplicably, all on her own, she begins leaving for school with a scrubbed face. The makeup was a phase, after all. I congratulate myself on not harassing her. It works. It *is* about trust. I have to let her make her own way.

But when she starts staying after school every day to watch basketball practice, I begin to worry again. I wonder who the boy is and why he isn't calling her at home. Some of those athlete types are unsavory, over-developed, too physical for their ages.

I can't stop wondering about her question: Why do I obsess about sex? Do I obsess about sex? Last night I dreamt about that author again. We didn't have sex, but we did play a highly erotic game of footsie under a restaurant table.

I hold my tongue for as long as I can, but Jennifer is leaving for Italy in two weeks. I imagine her confiding in Robert about her new boyfriend. I can't stand him getting information I don't have. I say, as casually as I can, "I'd like to meet your new friend."

Jennifer knows I'm fishing. "What friend?"

"The boy on the basketball team," I say.

Her silence convinces me I won't hear word one about the boy, ever.

But on Thursday the following week, she brings her new friend home after basketball practice. She's not a boy, but she looks like one. I've heard about this girl. She's the star on the girls' basketball team and a straight-A student. Jennifer introduces me to Ashley.

Ashley extends her hand, smiles with big dimples, then asks if she can help with dinner. Jennifer chimes in, "I invited Ashley to dinner."

I force myself to say, "Great."

Ashley's easy self-assurance both impresses and annoys me. She asks what I think of a couple ballot measures from last month's elections, then tells me what *she* thinks in no uncertain terms. As she talks, I wish I had cooked a real meal, rather than boiled pasta topped with jarred spaghetti sauce. Why does it feel like Ashley is trying to put me at ease? Jennifer seems entirely awed by the girl. After dinner, Ashley goes home to study for a history test. And for once, Jennifer goes to her room to study without any prodding from me.

I sit with my tea in front of the TV and wonder why Jennifer has introduced me to her new friend, let me in on this corner of her life. I wonder why Ashley makes me so uncomfortable, and I think of Rachel for about the tenth time this month.

Jennifer comes out of her room at ten o'clock. "Mom?" she asks. "Did you like Ashley?" I can tell by her eyes how much she cares about her new friend and this breaks my heart. But I'm scared for her. What is Jennifer doing now? "Yes," I say. "I liked her a lot."

Jennifer smiles and I'm gratified that my opinion means something to her. "Give me a hug good night," I say and she does.

By the next morning at breakfast, Jennifer has regained her defiant face, though it is still makeupless. I guess that she's gearing up to tell me something and I'm right. Just before going out the door for school, she says, "Mom, you should know. I'm a lesbian." The door slams.

I'm late for work, but I sit at the table another ten minutes, my coffee getting cold, struck motionless by a kind of terror. I imagine a gigantic emotional vacuum sucking my daughter away. If I stand up from the table my legs will collapse under me. I tell myself that nothing is wrong with being a lesbian, but that word causes a core of pain to throb inside me.

Then, finally, I decide: no, Jennifer is not a lesbian. This is just one more of her tactics to get my goat, to shock me. I even laugh, sitting there alone at the kitchen table, at my silly overreaction. She got me, finally found something she could stun me with. I vow to be a better mother, to be the adult, to give her the space she needs to go through her trials.

I remember one night in about 1972 when my father came home from work in a rage. At dinner that night he looked at each of us children before telling us his story of horror. That afternoon, he announced, a young couple was fornicating in Pioneer Square, right in the middle of downtown.

I was seventeen years old, liberated, and righteous. "Why," I asked my father, "do you care? What does it have to do with any of us if they want to express their love—"

Dad's fist slammed onto the dinner table. Plates bounced and soup sloshed. His temples, always our barometer for his anger, pulsed.

"Sam," my mother said.

Dad kept quiet through the rest of dinner, opening his mouth only wide enough to clamp onto another mouthful of food.

Why, I wonder now, does fornicating in public seem okay to a seventeen-year-old?


That night when Jennifer comes home after watching the girls' basketball team practice, I say, speaking as levelly as I can manage, hoping to communicate openness, "Tell me about Ashley."

Jennifer's lower lip trembles, reminding me of my little girl whom I haven't seen in years. Her eyes fill with tears.

I'm amazed, touched, and frightened. "Honey," I say, taking her hand.

"It's okay." But inside I'm panicking. Where's the rebellion? Is this real? Is she really a lesbian? Is it really okay?

"Boys are gross," she says.

So simple. So true. Yet I want to argue. I remember telling my own mother I hated boys and listening to her coax me back into the fold. My mother never denied boys' grossness. She made arguments for why girls and women must endure it. Why must Jennifer endure it? I remain quiet.

Jennifer whispers, "Have you ever been attracted to a woman?"

It's been so long since Jennifer has asked me a real question, has sincerely sought anything from me. I want to fulfill her trust. And yet, I never dreamt she'd ask this question. My fear takes over. I don't want Jennifer to be a lesbian.

"No," I say and hate myself for lying to my daughter. But instantly I rationalize: That was the early seventies. Sex in the seventies doesn't count. We all did everything. Sex was like candy, something to sample, nothing to take seriously. The nineties are very different.

Jennifer turns away from me, her face slack with honesty, her body small. I wonder if this, her thinking she's a lesbian, is because I've raised her without a man. I feel guilty. Then I remember that most of the children in this country are raised in one (female) parent households and they're not all gay. I want to retrieve Jennifer but I don't know how.

"Don't tell your father you've decided you're a lesbian," I say, and my voice sounds hard.

"I haven't *decided* I'm a lesbian. I *am* a lesbian." She wipes the tears away and I see the defiance mount in her face.

"Don't tell your father," I repeat.

"Why not?" Suddenly, she looks triumphant, realizing she can use this. "Because," I say. "He'll hold it against me."

"What's it got to do with you?" Now she's hot angry. This lesbian thing is another stab at establishing her own identity, and already I'm taking it, as if it were mine.

The house is absolutely silent. I pace from her room to mine and back again to hers. I touch the pictures of her friends up on her bulletin board. I see the new one, of Ashley. I consider putting on one of her CDs. I miss the thumping, shouting music.

I want to enjoy this break. Haven't I longed for it? My girlfriends from work promised to take me out a couple nights, show me how to meet men in the nineties. Sex sounds good, real good. But men sound exhausting. I look again at the picture of Ashley. "Mom, you should know. I'm a lesbian." Maybe it's true that children live out the lives their parents haven't had. Haven't dared have? My girlfriends at work would be shocked by my night dreams. That author and her toes under the table. I look again at Ashley and wonder why this self-assured girl got all the breaks — athletic ability, straight A's, good looks, and apparent sexual clarity — all by the age of sixteen. Here I am at forty, beached up on the dry rocky shore of celibacy.

I leave Jennifer's room. This silent solitude is scary. I'm afraid of what it will bring crashing up on my shore.

Besides that, it's hard to enjoy this time alone because it doesn't feel temporary. I hate knowing that he's fattening her up on *carciofini e funghi all'Olio e bistecca alla fiorentina*, famous art, and luxurious accommodations. She's having the time of her life. Robert is a fine listener if he wants to hear what you're saying, and he'll want to hear everything Jennifer says. He'll absorb her being. Melinda, the new wife, will do her best to ingratiate herself, as well. Undoubtedly she's wise enough to make it clear she's not trying to replace Mom. She'll show how respectful she is. Of me. Of Jennifer and Robert's relationship. I feel so lonely.

I call Mom. The phone rings fifty times. I hang up and go right out to get her an answering machine for Christmas. When I get home, I wrap the present, then try to think of something else to do. I wish I'd told Jennifer the truth.

In 1975 I was only six years older than Jennifer. Rachel, who was from Mississippi, was in my political science class. She argued fiercely and too often with the professor. Her parents had been deeply involved in the civil rights movement and Rachel had thought through politics. She wasn't swallowing whole what she called the "garbage" the professor fed us in Poly Sci 103. Sometimes she and I talked after class. When we discovered we both wanted to travel around Italy after graduation, it seemed natural to hook up.

I thought of Rachel as a radical and never considered the word *lesbian* until years later. She loved to talk and I loved listening to her fine southern accent, the way her words swung real low, got drawn out, then swooped up again. She wore her hair one inch long and walked "like a man," but no one at school ever bothered her because she was so smart. I told myself it was her brains that attracted me.

The first time, we were drunk. After a week in Florence, where she mentally seduced me with her exhaustive knowledge of art and history, we hitchhiked to San Gimignano, the tiny Tuscan town with thirteen watchtowers. We checked into the youth hostel, then set out exploring at five in the evening. Yellow light washed the cold stone walls. Blossoms spilled out of every window. We found a small *trattoria* and Rachel said, "I'm ordering for both of us." I felt a surge from my belly rush out to fill my fingers and toes. "Okay," I agreed. She ordered spinach with olive oil, steamed mussels, pasta with porcini mushrooms, and a liter of San Gimignano *vernaccio*.

Afterwards, we walked to the edge of town and climbed some steps to the top of the medieval town wall. The day's last sunlight buttered the rolling vineyards below. A mess of swallows, undoubtedly the descendants of generations and generations of San Gimignano birds, danced in the purpling sky. For no reason at all, I knelt and kissed the tips of Rachel's sturdy brown Earth Shoes. Then I grabbed her calves to pull myself back up to my feet. I grinned at her, like I was joking, but she didn't grin back. She looked at me with that look of endless knowledge that she often had, and didn't speak. *It's the overwhelming sensuality of Tuscany, I told myself, that's stirring this deep gratitude in me.*

As we stood looking out, a rain cloud drifted over us and a light sprinkle fell even as the sun shone a few yards away. Rachel put a hand on the back of my neck and ran it slowly down to rest on my behind. I turned to her. She held my behind in her two hands and pulled me against her. I kissed the hollow at the base of her neck and she undid my belt buckle and unzipped my jeans. A shudder of fear ripped through my body and I stepped back. I saw my own fear reflected in Rachel's eyes, and the sight of that smart, usually fearless woman looking scared shot love direct to my belly. I smiled at her, reached for her hands and put them back on the top of my jeans. Rachel eased my pants down to my calves and pushed me onto the cold stone on top of the wall. I lay back and my arm dangled over the drop-off. I rolled my head to the side, looking down the hundreds of feet to someone's garden below. The stone was icy cold on my bare buttocks. As she stroked my belly, then the curly hair between my legs, I let my knees fall open and lifted my behind off the wall, bucking for her hand. But she didn't give me her hand.

Rachel leaned down and put her mouth on me. She didn't taste and tease gently. She didn't eat me for my pleasure, she ate me for hers, sucking and licking hard. I slammed my hips up into her face, thrashing on the precipice of that ancient stone wall, coming immediately, and then again and again, until Rachel pulled back. The shock of her withdrawal nearly sent me flying off the wall, but she grabbed my arms and tugged me to my feet. Then I heard what had stopped her. People were coming up the wall steps. She squatted and grabbed my jeans, pulling them up to my waist. An old Italian woman dressed entirely in black, leaning on the arm of a younger woman, her daughter probably, watched me zip up my pants and fasten the buckle. Then I saw what the Italian women had climbed up to see. The most vivid double rainbow I'd ever seen arched directly over our heads. Rachel took my arm to steady me. I nodded to let her know I was okay, and we clamored down the rampart steps.

For a couple days I couldn't get over how fast it had happened. We hadn't even kissed, though I told myself I was glad for that. Having it be just sex seemed easier to accept. Finally, three days later when we talked about it, we agreed that a sexually free woman should try everything, try all the flavors of the rainbow, we laughed. *Rainbow* became our code word for sex.

The next time, we were exploring the perimeter of a castle. A hillside of wildflowers met the base of the castle's stone wall. We joked how the many colors of the wildflowers were like the many colors in the rainbow. With our backs against the rough stones of the castle wall, I opened small packages of prosciutto, black olives, purple grapes, crusty bread. Rachel wrapped a paper-thin slice of prosciutto around a fat grape and pushed it in my mouth, leaving her finger in with the meat and fruit. I chewed the food and sucked her finger until she pushed all the newspaper-wrapped packages of lunch aside and pushed me on my back, again.

A week into the time alone, I know that I have lost Jennifer. I can't compete with trips to Italy, with large clothing allowances, with the total understanding that apparently Robert possesses. I have no money to fight him in court. And anyway, if she wants to live with them, who am I to get in her way?

I'm amazed when she calls me. She says she is charging the call to Robert's credit card. She sounds distant. Not her voice, because the new fiber optics make long-distance phone calls from anywhere in the world sound like the person is next door, but emotionally distant. I wonder why she is calling. "What have you seen?" I ask.

"A lot of Michelangelo," she answers. "It's been raining. A lot of museums."

I celebrate that she sounds a bit bored. I want so badly to ask about Melinda. Even about Robert. Of course I don't.

"What are you doing?" she asks me.

I fake joy. "Christmas shopping, seeing friends. Oh, and I finally pruned the pear tree!" I laugh. I've been talking about pruning the outlandishly overgrown pear tree for five or six years. I hear myself sounding as if she's been in my way, as if I'm finally getting to live my life. She's silent.

"Is the food good?" I ask. "I remember the food being fabulous."

"It's okay. Daddy always orders too much."

Of course. Seduce her with opulence.

"Have you met any nice people?"

"No."

I am silent now, not sure why she called. I suppose Robert told her to. He would do that. Throw me a bone. It makes him look good, fair. He considers himself utterly fair.

"I better go," Jennifer says. "Long distance."

"Bye, honey," I say. "I love you."

I hang up and realize I sounded insincere. I love her so much. But I feel mean. I'm glad for their rain. Even more glad for the forced museums. Teenagers hate museums.

I thought I hated museums too until I saw them with Rachel. In Montepulciano we found a tiny two-room museum, the former home of a wealthy eighteenth-century winegrower. The museum was on a back street and the woman who lived across the way was in charge of collecting admission. We gave her a few lire and entered the first dank, musty room. A bunch of contemporary wooden tables were loaded with relics, some ancient and others only about twenty years old. We fingered the items, giggling because the museum was so hokey, and shivering because it was so cold. After unlocking the door for us, the woman disappeared behind her own door across the street, but she came back to check on us a few minutes later. She motioned to the next room, wanting us to move on. I supposed she was in the middle of her housework and wanted to be rid of us. But we giggled at her impatience. What did it matter if we lingered here? We'd paid our couple lire. Besides, Rachel became absorbed in trying to figure out what each little artifact had been used for. She'd be serious, then I'd suggest a lewd use for an object and we'd crack up. She picked up a big rusted pair of tongs and clamped one of my breasts with them. Just then, the woman returned a second time and shooed us into the next room. So we went.

Then I realized why she'd wanted us to move on: not because she didn't want us to linger, but because this second room was her real pride. She grinned widely and swept her hands out to express its magnificence. This had been the bedroom of the wealthy eighteenth-century wine-grower. The huge four-poster bed was covered with a badly mildewed brocade spread. Dark paintings of horses and beheaded men and gleaming swords covered the walls. The woman kept nodding her head forcefully, demanding we show our complete delight. We smiled, exclaimed in English, swept our own hands. Finally satisfied that we were now enjoying the part of the museum she thought worthy, she said in rapid Italian what we believed to be an encouragement to stay as long as we liked, and left the museum to return to her housework.

The room smelled dank and old. I couldn't imagine living without heat, without a daily shower. "It wouldn't be so bad," Rachel said. Then she wrestled me onto the bed. "What are you doing?" I asked, resisting her for the first time. "That lady."

Rachel could live and breathe history. I can only imagine what her fantasies were that afternoon in Montepulciano, she didn't tell me, but she stripped me and, still fully dressed herself, made love to me on that old musty bed. I was frightened, not liking how my imagination conjured up the Italian prison where they kept perverts. "Grab the top of the bed," she told me, and, still on my back, cold and naked, I reached both hands over my head to grasp one of the bedposts. She ran her fingertips over my nipples, then licked her fingers and brushed them across my clit. She stroked my belly lightly for a long time, pushing into the hollow above my pubic bone, grasping my pelvic bones, then stroking my belly again. I was dry, and still frightened, when she shoved her hand up me, hard. But when she pulled it out again, I groaned with the loss. My hips raised off the bed for her. She looked down at me lying with my hands over my head gripping the bedpost, my legs stretched apart, my eyes begging her, and asked, "Do you want it or not?"

I didn't know how to answer. I tried to say we'd better go, but my hips rose for her again. She placed her hand at my opening, then pushed it in, out, and in again, fucking me hard, though I was still dry with fear. Which was why it took me forever to come. I finally reached the edge of an orgasm when a small noise made me open my eyes. The museum keeper stood in the bedroom doorway, gripping the doorjamb, her mouth open as if she were trying to say something, looking horrified. I saw Rachel swing her head around and see the woman, too, but she didn't miss a beat pumping her hand in me. For a moment I felt my mounting orgasm begin to collapse, but in the next moment it roared upon me. The woman in the doorway gasped as I shouted my climax, sucking in that dank, musty air.

When I opened my eyes, she was gone. Rachel and I ran to the train station, took the first train going anywhere, and didn't feel safe until we deboarded, much to our delight, in Orvieto.

On Christmas Day, I bravely cook myself a roast. A whole roast. Mom is spending the holiday with Harry's family. She invited me, of course, and a couple other friends asked me to join their families, but I stay home, hoping Jennifer will call. She doesn't. By now, I figure, she's lost in the Tuscan pleasures, already accustomed to luxury. I wonder if she still thinks she's a lesbian.

After putting the roast in, I lose interest in cooking. I watch TV until the meat is done, several hours later. I carve off a few slices and eat them standing over the sink with a couple pieces of bread.

Then I decide to call Rachel. I find her New York City phone number in my college alumni directory. She answers the phone, "Yep?"

I falter and stumble through a reminder of who I am. She bellows out, "My god, where are you? Are you in town?"

I think I'm reassuring her when I tell her I'm in Oregon, far from New York, but she says, "Well, damn, that's another world." Her edges sound rougher. I bet she's gained weight. I wonder if her hair is still short.

We chat awhile. She readily comes out to me, and I tell her my daughter thinks she's a lesbian. She asks if I'm still married to "that Robert guy," and I tell her not on her life. She laughs and I flatter myself thinking she's pleased. Neither of us once mentions that it's Christmas Day and I like this. She tells me that if my daughter needs anything, references to gay organizations, a stable out dyke to talk to — at this she bellows her laugh again, as if referring to herself as stable is a big joke, and then sobers up fast and says — Jennifer can call her. I feel a surge of jealousy and want to tell her that I want to talk to her. I don't want to give her to my daughter. We hang up, saying it was great to talk, neither of us saying we'd like to talk again, and I cry. I cry and cry and cry.

The last time she and I made love, I cried, too. We'd taken the train to Rome. The next day we were flying home. We'd spent all our money and had to wait for the plane flight for our next meal. We planned on sleeping at the airport, but we both wanted one more night in Rome, even if it was on empty stomachs. So we wandered the streets for hours and hours, accepted two different invitations for drinks from men, then did some fancy talking and, in one case, running, to lose our dates. At three in the morning, we found ourselves in Campo de Fiori, Rome's best produce and flower market, exhausted. We tucked into a doorway, saying we'd sleep a couple hours before taking the train to the airport. Instead we soulfucked. It was bottomless, bass-note fucking, without humor, without our minds. The last time I came, I also cried, hard, the release from my chest and throat every bit as big as the one from my cunt. We were still kissing, our tongues down each other's throats, when the first fruit and flower vendors arrived at five. In the middle of the square, they built a fire with the wooden crates they used for carrying their merchandise. We warmed ourselves by their fire, using the Italian we'd learned during the summer to talk with the merchants, watching dawn lift the night. Then, dirty and tired and hungry, we walked to the train station. On the plane home, I told her that she was the most delicious flavor of the rainbow.

Rachel and I, having gone to live and work in separate cities upon our return from Italy, exchanged passionate letters for several months, always reporting on our rainbow experiences with others. Both of us slept with men, and I suspect she also slept with other women, though she didn't write me about that. I soon met and married Robert.

Jennifer returns from Italy looking worn-out. Robert and Melinda drop her off, do not come in the house, for which I am grateful. I contain my excitement at seeing her and ask about the trip. She is silent and glum. I wonder if she's figuring out how to tell me she's moving in with Robert and Melinda. I feel raw and electric. I finally blurt, sounding adolescent, "I guess you'll move in with your dad now."

Her head jerks up, surprised to hear the tears in my voice, my resigned tone. Tears fill her own eyes. She throws her arms around me. "I'm so glad to be home," she sobs. "I hate Melinda."

The gratitude that explodes inside me is bigger than fireworks, it's a million bursting stars in my chest. I hold my daughter to me. I vow to be honest with her. I'll do everything in my power to help her get through.

That night I tell Jennifer that I wasn't truthful with her. I tell her that I have been attracted to women and though I don't give her details, I tell her I had a lesbian (I'm surprised at how hard that word is to say) affair in Italy twenty years ago. Twenty years is nothing to me. To Jennifer, it's ancient history. She's fascinated and asks lots of questions.

Jennifer returns to school the next day. When she comes home, after girls' basketball practice, I ask how Ashley is. Jennifer doesn't answer me. After that first day, she comes directly home from school every day, apparently not staying to watch basketball practice, and sulks for two weeks. Though she won't talk to me about what's going on, she doesn't get angry at me for asking either. I wonder if Ashley has jilted her. I feel furious and consider calling the girl's mother and then realize how ridiculous that would be. I feel hugely sad for Jennifer. I know I am feeling her loss too deeply, that I'm really feeling my own emptiness. But still it hurts.

Then, at the end of January, Jennifer brings home a boy who is in her math class. Donald seems bright enough, but I don't understand why he doesn't fit, in Jennifer's mind, the "gross" category that all other boys are in. Or, at least, were in a few weeks ago. His pants, about three sizes too big, fall off his skinny behind. His shoelaces flap around his untied sneakers. His acne looks as though it could be cured with daily washing. Yet Jennifer speaks to him and looks at him with what appears to be longing.

That night, after Donald leaves, Jennifer and I share an anchovy, black olive, and capers pizza, which I notice she eats with relish. In my attempting-to-be-casual voice that Jennifer always sees through, I say, "I thought you were a lesbian."

My daughter shrugs. "I guess I'm not."

This time it's me who's silent. I feel as if she's pulled a chair out from under me.

She takes a big bite of pizza and with her mouth full, says, "But Mom, that doesn't mean I'm not happy for you. You know, the stuff you told me about that woman Rachel and the feelings those memories brought up for you? I think you should explore those feelings." My daughter swallows, looks composed and thoughtful as she adds, "But actually I do think I'm heterosexual."

"I see," I say, and reach for the phone. I don't know whom I'm going to call. Mom? Rachel? I hold the receiver to my shoulder. "Maybe," I tell Jennifer, summoning as flippant a tone as I can, "maybe this heterosexuality thing is just a phase."

"Your heterosexuality or mine?" she asks, and then when I don't answer, she smiles, tomato sauce adhering to her front teeth. "Maybe. I guess we'll see."

All at once, my seriousness and fears slough away. My daughter's sense of possibility, her ease with what can be, brightens inside me.

I've made a lot of mistakes in these fifteen years of raising Jennifer, but what a good girl she is, anyway. Fifteen years isn't much of a sacrifice for this love I feel right now. I put back the phone and get up to squeeze her to me, saying, "You're the very best, do you know that?"

"Thanks, Mom," she says, taking the last piece of pizza. "But if you do start dating someone, I want you in by midnight. Fair's fair."

# Hot Wheels

## by michon

She loves it when it's hot. Summer is made for her. She was born in summer when the sun was at its highest. Her body is made to receive heat.

She loves the heat so much that sometimes she just sits in her car that's been baking under the sun. The air is hot and humid and the steering wheel burns her knees when they touch it. The heat sucks the chill from her skin. It raises the hair on her arms and unravels the knot between her shoulders. She leans back, closes her eyes, and inhales/exhales.

Instinctively, she lifts her hand to her chest. It lies between her breasts like a wilted flower, absorbing moisture from her evaporating sweat. The pads of her fingers stick to her skin, but she pulls her hand up to her neck, leaving a yellow indentation where her fingers used to be. Her hand strokes downward, smoothing the creases in her neck; downward, crossing the ribs in her tank top, down to the bottom of her shirt. She reaches four fingers under, resting her thumb on top of the red cotton knit fabric. She draws spirals around her belly button with the uneven nail of her forefinger. The spiral forms a loop around her navel ring. She tugs.

It's heat wave hot, but she doesn't roll down the windows. She just keeps inhaling/exhaling her available stock of air. Feeling the heat of her own breath cross her bottom lip is like tasting the heat of her flesh. Sweat builds at the rim of her hairline and in the cleft of her upper lip, but she can't lift her hand to wipe it away.

She doesn't want to distract herself, but she opens her eyes long enough to look around and wonder if anyone can see her. If they could, would she mind? Feeling safe from exposure, she lays her head back, closes her eyes, and allows her thighs to sink into the synthetic fibers of her zebra-print seat covers.

Belly button: right above the round of her belly. Her hand fondles the button of her 501s, slips the cool metal through the denim slit. She pulls the flat metal zipper down between her fingers to expose/to release her black burgundy wine passion flower.

Sweat trickles between dark crevices. It mixes with the scent of African violet body oil in her pits and behind her knees. The fragrance hovers in the car cabin like the aftertaste of black coffee clinging in her mouth. Inhale.

She slowly lifts the weight of her eyelashes. A glimpse of the bright buttercup sun burns her eyes: close.

Fingers tiptoe down, curl around the spiraling vines of her engorged bud. Lift. Push. Squeeze. The bud grows, darkens, and blooms with the rhythmic swirling of fingers pressed against it. Her pelvis pushes forward on the seat and her thighs roll apart like the walk of a tumbleweed. Fingers swirl faster like the quick wrist strokes of blending creamy chocolate cake mix. Fingers slip between the ravines of the vulva; they slip inside like tongue slips into mouth.

Inhale/exhale/inhale/exhale/swirling/pulsing/throbbing/coming.

And she comes behind the shadow of closed lids flashing pink-purple-blue psychedelic circles. This ecstasy is like the slow flow of honey from a fallen jar. Lips slide and stick. Exhale.

She rolls down the window; warm, dry air rushes in. It cools the sweat caught in her brow. She looks into the rearview mirror. The buttercup sun stares.

# Las Rockeras
# Warm Up — Con Swing!

## by Maria Santiago

Sara was all nerves. This was one of the biggest concerts they had ever been asked to do, and now they were going to be late. She drove as fast as she could, given the conditions, which included a sudden tropical rainstorm, threadbare tires on the '71 Renault, and headlights that wouldn't work unless Teresa held the two little exposed engine wires in contact with each other.

"*Cuídate*, Sarita! There's a kid crossing the street up ahead. Slow down!" Without looking up, Teresa thrust her left hand out and, as she often did, tapped the horn on the steering wheel — the prototypical backseat driver, though sitting in front. "Slow down, *mi'jita*, we're not *really* late! You know how things go: they say get here at such and such a time, but they only say that 'cause they think that if they don't tell us to get there early, we'll get there late." It sounded complicated, but Sara understood perfectly.

"Teresa, hold those damned wires together, will you? Our lights just went off. Leave the driving to me and just keep the lights on!" Sara scolded. "Anyway, they're right. If they didn't tell us to get there earlier than we need to, we *would* get there late!" She was trying to relax, but every time they had a gig, Teresa would mess around until it was almost time to go. And then she would decide she had to wash her hair — a major task, given its length — or she'd realize she had no stockings without holes to wear with her black micro-miniskirt, or she would rummage through the clothes closet complaining that she didn't know what to wear, rejecting each of Sara's suggestions. Sara was a horn player and backup singer, and Teresa's lover. The band was Teresa's, and she was Cuba's most popular *rockera*, or rock musician.

Sara had grown up in New York City, but two years ago she had been persuaded to move in with her mother's family in Havana to "find her roots." The project had appealed to her then — and appealed even more so now that she'd found Teresa. But she never expected to play her beloved rock music here: she knew Cubans loved their salsa and other homegrown music, and she had also heard that the Cuban government discouraged people from listening to or playing "Yankee" music, especially rock, that long-haired hippie capitalist music that continued to overrun the world. But things had changed in Cuba during the 1980s, and though there was still a lot of antirock discrimination, both subtle and overt, Cuban kids were listening to rock on the radio, watching MTV International, and introducing rock to their parents, teachers, and peers.

Always an individualist, Teresa was one *Cubana* musician who had never even wanted to write or sing anything *except* rock, and she had worked hard for years to gather a band that could do justice to her songs. Now she was succeeding beyond her wildest expectations. Sara was the final prize, as far as Teresa was concerned. In Sara she had found a lover *and* an *Americana* rock sax player! During the band's year-old existence, the press had become surprisingly enthusiastic in its reviews, and they loved to interview the exotic Teresa. However, the one thing they were careful never to ask her was why, at age twenty-seven, she was not married. They didn't want an answer to that question.

Earlier tonight, Teresa had changed her top three times and then tried on several pairs of boots and sneakers. Finally, she had picked up the black leather boots and announced that she supposed they would do. Sara was still in *gringa* mode; after almost two years in Havana, she was still learning to relax and go with the flow of this tropical Latin culture. Few of the island's citizens seemed to have a sensible sense of time. *Well,* she thought, *I'll just have to keep working on being as mellow as Teresa and everyone else. Shit. The audience never expects a show to go on until at least half an hour after it's scheduled.* She sighed and turned into the parking area behind the theater.

As they tumbled out of the car, Teresa grabbed Sara's sax case, along with her own bag, which was stuffed with makeup, silver-studded leather wristlets, work papers for the band, her stockings and hairbrush, a tambourine, and who knew what else. Analise, the theater manager, and José, the stage manager, met them at the stage door, trying to hurry them without seeming to. "Your band is on stage doing the final sound check, Teresa. Do you need to check your microphone levels?" Analise murmured with an anxious smile.

"I'm sorry we're a little late. The car wouldn't start," Teresa lied smoothly. She smiled sweetly at Analise. "I don't need to check my mike. We did a lot of adjusting this afternoon at the rehearsal. Just tell Ramon, my guitarist, to check it. He knows what it should sound like."

José sighed loudly. "We've been holding the audience in the lobby, but we'll have to start letting them in soon, Teresa! It's almost eight o'clock and the crowd is too big to stay out there much longer. Can you be ready in fifteen minutes?"

"Sure. Let me just put my things on. Let's go, Sara, help me out, okay?" Teresa answered, and all of them knew that fifteen minutes would be more like half an hour. As they reached the dressing room and walked in, Teresa assured Analise that they wouldn't need anything and closed the door politely.

Sara had dressed for the show at home, and now began unpacking her saxophone, wetting the reed, and putting the horn together. Teresa tore off her jeans and pulled on her black panty hose and then her micro-mini. She slipped on her boots and found her leather wristlets in the bag. "I hardly have time to put on my makeup," Teresa grumbled as she began hurriedly to apply it.

"Yeah, and I don't have time to warm up," Sara responded angrily. "And whose fault is it? I was sitting there waiting for you, *como usual*, Teresita."

Teresa brushed her hair and didn't answer. She was pretty good at avoiding fights. Unlike Sara, Teresa hardly ever needed to have the last word. Her tactic was to win an argument by stoic silence. Sara watched Teresa brush her long, beautiful hair, which she normally just tied at the back of her neck, and then stand up and adjust the micro-mini over her ass, pulling it down as far as she could — which was only about three inches below her butt. Sara always felt a surge of desire when she looked at Teresa before a concert, even in this most femme of outfits, which Teresa called her "drag."

Teresa put on her wide black belt with the silver chains at the front, adjusted her blouse, and stared at herself in the mirror. She stretched her mouth wide, doing her vocal warm-ups during this last-minute fixing. Her voice held the low notes with a rich huskiness that Sara so loved. "How do I look, Sara?" Teresa frowned at herself in the mirror, always critical of her appearance just before a show.

"You look great, as usual. Let's go," Sara replied shortly, turning her back, suddenly angry again.

Teresa walked over to her. She grabbed Sara's shoulders and pulled her backward until Sara was leaning into her, then murmured in her ear, "*Discúlpame* — excuse me, love. You look beautiful, too — as usual." Sara didn't respond.

"You *do* have time to warm up, you know," Teresa continued, her head next to Sara's. "And I'm going to warm you up right now. Then, you will perform your sax solos *con swing*, like always. Swing, that quintessential American musical concept of "hot" combined with "cool," had occupied a treasured place in Cuban youths' hearts for years now; it was used to express more than just a musical feel: it was a way of facing life.

Teresa grinned, and reaching her arms around Sara, hugged her hard for a moment. Then, placing her hands possessively over Sara's breasts, she began to play with Sara's nipples and kiss her earlobe. Before Sara could break away, Teresa slid her tongue into Sara's ear and began to puff out warm, tiny breaths.

Sara turned around to face Teresa, pushing Teresa's hands off her, trying to disengage. "You're completely crazy, Teresa! They're going to come in here any second! *Déjalo!* Do you want to get us into more trouble than we can handle? Stop it!" she whispered urgently, trying not to laugh. But Teresa continued pressing her body against Sara's, pushing her up against the wall opposite the door.

"I'm going to warm you up, love, *relájate!* Relax! No one's going to come in; they'll at least knock first," she whispered as she took a handful of Sara's hair in her long, slim fingers and pinned her head against the wall. She leaned in to kiss Sara.

Sara squirmed. "You are too much, you crazy hunk! I'm going to get you back later!" Sara grabbed at Teresa's crotch, and Teresa jumped back, alarmed at this turn of events. But then she smiled wickedly and, leaning close, whispered into her lover's ear, "*Chica*, lucky I noticed this: your bra strap is twisted!" Sara frowned in concern and reached back to fix it. "No, wait," commanded Teresa. "I'm going to fix it myself. Don't touch!"

"Bully! Leave your hands off me!" Sara laughed again and tried to move away. But Teresa moved in quickly and pushed Sara's backside into the makeup table next to them. At the same time, she grabbed Sara's wrists and held them in front of her with one hand, using the other to swiftly pull Sara's pink tank top out of her pants. Reaching underneath, Teresa hooked the bra clasp in her fingers and snapped it open, all in a flash. Sara felt her breasts swing free and the bra hang loose under her top.

"Oh! *Coño, chica, no!* Not now, Teresa, not now!" Sara hissed. They struggled fiercely but silently until Sara found herself on her back on the makeup table, her legs dangling over the edge. Teresa, still grasping Sara's wrists, pushed Sara's arms over her head and slid her hand under Sara's top. Teresa lowered her face, and her lips pressed down on Sara's. Sara opened her mouth and Teresa's tongue slid in.

Suddenly Sara opened her eyes and twisted her face to the side. "Teresa, that woman — Analise? You're insane! *Chica,* someone is going to walk in *en ese momento!* Stop! Please, Teresa!" Teresa grinned down at Sara and put a finger to her lips.

"*Mi amor, te deseo!*" Teresa demanded ardently.

"I don't care if you want me, this is dangerous!" Sara struggled to get up, in a panic now.

"Sara, *yá no me jodas!* Forget about the *jodeado* door! Lie down!" Teresa demanded, and moved her hand over Sara's breast again, kneading her nipple between her thumb and middle finger, sending shivers up Sara's spine.

"Don't curse at me, Teresa! Someone's going to walk in and I for one—" Sara began, but Teresa's mouth stopped her right there and Sara gave up.

Teresa moved her hand over her lover's body and unsnapped the top of her jeans, then unzipped them. Sara felt her legs begin to tremble. Teresa's hand kept moving until Sara felt it inside her panties, the fingers resting between her cunt lips, the middle finger just inside her inner lips. She sucked on Teresa's tongue to keep from moaning out loud. Then Teresa's long middle finger pressed up into Sara, and everything between Sara's legs felt really wet, wet and warm and achy. As Teresa began thrusting her finger in and out of Sara's cunt, she continued holding Sara's wrists together and kept her tongue in her lover's mouth. She added another finger, and then a third. She fucked her, hard. Sara's hips began to rock on the makeup table.

"*Sera, mi amor!* Wait a minute," Teresa whispered, lifting her head up and releasing her lover's wrists. Teresa grabbed Sara's shoulder and pulled her body a few inches closer so more of her ass was off the counter. At the same time, she drew her fingers from Sara's cunt and moved her leg into Sara's crotch. Sara groaned, partly disappointed that the fingers were no longer inside her, but also excited by Teresa's muscular thigh pressing into her crotch. For a moment she wondered, *What the hell are we doing?* But her thoughts flew away after that.

"*Mi vida,*" Teresa whispered, leaning her mouth close to Sara's ear, "put your arms around me! Let's really make love! *Te deseo, te quiero.*" She continued whispering all kinds of things into Sara's ear until Sara's arms came up around Teresa's shoulders.

As Teresa's leg pressed rhythmically into Sara's cunt, Sara realized that Teresa hadn't actually taken her fingers away, but had only moved them. One finger was pressing fiercely, sweetly, on her clit. Sara was melting fast. She began to moan, trying not to let too much of the sound out. But she felt her orgasm beginning to build and she began holding her breath, in order not to scream out loud. Her knees began to straighten and the trembling in her thighs weakened her ability to resist anything.

Teresa had been alternately stroking Sara's hair and her cheeks with her free hand while they kissed. Now she moved her hand down and stroked her lover's breasts. Then, reaching around Sara's body and under her ass, she pulled Sara's pelvis tight against her own pubic bone, causing her finger to press even harder on Sara's clit, in just the right spot. The combination of sensations below her waist was finally too much for Sara and she exploded, arching her body into Teresa's. The flush on her face felt like fire, and Sara turned her head so she could gasp in more air. Teresa watched her from three inches above, and when Sara opened her eyes, she found herself staring into Teresa's mischievous grin.

"You warmed up enough now, love?"

Sara was about to reply when they heard a sound at the door. Sara bolted upright, gasping in fear. The doorknob rattled as it turned — then encountered the lock Teresa had secretly secured when they had entered the dressing room. As Sara looked at Teresa smiling over her, she swore silently to find an appropriate payback!

They heard Analise's voice, "Teresa! It's late! Do you need anything else in there? Can we go on now?" Her voice was plaintive. Sara peeked at her watch. Only thirty minutes had passed since they had come in! *This is a record, for sure,* Sara thought, smiling fiercely at Teresa.

"We're coming right now, Analise," Teresa called out. She reached behind Sara and fastened her bra, then helped her tuck everything back in and zip up her jeans. Sara's face was still flushed and warm. She looked at Teresa and saw that under her makeup Teresa was also flushed. Beads of sweat stood out on both their foreheads.

"I'm warmed up pretty good, Teresa, and how about you? How'd you ever think up this new warm-up exercise, anyway?" Sara joked as she picked up her horn.

"*Querida*, you inspire me to new heights of creativity. But I think that maybe this particular warm-up is a bit too strenuous to do right before a show. Maybe we should save it for before rehearsals or something." Teresa laughed as she smoothed out her clothes and gave herself a last glance in the mirror. She caressed Sara's shoulder and quickly kissed her on the tip of her nose. "Don't be mad at me about the door, lover!" she murmured as she opened it. "Come on, let's swing!"

They walked out and were led to the stage, where the rest of the band greeted them with great relief, but softly, since the audience, behind the curtain, was only a few feet away. Teresa walked over to stand in the wings so she could make her entrance after the band played the first song's intro.

"We thought maybe you had trouble with that old tin can of a car you have," Ramon whispered to Sara in the last moment before the curtain opened.

"Naw, Teresa just thought we both needed to do some extra warm-up exercises, and she got really involved. I kept telling her we'd be late, but she wouldn't listen. You know Teresa," Sara added in a whisper, and winked at her bandmate. Then they got the cue to begin the first song and there was no more time for talking.

# Locks and Keys

## by Tristan Taormino

I heard a scuffle of feet and some muffled voices, then the screaming in the next room stopped. Everything was quiet as I waited for the nurse to make his hourly rounds. When the door to my room creaked open, a flashlight glared in my face and I pretended to be asleep. I felt anxious and restless: exhausted from endless therapy groups full of the shared retelling of horror stories; frustrated by my overworked social worker, clueless shrink, and sleazy art therapist; and terrified of my intense emerging desire for Rob.

I could only imagine what brought her here. Me, I needed a safe place to be. With its richly colored mahogany furniture, wallpaper dotted with framed prints of old-fashioned drawings and maps, and plush pale gray carpet, the place looked more like a law firm than a hospital. I think it was because nothing was white; none of the furniture, sheets, towels, or clothes anyone who worked there ever wore were white. It could almost have been some kind of a dorm, with people walking through the halls all the time, except the people were all in a daze of some sort or another. Oh, and the doors to the outside world were locked, and none of us had keys.

When I first got here, they confiscated my sex life — copies of what the fortyish woman wearing a light green silk sweater called "sexually explicit material" — along with my razors, my vitamins, and the shoelaces from my Doc Martens. "Procedure," she said. Then she led me down a short, curved hallway to an empty, stuffy room that felt like a cross between my dorm room in college and a room at the Comfort Inn: two beds, two dressers, a private bathroom; everything painted mauve. She left me alone to "get situated." As I wandered through the overheated room into the bathroom to unpack what was left of my stuff, I caught sight of myself in the mirror. I brushed back the wisps of light brown hair that had slipped out of my ponytail into my face. My black roll-neck sweater brought out the shadows under my tired eyes, which looked gray instead of dark blue against my pale skin. As I lifted my sweater over my head, I felt a presence behind me in the room. I knew it wasn't the nurse, so I looked up into the mirror abruptly. The words, "Hi. I'm Robbie, your ... roommate," came from the lips of a tall, twentyish woman with a solid build and very short black hair. I was stunned into silence. Unwittingly, they had put me in a room with another dyke. I was feeling better already.

"Hi, I'm Allison," I said as I turned to face her.

"What are you in here for?" she asked directly.

"What?" I returned.

"You know, what are you in here for? That's the big icebreaker question around here. When John's girlfriend broke up with him, he just freaked, plus he's a major coke addict; Shirley's tried to commit suicide like twelve times; Bob is mildly schizophrenic, but I get along with him fine; Toshi is manic-depressive and has uncontrolled rage; Ellen has chronic depression; Phillip is suicidal; that chick Jane is just a mess." I looked at her, puzzled. "Sorry. I've just been here awhile and I know everyone's shit. They're all really more than that. And you?"

"What about you?" I asked, feeling bold.

Suddenly, she just shut down. I fixated momentarily on the matching thick, reddish scars on her wrists. The right healed incision was longer, darker, and looked more painful, though they both looked like they still hurt her. They looked familiar. Her body, which at first had appeared strong, now seemed to sag under some invisible weight. The little glint in her green eyes that had sparkled at me when she was playing the new neighbor had just gotten snuffed out. Her eyes left mine and focused on the mauve carpet.

"Oh, you know, long story, I..." Her voice drifted off.

I had clearly made the wrong move, and I sincerely regretted it. I searched for a way to bring her back to me, but the nurse in the green sweater returned, announcing, "Robin and Allison, it's time for group," and I followed Robbie out of the room. I then discovered that the curved hallway was actually circular; no matter how far I walked, I would only come back to the same place. I couldn't escape from anything.

People were sitting in a circle on the mahogany and gray print fabric couches. I tried quickly to figure out who was who according to Robbie's quick list. Little by little, everyone talked. Each had a story more disturbing than the last. Shirley's dad molested her for years, and now her husband had been beating her up for years. Toshi had this crazy family and a really unstable home life. John just cried a lot and got a massive nosebleed in the middle of his hysterics. Jane seemed learning disabled and heavily drugged on top of that. Bob began believing that the Devil was talking to him when he was sixteen. Ellen had been in and out of hospitals for twenty years and was ranting about her psychiatrist changing or not changing her meds again. I felt out of place and nervous; I just wanted to go back to my room, curl up with a pillow, and cry. But I was sharp enough to know that a mental institution is the *last* place on earth where you can act crazy, weird, or antisocial. Besides, I wanted to make a good impression, so I revealed a little: my ongoing struggle with chronic depression, my panic attacks and suicide attempts, my new sudden withdrawal. I felt more comfortable talking about my symptoms than about everything in my life that made me feel them. I wasn't ready to hash out my obsessive drive toward overachievement, my fucked-up eating habits, the terror of losing my father to AIDS, or my overwhelming feeling of being lost. Talking to them seemed strange; they were all on medication, from Prozac to Lithium. I felt like the sober designated driver at a weird Christmas party. When I listened to all my problems in my head, they sounded like the laundry list that Robbie had recited earlier or the plot of a bad TV movie that I would watch for the morbid thrill of it.

Robbie said nothing. I knew she had tried — maybe more than once — to kill herself, to tear herself open and let her blood flow, escape. I also knew that she too had a story. It could have been anything, but I was sure someone had fucked with her and really hurt her when she was young. She had a way of playing with her hair that instantly transformed her from a tough butch dyke to a small, scared tomboy. She sat and listened intently, all the while staring at me with her wicked yet strangely soothing green eyes, sending waves of warmth through my body. But when I looked into those eyes, I couldn't see her spirit, only a faraway passion; I didn't know what coursed through her veins and kept her alive. Whatever it was, it was trapped, along with all her feelings, way down deep in some tender spot where no one searched, where no one even ventured. She could not open up to these strangers, and she wouldn't cry in front of them. Her distant mystery attracted me right away; I longed to seduce the desires simmering below the surface of her skin. Yes, there were walls between us, but I could swear that her eyes were beckoning, "Come to me."

The creak of my bedroom door, the jingle of keys, and the bright glare roused me a little from my dream. The hourly flash of false daylight shined from the end of the nurse's arm directly into my face; then it was gone again. And I was alone, dying to touch myself. I could hear the object of my dream — which was really part memory, part fantasy — breathing in the bed next to mine. She certainly was a quiet flirt, never letting her guard down, never revealing too much of anything, leaving me — and my mouth — always wide open. I moved my hand down below the stiff blanket and reached under my satin panties. I slid my middle finger through my swollen cunt lips in one slick upward motion. I was dripping. For months, I had been so consumed by a very dark place, so emotionally, physically, and sexually drained, that my dampness startled me for a moment. It was good to feel my body respond to stimulation after so long. I moved my thumb up to my clit and gently swirled around my wetness. As I slid one finger inside my warm cunt, which was beginning to open wider, I began breathing heavier. I wanted more pressure on my clit, so I turned over on my stomach, pushing my ear against the pillow and blocking out all other noise except the sound of my own breathing. I pressed my fingers firmly against my swelling cunt, rubbing in a familiar rhythm I knew in my sleep.

Suddenly, I felt a presence standing over my bed. When I lifted my head off the pillow, I could no longer hear the other breathing in the room. Rob quietly slid into my bed and on top of me. I could feel her soft breasts and firm nipples on my back. Although her naked body was broad and strong, she did not crush me. She kissed the back of my neck gently, then licked my ear. My heart raced and my clit hardened under my slippery fingers. She playfully tugged at my long hair as she lapped at my neck. She reached her arms around my body and pushed my t-shirt up. Her rough hands explored my skin tenderly and cautiously. But when she discovered the metal ring protruding from my now extremely taut nipple, her touch became rougher, less inhibited. I squealed.

"Shhh ... If you're very quiet, I'd like to make you come," she whispered, then she covered my mouth and tugged even harder on my nipple ring.

The pain shot through my chest and directly to my pussy, but I held back the scream inside me.

"Good girl," she said. Her hand moved away from my mouth and down to my other breast. She grabbed both my breasts, digging her nails into my soft flesh, and I moaned as her hips pushed into my ass.

She moved her lips from my neck to a patch of sensitive skin between my shoulder blades and voraciously took it between her teeth. As she bit down, her hips pressed harder into me. I felt her hand travel downward to explore my ass. She lubed her fingers with my cunt juices and rubbed the opening of my asshole, darting halfway in and then out again. Grabbing at the pillow, I struggled to get out from under her and turn over. I wanted to beg her to hold me down and fuck me to death.

My movement startled her, and she paused and pulled back for a moment. "Are you scared, or do you want to wrestle?" she asked, kind of shyly.

"Neither," I said. I flipped over on my back, spread my legs, then shoved my middle finger deep inside my hungry pussy and pushed it directly into her open mouth. I was hoping she got the picture. The next thing I knew, she pulled a small plastic bag from under my bed and drew out a latex glove and a squished tube of KY.

"Where did those come from?"

"The hospital — I snuck them in for just such an occasion..." Coyly, she grinned — I think for the first time since I had met her — and snapped on the rubber glove. She squeezed a blob of clear jelly into her gloved hand and then paused seriously.

"Are you sure about this? I mean is this okay...?"

"I'm sure," I said, and I reached up and kissed her hard. She pushed my shoulders firmly back down, and I spread my legs as my head fell back on the pillow.

She moved her hands up my legs until she reached my swollen pussy. She tugged at my pubic mound and teased my clit with her fingernail. She carefully slid a finger inside my soaking wetness. She pushed in and pulled out slowly, then quickened her pace, adding a second finger. My hips rocked with her plungings as her thumb pressed hard on my even harder clit. Her tongue slid into my mouth as her fingers slid farther into my cunt. I bent my knees and opened my legs as wide as I could for her. She liked that, and pushed more fingers up my warm, dripping insides. I was full of ecstatic pleasure from her strong, fierce hand, a hand that was attached to her wrist with scars of pain. Her hands had touched too many things they did not desire; they had absorbed her past and been marked. They liked where they were now, though: one hand searched and grasped for a path deep inside me, while the other pulled at my nipple ring. She kissed the side of my face, and I could feel her breathing in my ear. I held her face in my hands and kissed her fervently, begging her with my mouth and my tongue and my teeth to fill me up. I ran my hands down the length of her back, clawing at her soft, wet flesh. Her hand moved diligently and delicately way inside me, drawing out from my depths slippery juices and quietly uninhibited moans. My hips moved in rhythm with her hand's motion as I came closer and closer.

This was not how I imagined our encounter would be, not how it played itself out in my head at night. The locks keeping in her desire were always clearly visible to me, as obvious as the circular hallway outside our bedroom door. But the keys to unlock her mysteries — they were harder to find. I wanted so much to touch her, to arouse a wetness from between her firm legs and awaken the same potent feelings she had drawn out of me. She needed to be touched, to be healed a little, to feel the tingle of pleasure between her legs that my mouth and hands could give her.

But instead, she was giving herself to me in a way I hadn't expected. She trusted me enough to put her painful past inside me. I wanted her to pull mine out. I closed my eyes tightly, holding in the terror of this huge orgasm she was leading me to. I was panting, writhing, letting her hand consume me for the moment, focusing on the way she stretched and filled me. Her coarse knuckles curled inside my wanting body until my starved cunt clenched around her fist, groping tightly. I came hard, fast, scared, alive. As Rob buried her face in mine, tears filled my eyes, ran down her smooth cheeks, and wandered down my neck. I opened my eyes and kissed her ears, gently licking the tears. "Thank you," I whispered. She laughed quietly, and I thought I saw a spark of light, like a sudden metallic flash at the curved edge of a dull and tarnished key. Just for a moment, the key was in my grasp.

# The Arroyo

## by Ronna Magy

We have always lived in the house down by the arroyo, as long as I can remember, in the place where the earth opens and water flows out onto the sand. Why was our house in El Casco built down near the place where the earth opens, you ask? The answer is simple. When my grandmother and her friends needed to wash clothes, they found water in the arroyo. They had no big river like in Rodeo, no river, no electricity, no washing machines. The women of our town found places where water came up from under the ground, and there they washed clothes. Now, as I look out my back window, I see their granddaughters, my friends Alta, Berta, Sonia, and Luisa, and their great-granddaughters bending over to scrub the clothes, pound them on rocks and recount the stories of the valley.

Some in my town say I who am an old woman, I whose hair is now gray and wild, was born of the long arroyo that stretches in back of my grandmother's house and I am part of that land. The arroyo meanders from narrow to wide to narrow like my mother's mouth, like a woman's womb, full and arched at the center, softened at both ends where water recedes and the land returns to itself. My mother said that on the day I was born, when her strength returned and the moon was full, she dripped the blood from the afterbirth down the banks of the arroyo and buried the sac that carried me there, deep in the earth. When the dry earth had been quenched with her blood and my blood, the arroyo opened larger, the way a woman's womb opens in the heat of love, and water poured up from under the ground into the hole and it was no longer dry.

The earth of that arroyo melded with blood from my core in a time when I didn't yet know I had memory, when my blood and my mother's were still unmingling. Inside that great cauldron of the valley, my mother's blood, the blood of my grandmothers, and mine were swirled by the winds that blow until only the truest elements remained, the black of iron and the red of copper. With our blood mixed under the earth, nothing could endanger the women of our family. *Mi abuela* told me we would always be safe from danger. The arroyo has sustained me with earth and water all my life, the way it has all the women of my mother's family. The arroyo and I have fed each other in the long slow way one comes to know a woman's body, from the first single caress at the back of the neck to the touch of a tongue inside the folds of the womb. When water flows up over the arroyo, it washes through El Casco, cleansing the land.

During fiestas we remember the dark time long ago when the land exploded in flame and what was old was transformed into what was new. A night when fire rode on torches through the town and dust filled the air. Down from the Sierras, across the rain-filled arroyos, down into the valley of El Casco, through the quiet night, the *revolutionarios* came, shouting, "*¡Viva Pancho Villa! ¡Viva la revolución!*" They carried young men off on the backs of red horses with flying tails and dust on their hooves. Cries of mothers filled the night as women stretched their arms to the heavens, imploring *La Llorona*, the childless night goddess, to give back their sons, but it was too late. The gray smell of smoke crept under every door, through the dusty streets, swirling after the horse riders. *Haciendas* of the *patrónes y tantos años de opresión* burned beneath the torches. Fiery flames licked the dark night the way green cornstalks cut into blue skies on summer days. Then, the flying horse riders swept back across the waters of the arroyos and south to San Juan del Rio and Durango.

The sun that next morning shone on homeless *campesinos*, my grandfather and his friends, searching for remnants of former lives. In the season when the beans began to send green shoots upwards, the farmers of El Casco divided what was left of the *haciendas*. Scavenging amongst old pieces of the *patrón's* house, they retrieved brick made by their fathers and formed new ones of mud and straw. Shouting, "*¡Tierra y libertad!*" their words echoed from brick to brick as they remade the houses and reclaimed the land.

Remnants survive today from the fire storm: old bricks, the old church wall, a bell that tolled for the Spanish *conquistadores*. That bell rings on Sunday mornings, when the night sand of the arroyo still closes our eyes and the sun has barely moved to replace the moon across the sky.

It is a part of the *patrón's* house we live in. High ceilings made from aging timbers point upwards to motionless white clouds. Bricks of brown mud and yellow wheat stalks, baked in the same sun since the revolution, form the walls. The bricks blister like tortillas cooked over an open fire, like the earth, cracked when the sun has been too long overhead, awaiting the rains of mid-June. Outside this window my grandmother sat making corn tortillas over the fire, and down by those rocks she washed clothes. In the fields my grandfather planted corn and beans and turned the soil between seasons of growing. My father, Arturo, grew up inside these walls, sat on that chair and ate the *masa* fed him with the old wooden spoon. He brought my mother, Dulce, to this house, and this is where I was born, on this side of the wall.

When I, Ana, was not more than a child, a girl playing with dolls made from cloth and corn husks with crosses for eyes, I played with Carolina, my friend who lived on the other side of the wall. Our *hacienda*, our house, our rooms, connected and divided by the same bricks. Carolina was taller than me and ran like a light breeze in summer, long hair and dark eyes shooting sparks back to the sun. I was older, a child of night enchanted by the perfume of jasmine, remaining in dreams of stars, moons, and planets far beyond waking.

In the morning on school days, my mother braided my curly hair, weaving the plaits straight as one does the heavy hairs on horse tails. By noon, the hair found its way free down my back, struggling out like a new plant searching for light and air at the surface. At school, Carolina and I sat next to each other, shared tortillas and beans and the stories of El Casco: a *serenata* under the window of Guadalupe Cruz when Javier Ortega sang the most beautiful of *corridas*, a love between married Estella Ramos and Oswaldo the bus driver. After school, Carolina and I ran the dusty streets playing *al escondido*, hiding and looking behind doors and high cactus for each other until we reached the *kioska* in the plaza, where my sister, Sylvia, went on Sundays and walked in a circle of young girls waiting for flowers in the hands of young men.

Carolina and I were the best of friends. We told each other the secrets of girls and laughed at old men snoring in the plaza. We carried each other's books as we walked and sometimes we held hands. Perhaps we were always more than friends.

One time my father drove our family and Carolina's to *el carnaval* in Jalisco in his truck. "Let's go! Let's go! Don't you want to go?" Carolina

jumped up and down, pulling on everyone's arms until excitement overtook her body. When her face turned the red of a matador's cape, her
mother plied a wet cloth to her forehead, saying, "*Cálmate, m'hija.* Wait
until we are there."

At *el carnaval*, a *torero* in his *charro* suit waved the red cape in front of the
bulls, and Carolina and I imagined flying off to faraway lands. "We'll go
to Spain," Carolina said, "where women dance in red silk dresses and wear
black lace *mantillas.*" And I, too, dreamed of arching my back to the *fla-
menco, castañuelas* between my fingers, the sound of music filling my soul.
My heart beat faster when *las charras* paraded on horses dancing and bowing in the ring and the audience shouted, "*¡Bravo! ¡Bravo!*" We clapped and
clapped until tears came. Sweet *chocolate* filled our throats and *ranchera*
music from *los tamborasos* filled our ears, making the feet on the ends of our
legs dance. Our arms laced round each other's necks.

For days after *el carnaval*, Carolina and I played *torero* and bull outside on
the patio, one of us fluttering a flowered tablecloth in the air, the other
charging. We played until we were tired and then, exhausted, we sat on
the rocks by the arroyo, leaning on one another as we dipped our toes in
its waters.

My mother, Dulce, told me that when she first saw my father, the dust
still flew off horses' hooves. My father had ridden six hours to a dance in
San Luis del Cordero. Young women stood in a dark corner on one side
of the church under the dim light of kerosene lamps. Young men shuffled
their feet across the room, hands in their pockets. For a while, only
shadows danced on the walls. My mother could barely see the eyes to
which my father's face, straight hair, and body connected. His silver-toed
boots glistened in the light and his mouth smiled at her from under his
hat. Looking into her eyes, his voice asked, "Would you like to dance,
*señorita?*" She shyly said, "Yes," and they danced *un bolero*, moving back and
forth under the old lamps.

Her friend Mercedes whispered to her, "He likes you." And my mother said, "Are you sure?" Mercedes nodded. After that he rode to her on
weekends in jeans and cowboy boots. You could see them dancing until
the floorboards wore thin under their feet and the music of the dance was
one with their souls. When friends saw them walking, long after the
dance, music still played in their hearts and their feet took up a rhythm
only the two of them knew.

Riding to San Luis on horseback with compliments and gifts in hand, my father's uncle and a friend spoke for my father to my mother's parents. The couple was married in San Luis, my father bringing my mother back to our church for a reception in the courtyard next to the old wall. The old bell chimed the celebration of the event all over the valley.

When I was a child, my mother and I sat in front of the fire at night mending my father's brown pants and work shirts, patching the knees and worn elbows. My mother told me of stealing kisses with him down by the arroyo, away from the eyes of her parents, as the moon rose. Their fingers laced together as they kissed in the darkening light of the evening sky. A moment in time long after the arroyo had been formed, it was still before I was born.

On hot summer evenings Carolina and I met secretly outside to smell the perfume of night jasmine and gaze at the heavens. Around us were the sounds of horses and the low growling noises of dogs. We giggled as girls do, pointing up at stars shooting across the sky, watching their magic twinkle fall on the glistening watery surface, dark shadows against darker water.

Our mothers warned us about *La Llorona*, the woman spirit who waited by el río Guadalupe to replace her dead children's souls with those of the children of Abasolo and El Casco. The mothers of our town told children not to go outside after dark, but we didn't listen, for the sparkling waters of the arroyo drew us out to her. Walking to the water's edge, we marveled at our reflections, tossing small stones into the water.

A cry in the night from the coyote against the silence, a noise in the sand behind us, and our minds filled with dread. Another noise in the bushes and our arms clutched each other's waists. A large rattler slid in and out through the sand near us, and then moved on. Carolina sighed and I heard her relax. "I was so scared!" she said. "Me, too!" Our hearts were pounding. We both giggled, standing at the water's edge. "What if *La Llorona* had come to take us?" she asked. I answered, remembering *mi abuela's* stories, "As long as women's blood is mixed in this earth, she cannot have us," I said.

We stood listening to the sounds of our breaths, chests rising and falling, arms encircling waists, legs touching, as the fear died away. A warm sensation rose in my body; the stolen kisses of my mother and father at the arroyo flooded my memory. I kissed Carolina, felt her mouth on mine. Her lips held the flavor of sweet chocolate. We kissed again and held each other's faces and hands until darkness took away our vision and we could no longer see. Our caresses were magic, the touches of daughters become women. Her skin felt of carnation petals and rose flowers.

For many nights after that, we waited for our parents to fall asleep, then went outside, snuck across the patio, and met down by the arroyo, the mother who had protected us from *La Llorona* and brought us to each other. There, rubbing our soles along the hard granite rocks, we pressed our bodies together, breasts and stomachs and legs touching. There was the caress of hands and the softness of lips, loving moments when there was no knowing of time.

Now, in my bed on Sunday mornings, grains of sand in the sheets take me back. I remember Carolina, the softness of her tongue on my lips, her hand caressing my breasts. In that churchyard, I watched her long wavy hair and bright brown eyes the color of a horse's saddle. Carolina, oldest daughter of five, whose mouth was soft against mine and whose slender feet were the size of my own. Sitting next to me at mass, she kicked her feet against the pews and both of us giggled. Down at the arroyo I knew the feel of her body under my hands.

I remember a later time when Carolina and I ate together down by the arroyo. We spread our food on a coarse tablecloth she'd sewn, the stitches forming pink and red flowers on the fabric, red dust and sand weaving itself into the fibers. A few summers had passed and our breasts had swelled the way carnation buds become full and push up just before opening. Now, both of us squatted, bleeding into the brown sand, a connection between us and the earth. We fed each other sections of orange, licking the juice as it dripped down the sides of each other's mouths until nothing more than a damp sweetness remained between our lips. Her kisses then were soft and sticky on my lips, like the silk tassels of new corn. Her hair held the sweet smell of the earth after summer rains. My mouth found its way down from her lips to her soft breasts to the sweet brown of her nipples, and I sucked on her the way I had on my mother, resting in that softness until the sun was low.

In the year of the big drought, when no rain had fallen for months and the land became grooved like old skin, Carolina and her older brother, Miguel, moved away from me, away from the arroyo of El Casco, away from the land that drew us to one another. She went to the city, to

Durango, to live a new life with her *madrina*, Señora Petra. The old blue
pickup truck was piled with her things, things I'd known all those years.
Like a cornstalk uprooted before its time, she was pulled from our love.
She learned to work in her *madrina's* stall at the *mercado*, a table with poles
draped with fabric walls. Carolina sold oranges, bananas, and apples, and
made a little money to send back to her parents in El Casco. I remember
the moment when our arms wrapped round each other, and her sad smile.
She did not want to go to the city; her heart was here. I could not pre-
vent her from leaving, could not stop her tears.

I visited her there once a few years later. It was after she and her
brother had saved enough to move her family to the city. We walked
through the market sampling food and talking of El Casco. I told her of
the seasons of planting and the love stories of our town, of the arroyo and
how it had swollen with the rains. She talked of the cost of fruit, showing
me the best and most expensive, told me of the merchants and what sold
for the highest prices in the stalls. She became a child of Durango, a child
of markets who talked of money and sales in a way that separated the
apples from the trees, a child whose dreams became displaced by glam-
orous voices and city rhythms. I knew her then, but then again, I did not.
Her time was filled with young women and men of the city; our friendship was not the same. We no longer touched the way we had at the
arroyo. What had been had been.

Now that my hair is long and gray and flies freely in the summer
breeze, I tell you these remembrances, these love stories of El Casco. My
mother and father are gone, and many have moved south to Durango or
crossed *la frontera* for *El Norte*. The waters of the arroyo still sustain my
body and the sands mingle between my toes.

When I remember my youth, I still dream of Carolina. For me, there
are the memories. Does she think of me, you ask? Or did she forget me as
lovers forget one another, fading into the moments of time? Did she, after
she moved to Durango and became a woman, remember the earth of El
Casco and the places where the earth opens its lips and floods with the
moisture that comes in a time of passion? Does she smell our love in the
soft kisses of others on nights when sweet blooming jasmine overpowers
her senses and holds her within its arms?

I think she does. I know she does, for when I walk the arroyo each
night sleepless, when the sands shift under my feet and my toes find the

hard granite where we rubbed our feet and touched lips and bodies together as younger women, I feel Carolina is still of that earth. Sometimes I think she is a lost soul wandering out there each night, waiting, whispering, calling me back to the arroyo, the place that witnessed our love.

Parts of young Carolina and I are buried in this earth: our blood, our kisses, our youth. Our spirits float over the night-sparkling waters of the arroyo, calling the young women of El Casco to join us at the place where the earth opens from narrow to wide to narrow and the water flows up and onto the sand, to feel the touch of women and know the depth of women's love.

Today, I look out my back window and hear the voices of Alta, Berta, Sonia, and Luisa. Their sounds carry up from the deep place of the arroyo through the window and into my kitchen as I place the cloth Carolina gave me long ago on the old table made by my grandfather. Smoothing its creases under my hands, a voice inside me notes holes to be sewn and seams to be mended. I trace the remaining red and pink flowers with my fingers, rubbing the frayed edges. I want to preserve and care for it and my memories of Carolina and the arroyo of my youth.

# Me and My Appetite

## by Lesléa Newman

I was sitting with Angie at Dunkin' Donuts taking my time, as neither one of us was in a big hurry to get to work. Angie was having black coffee and an old-fashioned but I was going for broke: a hot chocolate with whipped cream and two mocha-frosteds. Gotta do something to spice up your day when all you have to look forward to is eight hours of sitting in front of a computer terminal with no one saying anything to you except "Don't your eyes kill you, looking at that screen all day?" or "I don't know how you do it with those nails of yours."

Angie and I don't talk much in the morning. It's bad enough to have to be up and dressed before noon; at least Angie understands it would be too much to expect me to be civil about it. We just meet at some dive before work to fortify ourselves and give each other the once over. You need a girlfriend to tell you if your seams are straight, if your earrings match, if your slip is showing.

We finished our donuts and whipped out our compacts and lipsticks in one smooth motion, like a dance. Angie tends toward orange, which you can only get away with if you have beautiful bronze skin like she does. I go more for pinks and reds. We flipped open our compacts with our left hands and swiveled our lipsticks up with our right. As I was outlining my upper lip, I saw Angie's eyes leave her mirror for a split second to glance over my head and then return to her reflection.

She finished doing her mouth, and scraping at a smudge on her chin with her index finger said, "Don't turn around, but we are being admired."

"By who?" I asked, moving my compact a little, like a rearview mirror that needed adjusting.

"By whom," Angie corrected me before rolling her lips inward and pressing them together to even out her lipstick. "By that young man at the counter." She pointed with her eyes.

I lifted my mirror for a better view. Crew cut, leather jacket, white t-shirt. "Christ, he looks all of sixteen," I muttered, patting a dab of powder on my nose. Angie put her works away and swiveled in her seat. "You ready?" she asked, lifting her jacket off the back of her chair.

"Yeah, yeah." I was still fiddling with my face when our not-so-secret admirer turned on his stool to reach for a napkin and there in his profile was just the faintest outline of breasts. I gave a little gasp. Our he was a she.

"Girl, what is so fascinating about your face this morning?" Angie was on her feet, one high heel tapping with impatience. "Are you coming or what?"

"Or what," I said, catching the little butch's eye in my tiny mirror. Her face was openly curious and I gave her a little wink that said, *Hold your horses, baby, I'm coming.*

"Angie." I put my compact down. "Will you please tell Mr. Franklin I have car trouble and I'll be a little late?"

"What?" Angie looked at me and then over my head at the counter for a minute. Angie knows boys don't interest me in the least, so she must have seen what I saw because she sighed and shook her head. "That's the third time this month, Sally," she said, giving me one of her tsk-tsk-tsks. "What do you want to go playing with her for, when you got a good woman waiting for you at home? And besides, Sal, she's jailbait."

"I'll make sure she's of age," I said, like Angie was my mother. "And anyway, Angie, variety is the spice of life and I can't help it if I have a hearty appetite." Angie has never understood this. Hell, a woman who always has a plain donut and black coffee for breakfast can't possibly understand the pleasures of jelly-filled, coconut-dipped, chocolate-frosted, or vanilla creams. Luckily Angie doesn't have to understand. The only one who has to understand is Bonnie, and she understands just fine. Bonnie is a dream come true. She doesn't mind sharing me as long as I follow the rules: not in our house, not in our car, no staying out all night, and no follow-up phone calls or love letters. And most important of all, Bonnie doesn't want to hear about it. Angie thinks we're nuts and she's always throwing me that Paul Newman crap — why go out for hamburger when you've got steak at home — but hey, it's worked for me and Bonnie for thirteen years, so who is Angie to knock it?

"So, what is it this time?" Angie picked her pocketbook up off the table. "Flat tire, muffler problems, fan belt, carburetor..." She counted off the possibilities on her long orange nails that glowed under the florescent lights.

"Umm ... let me think." I tried to remember what I had told Mr. Franklin last time. I really should write this stuff down.

"She's waiting," Angie said, tapping her foot again. "She just got a refill."

"Oh, just tell him I'm waiting for Triple A to come give me a jump start. Everyone knows that can take all day."

"You won't have to wait all day to get jumped, believe me." Angie fluffed out her hair and gave me a little wave. "Don't do anything I wouldn't do."

"Oh c'mon, Angie, I want to have some fun."

*Fuck you*, Angie mouthed. Then she blew me a kiss and was gone.

I lifted my compact and opened it again to check out my affair du jour. I caught her reflection in my mirror and ran my tongue lightly over my lips. Her eyes widened. Then I snapped my compact shut and rose as if I was leaving. I lifted my coat from the back of my chair and folded it over my arms, but instead of walking toward the door I merely lowered my butt onto Angie's still-warm seat, so that now, despite the fact that we were across the entire restaurant from each other, my girl and I were face to face.

"More coffee, miss?" A waitress appeared with a fresh pot.

"No thanks. I will have another donut though."

"What kind?"

I didn't hesitate. "Vanilla cream."

My baby butch was watching me for a sign but I wasn't ready to give it to her yet. The waitress brought my donut over and it looked luscious: two light brown golden cakes joined together with sugary white cream swirled inside and overflowing the top in a tantalizing peak. Even though I'd already had two donuts, this was a challenge worth rising to the occasion for. And like I've already told you, I do not eat like a bird.

Without taking my eye off the girl in the wings, I darted my tongue out and licked the white cream once, and then once again. Through the din of coffee being poured, cash registers ringing, and newspapers rattling, I could swear I heard that butch moan. I dabbed my middle finger into the cream and then put it into my mouth up to my first knuckle, sucking gently and rocking my finger in and out of my mouth ever so slightly. My girl slid off her stool a little and then regained her balance,

propping herself up with her elbows on the counter and resting her helpless head in her hands.

I looked at my donut, licked my lips, and then, locking eyes with my baby
butch, I brought that donut up to my mouth and proceeded to lick and suck
the creamy filling out of that pastry with as much passion as I've ever felt in
my entire life. My little dyke leaned forward wild-eyed, half rose out of her
seat, and practically did a somersault headfirst over the counter.

When I was done, I patted my mouth delicately with a napkin, and without bothering to reapply my lipstick, I opened my purse for a cigarette, which
I placed between my lips. At last my poor baby knew she was welcome. She
bounded across that greasy floor in two seconds flat, flicking her Bic.

"Sit down," I said, accepting her light and gesturing to the empty seat
across from me. We looked at each other for a minute. Her eyes were burning. "You look mighty hungry," I said, delighting in her blush. "What's your
name, lover?" I asked, putting my hand on top of both of hers. She was hanging on to Angie's empty pink packet of Sweet 'n Low for dear life.

"Sonny," she breathed, interlacing her fingers with mine.

"Sonny," I repeated, kicking off one shoe. "With an *o* or a *u*?"

"Oh," she moaned, as my bare foot rode up her leg underneath her
jeans. I took off my other shoe and caressed her firm calves with my feet,
silently thanking the Goddess that I had worn slingbacks that morning.
Some of my shoes have so many buckles, even Houdini would have a hard
time getting out of them.

Sonny's calves felt firm, like she worked on her feet all day. "You want
some of my donut, Sonny," I said, for it was a statement, not a question.
The poor girl could only nod. "C'mon, then." I put my shoes back on and
rose. Sonny was at my side in a second. Someone sure raised her right.
She helped me on with my coat, standing behind me while I took my hair
out of my collar and gently teased her face with it.

"Where we going?" Sonny asked, eager as a puppy, as we left Dunkin's.
"You got a car?" I asked.

"Yeah," she said, half turning, "but it's a few blocks back that way."

"Never mind," I said. I didn't need her car; I needed to know she was
over eighteen, though to tell you the truth, I don't know if I could have
turned back at this point. "You're old enough to drive?" I asked, putting
my hand on her arm. "How do you keep looking so young and handsome
like that? Your skin is soft as a baby's." I traced her blush with my index
finger.

"I don't know," she mumbled. "Just lucky, I guess."

"Oh, you're lucky," I agreed, taking her arm again. "Real lucky. In fact," I purred, stroking her arm through the sleeve of her leather jacket, "you have no idea how lucky you are."

I steered her toward a door, which of course she pulled open for me. "The Easton Mall?" Sonny was puzzled.

"Do you care?" I asked, looking around. "I mean, are you in a hurry?"

"No," Sonny said, and I stopped walking to thrust my hands onto my hips, pretending to be insulted.

"I mean yes," she stammered, mortified at offending me. I shook my head and rolled my eyes, as if I was disgusted that all she ever thought about was sex.

"Yes and no." Sonny was helpless, which is just the way I wanted her.

"Good." I started walking again. "I didn't think you'd mind if I picked up a few things."

I steered her through the light crowd of young mothers pushing strollers, junior high kids cutting school, and bored housewives looking at dish towels, until we came to Macy's. We passed Housewares, Juniors (where I paused briefly to admire a teal suede skirt), and Sleepwear until we came to Lingerie.

"Now, let's see." My hands swam through the racks, gliding over satins and silks. "What do you think of this?" I held a black long-sleeved, button-down nightshirt, cut like a man's pajama top, up to my chest.

"Oh no," Sonny said. "That's all wrong for you."

"Really?" I pulled my hand away from my body to study the outfit at arm's length. "You pick something out, then," I said, pretending to be disappointed as I hung the monstrosity back on the rack.

"How about this?" Sonny lifted a hanger full of red lace and feathers and held it toward me. "I've got a charge card here," Sonny boasted. "I'll buy it for you."

"Silly girl." Butches don't know the first thing about shopping. "I have to try it on first."

"Oh." She looked disappointed, but her face lit up when I said, "Find a size fourteen and I'll meet you in the dressing room."

I took off my coat and waited for Sonny. I didn't have to wait long.

"Here," she said, proud as anything. I took the negligee and pushed her gently, my hand against her chest. "Now you wait out there until I have it on and then you can tell me what you think."

I closed the curtain between us and called, "Now don't go 'way," as I let my skirt drop to the floor in a puddle at my feet. Sonny could only see me from the knees down, but I was sure her eyes were glued to the ground as I let blouse, bra, slip, stockings, and panties pile up in a heap. I stepped back into my heels and slipped the teddy over my head. It fit perfectly: the lace cups lifted and squeezed my breasts to maximum cleavage and the sheer material fell over my torso in silky folds, ending in a hem of feathers dusting the tops of my thighs.

"Come in," I sang from behind the curtain.

Sonny stepped inside and slumped against the wall, her watery knees buckling.

"Do you like it?" I breathed, twirling around so the teddy flared out, giving Sonny a peep show of my glorious bush and derriere.

"You look beautiful." Her voice cracked. "Shall we wrap it?"

"I'm not sure." I turned away from her to consult the mirror. Sonny stood behind me, her reflection drooling. "I'm not sure about this strap," I said, shrugging my shoulder a little, which caused the strap to slide down my arm. "Can you adjust it for me?"

Sonny stepped forward and her trembling fingers touched my flesh at last. I caught her hand and moved it from my shoulder to my breast. She caught her breath in a loud gasp and I had to shake my finger at her. "Shh," I whispered. "We don't want a flock of salesgirls in here asking us if we need any help, do we?"

"Hell no," Sonny whispered back as she started to shrug off her leather jacket.

"Leave it on." I pulled her to me in a full body hug and gently nudged her head down to the nape of my neck. She nibbled her way down to my nipple, spent some time there, and nibbled her way back up again in search for a kiss on the mouth, but I save these two lips for Bonnie so I just lifted the naughty nightie up over Sonny's head and from then on, there were no complaints. Sonny licked and sucked my entire body until that cream-filled donut had nothing on me, let me tell you. I was just about to explode when we heard footsteps that stopped right outside our dressing room. The voice that belonged to those sensible shoes asked, "Are you finding everything you need?" to which Sonny replied, "Oh yes," and proceeded to find them all over again.

Finally Sonny came up for air with a sticky grin. "Yum yum, " she said, wiping her mouth on her sleeve. "Finest breakfast I ever had."

I laughed. "I like a woman with a big appetite," I said, watching the lust stream from her eyes.

"What are we having for lunch?" Sonny asked, imagining, I'm sure, spending the rest of the day, if not her life, with me.

"Well, let's see," I pretended to ponder. "Why don't you see if this outfit comes in powder blue?"

"But red's definitely your color," Sonny said, a little whine creeping into her voice.

"Variety's the spice of life, sugar." I opened the curtain and shooed her out. "Light blue, baby. To match your eyes."

"Okay." Sonny took off and I got dressed fast. I had already made sure that the teddy only came in red and black, so I had a little time, because if I knew Sonny, she would rather die than come back to the dressing room empty-handed.

I straightened myself out and peeked out from behind my curtain. I could see Sonny with her back to me shaking her head as some poor saleswoman held up a light blue, full-length slip that was close, but no cigar. Grabbing my chance and my purse, I slipped out of the fitting room, out of the store, and out of the mall, and ran down the street toward the office, which is no small feat in three-inch heels.

I was only an hour and twenty minutes late for work, which wasn't too bad, considering. I passed Angie at her desk and hissed, "Meet me in the bathroom."

"Do I smell?" I asked when she came in.

"Pee-yew!" Angie wrinkled up her nose. "So tell."

I told, with Angie shaking her head and interjecting "unh-huhs" in all the right places. "So you left the poor girl all alone in a lingerie department with a salesgirl trying to make her quota?"

"Yeah." I filled a paper cup with water and took a long sip. "You know how heartless I am."

"So that's it for Dunkin' Donuts." Angie folded her arms. "You know Sonny'll be there watching for you every morning for at least a month."

"I know." I tried to do something with my hair but my reflection said, *Freshly fucked*, no matter how I combed it.

"And we can't go to Denny's anymore or the International House of Pancakes either." Angie shook her head. "Sally, what am I going to do with you?"

"Feed me toast and coffee in the car," I said, and Angie laughed. "That would be the only way to keep you out of trouble."

"Did Franklin say anything?" I touched up my lipstick.

"Nah, but we better get back to our desks." Angie looked at her watch. "Only an hour until lunch."

"Thank God. I'm starving."

"You and your appetite." Angie led the way out. "You want to grab some chow mein at that place on Fifth Street?"

"I can't," I said as we walked toward our station. "Remember the redhead?"

"Oh God, here we go." We stopped at Angie's desk. "What about the pizza place on the corner?"

"No good."

"The deli on Third?"

"Unh-unh."

"The Taco Villa on Forest?"

I shook my head.

"Sally!"

"What can I say?" I shrugged helplessly. "Me and my appetite."

"We better go to my house for leftovers," Angie said.

"Sounds good. What'cha got?"

"Sally, what do Bernice and I always eat on Wednesday nights?"

I didn't even have to think. "Spaghetti."

"So that's what we got."

"I'll take it." I'll never understand Angie and Bernice. Seven years together and they eat the same thing every week: pot roast on Mondays, chicken on Tuesdays, spaghetti on Wednesdays ... Don't they ever want anything different? There's no accounting for taste I guess. And anyway, who am I to judge? And besides which, Angie makes the best spaghetti sauce this side of the Mississippi. I'd do anything for a serving of it. Even leave Angie's girlfriend, the beautiful buxom butch Bernice, in the capable hands of the chef.

# Bridging the Gap

## by Anita Loomis

A t ten o'clock, the last woman bows at the door of the karate school and heads home in the warm summer night. The dojo hall becomes quiet and centered. I love this moment, this instant when all the sweat and frustration and fear and challenge of training wraps itself up into a perfect present. This silence is deep and satisfying, the quiet of exertion well played out.

I wonder who is more satisfied after a hard karate class: the student who found more strength in herself than she imagined she had, or the teacher, the sensei, who helped her student up or over or through whatever was holding her back? I like helping women become powerful.

It can be daunting though, seeing the expectation in my students' eyes, knowing the trust that is handed to me. It is a responsibility that calls for clear boundaries between student and teacher, for a certain restraint, a line between formality and friendship, for a gap between all the sensory information I take in while teaching a room of twenty-five sweating women and the thoughts I allow myself to pursue in my own private time. Like this time, right now.

I click the lock on the dojo door, rub a smudge left on the glass by a showered but still sweating hand with the tip of my white uniform, and give my black belt a habitual tug. I can feel the endorphins in my system from the hard physical activity. It's the only high I allow myself anymore. In truth, it's the only one I want. The cocaine always left me feeling worse and worse about myself. The karate, ten years of it and now three years with my own school, always leaves me feeling better. I breathe in my accomplishment, breathe out my satisfaction.

I mentally review the progress of the students who have just left for the night. Karla, a tiny blond former ballerina, has finally started to let her strength show. Her kicks are snapping out and back with a speed and grace far more beautiful than a partnered pirouette. Georgia had a little breakdown when Mica swept her feet out from under her during sparring. Well, she'll have to learn to pick her feet up and get out of the way. And Mica, just grinning and helping her up, holding out a gloved hand like a gallant gentleman who had inadvertently tumbled a lady from her carriage. Mica, grinning that smile that doesn't come from her mouth, but instead from her ice blue eyes. Mica, who is so courteous and correct in all the formalities of teacher and student, answering, "Yes, Sensei!" to my corrections to her punches. All the time, those eyes bright, her mouth parted, sucking in air through a little gap in her teeth, the slightest rise of pink on her porcelain cheeks, a slip of sweat above her lip. Mica.

I've seen crushes in the eyes of fifty adoring karate students. The admiration in their faces. The blushing when called on to demonstrate in class. And I recall my own intense fascination with my sensei, my teacher. Despite ten years of training with her, I still feel the heat rise when she gently corrects my alignment with her hand on my back.

You love your sensei. You can't help it. And you know it and she knows it and it never gets acknowledged in words. It just is and you leave it at that. That gap. That gap between the rising heat and the cooling distance of the teacher. It's appropriate. It's necessary. It's generally not too frustrating.

I flick out the lights on the training floor. Walking across the room in the half-light thrown from the locker room, I can see myself in the training mirrors. Some women have trouble with that part of working out — looking at themselves in the mirrors. But I have to admit I like it. I didn't always. I watched myself change in the mirrors of my sensei's training hall. I watched myself slowly transform from wobbly to balanced, from fearful to fearsome, from ashamed to proud. I am still surprised by what I see in the mirror, by the woman I have become. I can see my thigh muscles contract under the thin white fabric. I smile, remembering that when I first began training in the martial arts, I had naively chirped that I liked the baggy uniforms because no one could see my body. Then I started being intensely aware of the way other women's bodies shaped the pants and the midhip kimono-style jacket, of the well-defined forearms emerging from crisply turned-up sleeves, of the open expanse of a smooth sternum showing sometimes more, sometimes less as we kicked and punched in partnered exercises. I could look at myself in the mirror, but I had a difficult time looking the other women in the eyes. All those beautiful eyes.

My first lover was a woman two belt levels ahead of me. Trying to get through classes with her after we broke up was a disaster. I know from painfully direct experience not to involve myself with a student who is my junior.

I shake off the memory with a toss of my short dark hair. I turn and stand, facing the mirrors. *Who do you get involved with then?* I ask the question silently. Between running the school and teaching part-time at the college, I have little time for meeting, let alone fucking, any dykes not connected to me as a teacher. I sigh. *You love it though, don't you?* Yes, I do.

Taking a deep breath, drawing in my *chi*, my life energy, I begin to move through a meditative movement form, shifting from stance to stance. Breathe in, move your leg, breathe out, sink your stance. Breathe in, shift, breathe out, sink. I feel myself break into a light sweat in the humid night. Untying my uniform top, I drop it on the floor and pull my sports bra over my head. One advantage to having your own dojo: you can train half-naked. I can see my strong shoulders, small breasts, dark nipples. I'm lean now, with an athlete's body. Very different from the self-conscious twelve-year-old who won the sack-jumping contest at sleep-away camp with her strong, hairy thighs stuffed into a burlap bag! That was the first time I felt powerful, but it was quickly attached to a certain monstrousness. When I quit changing my chunky-sized blue jeans under my sleeping bag and tried wearing shorts like the rest of the girls, my counselor suggested I borrow her razor.

I am moving through my workout swiftly, a dripping sheen of sweat covering me, when I see a figure block the light from the locker room doorway. There's a body in the doorway. With years of self-defense training literally under my belt, I whirl around to face the doorway. With my arms out in a strong guard, legs planted, I let out a deep, loud yell like an eagle about drop out of the sky. "KIIAAII!"

"Sensei?" says the body.

"Mica?" says the sensei, naked from the waist up.

I see my students naked or half-naked all of the time in the locker room. I carry on serious conversations with women who are wearing only towels wrapped around their dyke waists. I usually shower later on, alone.

This time it is my student who is fully clad, in a snug pair of Levi's and a white t-shirt. I see the flash of an ear cuff. She is barefoot, though I hadn't noticed her shoes, usually a pair of motorcycle boots, on the shoe rack by the front door. Her curly brown flat top is still damp from the shower. I can smell lotion — no, not lotion, cologne? Mica is wearing men's aftershave. I feel my nipples harden, involuntarily on my part, voluntarily on theirs.

Mica takes a step into the training hall, bowing deeply to the spirit shrine and then to me. I think I see the slightest smile in her eyes as she bends down, though her form is absolutely correct.

"I wanted to speak with you about a problem I'm having in class." She takes one or two steps toward me, bridging the gap between us, entering my space. I find myself momentarily rooted to the floor. *Move your feet, counter, evade, get out of the way.* I am silently reminding myself that the woman who first crosses the distance toward her opponent has taken control of the fight.

Mica continues her slow walk toward me. I notice that jeans do not hide a woman's thigh muscles, either.

The critical distance, the distance necessary to throw an effective kick or punch, is swiftly decreasing. I reach down for my wrap top. Pulling it around me like a bathrobe, I discover that my hands are shaking, my fingers too clumsy to tie the side knots. I let them be, rather than show my lack of composure at being caught off guard.

"Certainly, I can talk with you. I hadn't realized you ... or anyone, was still here." Gathering up some shred of self-discipline, I walk past Mica into the locker room. The combination of soap and aftershave and damp hair makes me take in a deep breath, which has absolutely no calming effect whatsoever. *Keep walking,* comes the silent voice in my head.

"I stayed in the whirlpool a bit longer. It keeps me from getting too sore, and I'm trying to nurse an injury." Mica is right behind me. I can feel her breath, cool across the back of my neck.

"An injury?" I cross to my locker, pull out a towel, and begin to mop my face. "From class? Is that what you wanted to speak to me about?"

"Yes, it's the strangest thing. Sometimes I feel it, sometimes I don't. Sometimes it feels like I've been kicked right in the chest, right here."

Mica reaches out, takes my hand, and places it directly over her left breast, or heart chakra, or whatever you want to call it. All I can feel is a hot flash pass between us like lightning in a heat storm. I drop my hand.

"You know the feeling, don't you, Sensei? It's right here." She slips her hand past my cotton top and rests it directly on my incredibly tight left nipple. The lightning flashes right out of her eyes this time.

*Move your feet, counter, evade, get out of the way. The woman who closes the gap has the advantage.* Karate tips reel through my brain as unheeded as they would be by a brand spanking new white belt. My feet do not move. Another deep breath brings Mica's smell right up into my face.

Some decisions take years to arrive at. Deciding to become a martial arts teacher began to happen five years after I started to train. All the while I took classes, I insisted that my real goal was to become the best, as in most famous, sculptor in the Western world. Thinking it was what I wanted, I crashed along in the city's fast lane. Gradually I've discovered that life in a lefty college town with my own dojo and only a co-op art gallery suits me just fine. I'm miles away, two thousand miles to be exact, from my days of booze, drugs, and girls, girls, girls. I only miss the girls, girls, girls.

Some decisions take a lifetime, others just a split second. Here is a beautiful woman with her hand firmly planted on my very aroused tit. I decide brutal honesty is the best policy and also an effective counter-move. I summon up my best teacher's voice. I prepare myself to deal with her disappointment or anger. I look directly into Mica's ice blue lightning eyes.

"Yes," I say. "I know the feeling."

The most enormous grin spreads over Mica's face, sun behind storm clouds.

What did I just say? Didn't I just say, "No, that's in your imagination. I'm your teacher, not your lover." Hadn't I said that? Wasn't that the truth?

Mica's face is so close now I am reminded that she is about three inches taller than me. Then she is bending over my neck, kissing my shoulders, pushing back my uniform top, revealing my bare torso. She has both hands on my breasts now and her tongue way down my throat. Somebody is moaning. I think it is me. Mica moves behind me, helping my arms out of my sleeves where my elbows seem frozen, permanently bent. She has her hands on my rib cage now, is speaking into my hair.

"You are the most stunning thing I have ever laid eyes on. I've wanted to fuck you since the first time I walked into this school. Hot, that's what you are. The hottest fucking sensei to ever wear a black belt." It's butch talk, and oh, my, have I been missing that sound. Her hands are on my waist now, tugging hard on the aforementioned belt. Then her tugging stops and she begins to untie my belt gently, her arms still wrapped around me.

"This will have to come off though," she says, unwinding the well-worn fabric from my waist. "That wouldn't be respectful, fucking your sensei.

That wouldn't be right. No, better to fuck a woman naked. No belts. No uniforms. No formalities."

Mica's hand reaches past my shoulder and hangs my black belt over the top of my locker door. I can feel the dampness between my legs, that aching, tugging feeling as my cunt opens up, waiting.

She holds me to her with one hand. I hope she's planning to put the other hand down my pants. I want her to. I want her to so much. I close my eyes and lean my shoulder blades back against Mica's t-shirt. I hear a zipper go down.

"Just in case you're not sure we're on equal ground here." Mica turns me around, pushing me down onto my knees, pressing me into her cunt fur, curlier and damper than her flat top. Someone is moaning again, it must be me. I grab Mica's ass and bury my face in her crotch, trying to pull down her jeans, trying to get my tongue in her slit, licking at her belly. Breathing in Mica, breathing out lust.

Mica, however, has more countermoves than a lay back fighter, the kind of opponent who hits you just before you land what you thought was a sure punch. She pushes me backward until I'm lying on the floor of my own locker room. Holding me by the scruff of the neck like a baby kitten, kneeling beside me, she zips up her jeans and pulls the drawstring on my pants. She slides her free hand over the outside of the fabric, taking a firm grip of my entire pussy. "Take these pants off. Underwear, too." She releases her hold on my cunt to pull a latex glove out of her back hip pocket. Still with a firm grip on the back of my neck, she slips the glove onto her right hand, pulling it down with her teeth. With her teeth!

I scramble out of my pants as fast as possible and find Mica on top of me fully clothed, my bare ass against the cool tile. I'm not pinned. I could get up. I think.

Mica's fingers are separating my labia, playing with my clit, using my own wetness to slide quickly and firmly. "Uhh, unnh." When did I become such a moaner? I'm groaning deep in my throat. It feels good. So fucking good.

"Please put your fingers in me, please," I beg her, arching my back, trying to get my hole under her hand. "I want you. I want all of you in me."

Mica drops her tongue down my throat. The heat storm in her eyes is getting intense. "All right, honey, but next time I'm taking you home and using my biggest dildo on you."

One, two, three, four fingers plunge into me and come up wet. My cunt starts pounding. Breathe in, breathe out, huh, huh, huh, huh. I'm heaving my hips now. Wrapping my leg around Mica's denim-covered thigh.

She is still talking. "That's it, sweetheart, take it. Take all you want." And she's dry humping me through those butch Levi's. I'm stuffed as full as I can get when she grabs my nipple hard and I go right over the edge, wave after wave of pussy contracting like it will never stop.

Mica throws her head back. "Ah, baby, that always makes me come," she says, pinning my thigh. I swear I feel her clit pulsing as she arches back. I get to stare without reserve at her mouth, her teeth, her skin.

Like thunder moving off into the distance, Mica moves off of me, gently extricating herself from my cunt a finger at a time. She puts her hand close to her face and breathes in. "That was sweet," she says, her whole body smiling, stretching out beside me. She pulls me to her and I roll onto my side. My eyes focus on the locker room benches. Underneath one I can see Mica's gym bag stuffed full of sparring equipment. Tucked next to the bag, far from the shoe rack out front, is a pair of well-worn but carefully polished motorcycle boots.

I smile. "How about another round in the whirlpool?" I suggest, this time bridging the gap on my own.

# Dear Kris

## by Susan Fox Rogers

Dear Kris,
  It's Sunday morning here in Highland Corners. I just got home
after brunch in town with Tara, a woman I met at the bar last
night. I guess I picked her up, but she was the one who invited me back
to her place for the night. I'm not telling you this to make you jealous; I'm
telling you this because all night long I was looking for you in that smoke-
filled bar. And when I was with Tara, I wanted it to be you lying on top
of me, making love to me.

  I didn't get dressed up to go out, didn't feel up for it. And really,
the only person I want to wear a skirt for is you. I was in jeans and a
t-shirt, my tomboy look. The way I looked when I met you. But you
saw that I was more femme beneath the pants, and I saw you were
more butch beneath your long hair. I hope your hair is still short and
so soft.

  I noticed Tara right away because she was new to the bar, and because
with her slicked-back black hair and black pants riding low on her hips,
she looked more butch than any of the other women there. She was leaning against the bar, smoking a cigarette and watching people dance, when
I walked over, ordered a beer, and smiled at her. She smiled back, and I
asked her for a cigarette even though I try not to smoke anymore. I held
her hand in close when she lit my cigarette for me.

  "I'm June," I said. You taught me how to flirt. Or rather, I learned from
watching you.

  "Tara," she said. She winked at me and I smiled and looked away.

  She and her lover of eight years had just broken up. It was her first
night out at the bar after four months of sitting at home crying into her
beer. When I heard that I thought: *relationships never last, why do we think that
each one will?* And at the same time I thought: *Kris will always love me; I will*

*always love Kris. We will last.* I'm sure this makes you laugh, since the last
thing you heard me say is no. But let me finish.

Tara asked me to dance, and on the dance floor she held me tight. I
liked the way she moved, but I kept wishing she was an inch taller, as tall
as you are, and that she would subtly roll her pelvis into mine the way you
used to. Whenever you did that I wanted you, there on the dance floor.

When she asked me to come home with her I didn't hesitate, because
my body was just aching to be touched. I haven't made love with anyone
since you left. And when Tara touched me I knew why I had been sitting
home these past three months: I don't want to be touched by just anyone.
She made love to me very nicely, touched me gently. But, later, as I lay in
her arms, she had to ask, "Did you come?" I knew she wasn't feeling my
body, but was making love to me as she made love to every woman, as she
made love to her partner of eight years. The first time you made love to
me I knew you were touching me and only me. Do you remember our first
night? We were in your apartment in New York City. The moonlight was
shining in through the windows that looked out over Tompkins Square
Park. I sat on top of you, slowly pulled my shirt up and over my head,
then unsnapped my bra. I could feel you watching me, saw a slight smile
as you liked what you saw. I held my breasts, lifted them, gave them to
you.

That night, all I wanted was to feel your weight on top of me, but later
you told me you were afraid your weight would be too much for me. You
learned I am stronger than I look. So you lay next to me in your t-shirt
and boxers and gently touched me. Your fingers felt like magic as they
made me come once, twice, made me want more, your lips on my body.
I still laugh to think that you used only your hands because you didn't
want to scare me. Was I really so much of a country girl? I thought you
were practicing some version of safe sex, but I now think you did it so I
would want to come back for more. And I did.

While we were in the city, everything was fine. You could be who you
are, a freak you said, but in New York everyone is a freak. You could dress
how you wanted, and I could be with you without shame. When we went
out, I was so proud because I was holding your arm, and I knew that most
of the girls wanted to be me. But once we moved to the country, where I
come from and where I belong, things changed. I wasn't proud anymore.
When you slipped on your suit I wanted to ask you to change, to wear
jeans like everyone else. But I knew asking you to change would be ask-

ing you to be someone different, would be to say: *I don't like who you are.*
And I loved you, loved you so deeply my bones hurt when I thought of
you. But I wasn't proud enough, or strong enough, to stand by your side.
And that's when our troubles began.

I remember so well the first time we dressed up to go out. I came over
to your place. I asked if I could watch you dress, but you said no, you
wanted to surprise me. You bought the suit by yourself, came home smiling like you had just bought the world. I can only begin to imagine how
happy that suit made you, what it meant to you. You showered first, leaving the bathroom steamy and sweet smelling. You may have the roughest
hands, but the rest of your body is as soft as a baby's. I showered and
changed, slipped on a new black dress, the one with no back and thin
straps. I put on my high-heeled shoes and lacy stockings. When I stepped
out of the bathroom, I was weak with heat and excitement.

Your back was turned to me. You were selecting more music to play
while Aretha softly sang. I watched you from behind, broad shoulders,
trim waist, long beautiful legs in pleated pants. You didn't know I was
watching. Then you turned around, stopped, and looked at me leaning
against the doorjamb. I watched your face slowly flush, the excitement
come to your body. You smiled, then walked over, took me in your arms,
and kissed me gently on the lips. "You are the most beautiful woman in
the world," you told me. "And you are the most handsome," I said.

When we went out that night I had eyes only for you. But you said you
saw people noticing us. I know they had to have liked, must have
admired, what they saw. I know that we were so beautiful together. In the
country, people noticed us, too. But it was different. People made fun of
you, called out at you, at us. Even the lesbians thought we were weird.
Maybe they were jealous, or curious, but they were mean in their jealousy.
I wanted to be happy standing next to you, to have fun when we went out.
But what we started to do was stay at home, hide. That's not how I want
to live.

When I went out last night, I realized how long it had been. It felt good
to listen to the loud music, see women holding women, kissing women. I had
to keep myself from staring, it seemed so wondrous and new. As I leaned
against the far wall, watching women and men dancing together and apart,
I thought of us together in bed. I thought of when I bought that black leather
harness and the purple dildo just for you, just for us. You looked shy and
excited at once as you watched me carefully strap it on you. When I slid in

the dildo and tightened the leather straps, your stomach jumped and you began to sweat. I watched your face, intent and amazed at your own reactions, as I took your cock in my hand, then ran my tongue along the purple shaft. You groaned and said, "This feels too good, too real." I smiled, leaned over, and sucked you. Your hips moved slowly, wanting more. "Tell me what you want," I teased. I wanted to hear you ask.

"I want to be inside of you. I want to fuck you."

I climbed on top of you, took your cock in my hands, then rubbed the tip against my wet and open lips. Slowly, I let you enter me. We both hesitated, then took light, quick breaths when you were fully inside. I smiled and rotated on your cock, amazed at how good it felt, how much it felt like you inside me. I could never use that dildo with anyone else.

You were so playful but serious, always asking if you were hurting me when, excited and wanting to be deeper inside of me, you rocked your hips. "You could never hurt me," I always told you, "even though you are bigger, stronger." You are the gentlest person I know. You always had a sixth sense, a feel in the tips of your fingers or the shaft of your cock about what my body wanted, how you could please me, or please me one more time. I was the luckiest girl.

I felt the most lucky the night you let me touch you. I know you had never let anyone touch you before, but you trusted me, my hands, heart, and lips, to treat your body with respect and love. I was so scared touching you, so I traveled slowly down your body, tried to let love come out of my hands and caress you, heal the wounds I knew of and those I could never know of. You cried the first time I touched you.

Before you left, you asked me to marry you. It wasn't the first time, but I knew it was the last time you would ask. You couldn't wait any longer; you had to know if we were going to be together. You want to be married, to have children and a home. It's not really a lesbian life you want, one of small apartments and a list of ex-lovers. You want a traditional life where you work hard and love well, grow old together in comfort. I didn't understand that, but now I see the beauty in it. The first nights after you left, I had a bath drawn for you, dinner in the oven, and a pair of clean boxers waiting. I loved being your wife, even though I could not have said that then. It went against everything I believed in, everything I thought and had learned. Being married, getting married, seemed too traditional. When you asked me to be your wife, I wasn't even sure I could be your girlfriend. It had become too hard. So I said no.

Things seem so progressive now, with gay and lesbian issues on the front page of the *New York Times*. But will our world allow for people like you, for a love like ours? I hope some day. And in the meantime, I guess we have to live in one of the big cities. I know I said I never would or could move back. I will never love it, but I can love you there and that makes it safe. Safer than country roads and clean air.

I'm writing this letter, and I don't know where to send it. You left three months ago. You must be in the city, where else could you go? I'm sure you're doing well, and I hope you're not too friendless. But I imagine that your life is simple, that you work, then come home at night to a small apartment somewhere in the city. I just pray you're not coming home to someone in that apartment, someone who will touch your heart and iron your shirts. I want to be the one to do that. So I'll send this letter to places you might go and hope it lands in your hands. And I'll keep sending it until it does.

I love you. Yes, I want to marry you.

June

# Love Ruins Everything

## by Karen X. Tulchinsky

"I think we should become nonmonogamous," Sapphire announces over seafood curry at our favorite Thai restaurant in the Castro. "What!?" I say. A piece of curried prawn lodges in my throat.

Sapphire puts her fork down and sucks in a deep breath. "I've wanted to talk to you about this all day."

I swallow hard, trying to move the prawn farther down. "You have?"

"I've been thinking about it."

"Since when?"

She picks up her fork and turns a piece of eggplant over on her plate. "Since yesterday."

"Yesterday? What happened yesterday? I thought you went shopping."

"I did."

"For groceries."

"I did."

"At Safeway."

"Nomi, I did."

"And then you came home."

"Right." She puts down her fork abruptly. It clatters against the plate.

"And while you were shopping you decided we should be nonmonogamous?"

"Yes. No. Well ... not while I was shopping. I don't know when. I just did."

I fold my arms across my chest. "Who is she!?" I yell, a little on the loud side.

"Nomi." She looks around the restaurant nervously. "Lower your voice."

"Why!?" I shout even louder. "I've got nothing to hide." Sapphire hates it when I make a scene in public. Her proper WASP upbringing is deeply ingrained in her suburban middle-class psyche.

"Nomi. I won't discuss this if you keep shouting."

"Who's shouting?" I yell. Both of the sweater-fags at the next table look over in our direction and raise their eyebrows.

Sapphire throws her napkin on the table and stands. "I'm leaving," she says in a stage whisper. By this point everyone around us is listening. I know they are half hoping she will throw wine in my face or slap me. It would make for a better story when they tell their friends about it later.

"Sapphire." I laugh sardonically. "Come on. Sit down. You haven't finished yet."

She shakes her head and leaves the restaurant. I signal for the waiter.

By the time I pay, wait for my change and the rest of our food (which I'd asked the waiter to wrap up), and run up the hill and open the door to our apartment on States Street, I am out of breath and dripping in sweat. I fling the bag of food onto the kitchen table. Sapphire is lying on the couch in a knee-length t-shirt from Gay Freedom Day 1991. She flicks through the channels on television. Simon, her gray tabby, and the girls, k.d. and Melissa, two pure black kittens she recently brought home from the animal shelter, run into the kitchen to investigate the take-out food. I open the fridge and pop the food onto the top shelf. When I get back into the living room, Sapphire is watching *The Simpsons*. I stand beside the TV and watch her.

"Are you going to sit down?" She is still angry, although it occurs to me that I should be the angry one.

"Are you going to talk to me? No one can hear us now," I say icily. It drives me crazy that she is so uptight. I come from a family that screams and carries on in public all the time. To me, it's as natural as breathing.

She shuts off the television and sits up, to make room for me on the sofa. I go over and sit beside her, cross-legged, facing her.

She takes my hands and looks at me with a sweet, loving look, the very look that made me fall in love with her in the first place. "I don't want to hurt your feelings, Nomi. I love you. It's just that ... I've always gone right from one relationship to the next, with no space in between. I've never really been single, and I don't know how to date."

"It's not all it's cracked up to be."

She sighs. "Maybe so, but I need to find out for myself, and I don't want to break up with you to do that. I just want to try my hand at dating. Can you understand that?"

I turn away from her and sulk. "Sure I understand. You're bored of me and you're looking for someone new."

She leans forward to look in my eyes. "Nomi. I am not bored with you."

I turn to face her, but fold my arms across my chest. "If you dump me for someone else I'll kill you."

She kisses me on the lips. "I'm not dumping you."

"I'll shoot you. I don't care if I spend the rest of my life in jail. I'll do it," I threaten.

"Come here." She puts her hands on either side of my face and draws me to her for a kiss.

Three days later I'm walking down Castro Street. It is a warm, sunny day in November. The fog has lifted for the first time in days. I'm supposed to be at work, but I faked a dentist appointment so I could do some shopping. I am carrying a bag of groceries, my gym bag, and a bunch of cut flowers for Sapphire, all of which slip from my grasp and slide to the dirty sidewalk when I see a huge straight guy with a buzz cut, baggy pants, and a baseball cap lean forward and French-kiss my girlfriend. I stare at them for a moment, while everybody else stares at me.

"Hey, lady," shouts an adolescent boy. "You dropped your stuff."

The lovebirds break apart. Sapphire's eyes are soft and dreamy, like she is enjoying being mauled by the straight guy. I stand, transfixed, unable to move a muscle. The guy moves to one side. Sapphire's eyes connect with mine. She stands up straight, at attention, like a kid caught smoking cigarettes, or stealing money. I glare at her with pure contempt. She rushes toward me. Tears start streaming down my face. I turn and start to walk quickly away from her, leaving my parcels on the ground.

"Nomi," she yells. "Stop!"

I keep going.

"Nomi! Wait! Let's talk about this."

"What's to say!?" I yell over my shoulder. I'm breathing heavily, from walking uphill.

"Nomi. What about your stuff? You can't just leave it here."

"The hell I can't," I say. I know she has stopped to pick up the groceries because I don't feel her behind me anymore. I walk right past our street and keep walking. And walking.

"I knew it," my mother says, when I call her in Toronto and tell her about me and Sapphire.

"What? What did you know, Ma?"

"I knew it," she repeats. "I knew she wasn't a real lesbian." There is a tone of smug satisfaction in my mother's voice, like she's just solved the bonus phrase on *Wheel of Fortune.*

"Ma. What do you mean a 'real lesbian'?"

"I always thought she was very feminine."

"Yeah? She was — is. So?"

"So? So, she probably really likes men."

"Ma, that makes no sense. Feminine doesn't have anything to do with it. Anyway, since when are you such an expert on lesbians?"

"I learned everything I know from you," she returns. "Oh, and a little from Phil Donahue, too. Did you see the show about lesbian serial killers?"

"Ma, don't start with me. Please. Are you listening? Me and Sapphire are breaking up. It's just like a divorce, Ma. I'm very upset. I'm a wreck. I want sympathy. I don't want Phil Donahue."

There is silence and I know she is nodding her head. I can picture her doing it. "You're right, Nomi. What was I thinking? I'm sorry. Can you forgive me? How are you doing, dear? Do you need anything? Why don't you come home? You don't need to stay there now. You can stay with me. It'll be fun. We can have pajama parties."

"Ma. I'm too old for pajama parties and so are you."

"You're never too old for a little fun. Remember that, Mamelah. It's very important."

"I'm staying here, Ma."

"What's to stay for? Why don't you come home?"

"This is my home, Ma. I live here now."

"Okay. You can't blame me for trying. So? Tell me. Are you okay for money? I'll send you a little something to help out."

My mother the millionaire. We weren't exactly the Rockefellers when my father was alive. Now, my mother gets by on a small monthly pension from an insurance policy my father left her. "Since when are you so flush? What? Did somebody die?"

"Nobody died. It's Murray."

"What? He gives you money?"

"Watch your mouth, young lady. I'm still your mother."

"What did I say?"

She ignores my question. "He takes me out three, four times a week for dinner, Chinese, Italian, steak, you name it. So? My grocery bill is a little smaller these days."

"Oh."

I pack a small bag and go to stay with my friend Betty. I can't bear to be at home.

"It's Sapphire again." Betty stands in the kitchen doorway, holding up the phone receiver. "What do you want me to tell her?"

"Tell her to go to hell!" I holler.

Betty talks into the phone. "Did you hear that? Uh huh. Okay. Yep. I'll tell her." She goes back into the kitchen, hangs up the phone, and comes into the living room with two cans of Bud Light. She hands me one. I screw up my face, but accept the beer anyway and take a big swig. "How can you drink this stuff? It's terrible."

"You don't seem to mind." She sits beside me on the couch. "Do you want to know what she said?" Betty picks up the remote control and switches her thirty-inch TV screen on. Stereo sound emanates from the speakers. I watch in silence while she flips through the channels. She stops on *The Simpsons*.

"I hate this show," I announce, bitchily.

She looks at me like I've lost my mind. "You love this show."

I shrug. "I hate it. So? What did she say?"

She looks at me, hard, in the eye.

"What?" I say, unnerved by her stare.

"You're not going to like it."

"So? What else is new? Tell me what she said."

"She says she never meant to hurt you. She never meant to ... are you sure you want to hear it?"

I beat my fist on the armrest. "I said I did! Just tell me."

She sighs. "Okay." Betty spits the next part out fast like she can't wait to get it out of her mouth. "She says she never meant to fall in love with Richard. It just happened."

This is too much for me. I leap up off the couch. A stream of beer shoots from the top of my can and spills onto Betty. "Richard!? Richard? Just happened? Oh great! That's just great. It just happened," I repeat, as sarcastically as humanly possible. "How fucking original? Isn't that fucking original, Betty?"

"Not particularly." She lifts her butt up, reaches into her back pocket, pulls out a blue bandanna, and mops the beer from her face and chest. Her black cotton t-shirt has soaked up most of it.

"I can't believe this." I sink back down onto the couch, slam my beer can on the end table, put my face in my hands, and begin to cry. Betty leans over, rubs my back, and drinks her beer.

On Betty's living room sofa, I toss and turn all night. The next morning Betty pokes her head in. "I'm going to Cafe Blue for a cappuccino," she says. "Wanna come?"

I pull the covers over my head. "No!" I yell. "I'm never going there again. Me and Sapphire used to go there every Sunday morning."

"Well, it's Saturday," Betty says.

Betty saves us a table outside on the patio while I go inside to get our drinks. I balance two cappuccinos in one hand, a gigantic piece of chocolate cake in the other, and a recent copy of the *Bay Times* under my arm as I squeeze my way through the narrow, crowded cafe. I am almost at our table. I try to push past an unusually tall man, and somehow, when I look up, I am standing face-to-face with Sapphire. The tall guy, of course, is *him*. Richard. There is one brief second when I consider throwing hot coffee in Sapphire's face. I know she knows what I am thinking because her eyes grow wide and she looks at the cups and then looks back at me.

"Don't you just wish I was that immature?" I spit.

She puts her hands out in front of her. "Nomi. Please. Can't we just talk?"

"About what?" I thrust both cups and the cake into her open arms. I don't look back when I hear something crash to the floor. Betty follows me outside.

"Okay. So coffee was a bad idea, Nomi. But you know what I would do?" Betty paces back and forth in her living room. She has been nagging me to go out. All I've been doing is moping around her apartment. I think I am getting on her nerves.

"What?" I push a pile of silver paper clips to one side of the coffee table and a pile of brass ones to the other side. Lately I have taken to sorting through Betty's junk drawers. It settles my nerves to put something in order, even if it isn't my life.

"Go out. Get laid. Have fun. Believe me, there's nothing better for heartbreak than sex. Nothing." She crosses her arms in front of her chest.

"What is this?" I hold up a small metal object that might have once been a plastic key chain. It is covered in some sticky pink goo which looks like bubble gum that is so old it has melted. Underneath, I can faintly see an illustration of the Golden Gate Bridge.

Betty lunges forward, grabs the object out of my hand, and throws it into the garbage can. I decide to go out soon, if for no other reason than to make Betty happy.

Later that night, Betty goes out and I rent *Moonstruck*, the only movie I can stand to watch. I pop it into Betty's stereo VCR, open a can of Betty's Bud Light, pull Betty's brown and blue striped down quilt over my legs, and settle in for the evening. After my third beer, my favorite scene comes on. It is late at night in New York City. Cher, as Loretta Castorini, and Nicolas Cage, as Ronny Cammareri, are outside of Ronny's apartment building. There is a light snow falling and the new lovers are arguing.

"Love isn't perfect," Ronny says. "Love breaks your heart. Love ruins everything."

I know the scene word for word, expression for expression, frame by frame. I say the lines right along with Ronny, and just like him, I leave the *t* off when I say the word "perfect" so it comes out sounding like "perfeck."

"We're not here to make things perfeck. The snowflakes are perfeck. The stars are perfeck. Not us. Not us. We are here to ruin ourselves and to break our hearts and love the wrong people, and — and die."

A single tear forms in my eye and rolls down my cheek. I never thought that our relationship was perfeck, but I thought we had a good thing going. I miss Sapphire even though I hate her. I drift off to sleep as Dean Martin's voice sings the theme song:

*When the moon hits your eye like a big pizza pie, that's amore.*
*When you dance down the street, with a cloud at your feet, you're in love.*

I fall into a deep sleep. I dream I am lying in a big old four-poster bed and all around me are scantily dressed women whose sole purpose in life is to make me happy. One is kissing me. Another is rubbing my feet. One is in a corner fixing me a drink. The other is paying my rent. It is a lovely dream that has a multimillion dollar budget and a cast of thousands, all of them beautiful. Sapphire walks in, wearing a black negligee. She leans over and pours small kisses all over my cheeks. It is just like old times. I pull her on top of me and we kiss. She touches me everywhere with silk fingers. I feel a peace I'd almost forgotten.

I wake to the sounds of keys jingling in the lock, followed by giggling. Betty and some woman I don't recognize creep into the apartment, trying, quite unsuccessfully in their intoxicated state, to be quiet.

"It's okay," I announce. "I'm not sleeping."

There is silence for a moment. Then, "Hi, Nomi. Sorry to wake you."

"I wasn't sleeping." I pull the covers over my head as they make their way to Betty's room, which is one paper-thin wall over. I try not to listen while they have sex. With my head under the covers, I feel like I am in a cave. It is pitch-black. My heart hurts. It beats against the inside of my chest, cruelly. Quietly, with resignation, I cry. I try to figure out how my life fell apart so quickly. I fall asleep to the muffled sounds of Betty and her friend.

The next morning I decide to take Betty's advice. After all, I have been living with her for a couple of months now. Last week, we traded in her old green sofa for a large pullout couch and I began paying half of the rent. I ask Betty for help getting back into circulation. It's been a long time, and Betty knows everyone. She fixes me up with Alison, a woman she works with at the Big O, a woman-positive sex toy store in the Mission. On my way out the door, Betty informs me that Alison is just barely out of the closet. She has been with one woman so far, once or twice. "She's a little shy," says Betty.

I pick Alison up at eight and take her to see *Forrest Gump* with Tom Hanks. Halfway through the film I reach over and take her hand. It feels nice to touch someone again, but I am acutely aware that the hand does not belong to Sapphire. It is thinner, and her grip is weak. As the movie ends, tears roll down my cheeks. I pretend I am sad about Jenny, Forrest Gump's girlfriend who dies in the end of the movie, but really, I am thinking about Sapphire. I feel lonely and strange. I am not sure why I am out on this date. I fake a smile and suggest that we stop at the Cafe, a local dyke bar, for a drink.

At the door, Alison gets asked for her ID. I know she is younger than me, but it has not occurred to me to ask how much younger. Suddenly I feel old and my whole life seems ridiculous. I never should have listened to Betty, I decide. I don't want to date other women. I want Sapphire. I am about to suggest to Alison that I take her home when the bouncer gives back her ID and nods okay. Alison smiles. We go up to the bar, where I buy us each a drink. We sit on stools at an empty table by the window that overlooks Market Street.

I discover we don't have much to say to each other. I am new at dating after all this time, and she is just new, period. I scramble for small talk. We discuss the movie, the weather, our jobs, the community. After two drinks I am actually enjoying myself. I start to think that maybe Betty is right. Maybe an affair would be just the thing to lift my spirits. I lean forward and kiss Alison. Her lips are soft, but her kiss is tentative. I move closer and kiss her again. A quiet rumbling of desire stirs in my belly. It has been months since I have kissed anyone and three years since I have kissed anyone other than Sapphire. The DJ puts on "Mighty Good Man" by Salt-n-Pepa and En Vogue. I ask Alison to dance. We find a corner of the dance floor. I watch her move. Her hips sway from side to side, her long brown hair bounces behind her. She is wearing a low-cut top. Her breasts are round and full. They press against the black spandex of her shirt. She looks more attractive by the moment. I move in and put my arm around her waist. She puts her arms around my neck. We dance tightly together for the rest of the song, her body rubbing against mine. I notice how different she feels than Sapphire. She is smaller around and a little taller, and she moves slower.

I lean forward and kiss her. Her tongue is inside my mouth. Her soft breasts push against my chest. Her fingers run through my hair. I can taste rum and Coke on her tongue. We kiss until the song ends. Then, I pull back and look at her. She grins.

"Let's go," I say.

She looks startled, as if I have said something odd. "But we just got here."

"Yeah, but I think we might be more comfortable at your place."

"Oh." She looks disappointed, like a kid being asked to leave the sandbox.

"You are going to invite me back to your place, aren't you?"

"Okay," she shrugs.

She lives in a small studio with a pullout couch, one of those big old clunky ones that you can still pick up at secondhand stores for twenty-five bucks. Her apartment is on the ground floor of Haight Street, near Ashbury. You can hear cars rushing by, people yelling, buses, music. Her barred windows are covered in grime. The floor is sticky. There are four hundred dishes in the sink and the apartment smells like cat piss.

"Oh, damn," she says when we enter. She rushes over to the bed and feels the sheets. "Not again."

"What?" I stand in the entranceway.

"My cat's neurotic. Whenever I'm out, she pees on the bed."

"Oh." I laugh, even though it isn't funny. "Come here."

I grab her arm as she tries to rush pass, pull her to me and kiss her. In spite of her anger, she kisses me back. I put my hands around her waist lightly. She moans and I slowly reach up under her jacket toward one of her breasts. Her hand shoots out from nowhere and grabs my wrist, stopping me.

I pull back. "What?" I say softly.

"Uh..." She puts her head down. "It's just that ... uh..."

"What?"

She looks into my eyes, hers dreamy with lust. "Kiss me."

I do what she asks. We kiss for a long time standing in her kitchen, my back up against the fridge. We grope each other over our clothes. My nipples are hard. I am getting wet. Desire pounds against the impenetrable fortress I have had around my heart and body since the day I saw Sapphire kissing that man in the Castro. I slip Alison's jacket off her shoulders and toss it onto a nearby chair. I reach up for the small buttons on her sweater and undo the top one. Again her hand shoots out and grabs my wrist.

"What? What's wrong?"

She looks down again. "Look. Maybe you'd better go."

"Go? But I thought you said..."

"I did, but I'm ... just not ready."

"Not ready?"

"You know."

"Oh." I drop my hands to my sides. "Oh," I say again. "Are you okay?" I try to see her eyes, but her head is down and her long, straight hair covers them. I think maybe she is crying but I can't be sure. "Well, okay. I'll go then. Uh, if that's what you want. That is what you want, right? For me to go?" I want to move her hair so I can see her eyes, but I am afraid to touch her now. She does not answer out loud. She simply nods. "Well..." I search for something to say. "I'll call you, okay?" I back away toward the door until I feel the handle, open it, and quietly let myself out.

A few weeks later Betty's new girlfriend BJ introduces me to her friend Mimi, a lesbian librarian who is a few years older than me and coinci-

dentally, also recently divorced. She still lives with her ex. I don't know
how she can do it. I can barely stand the thought of Sapphire, never
mind the sight of her. I call up Mimi and ask her out. On the afternoon
of our date, she leaves a message on my machine saying that she was up
late the night before and is too tired to go out, could we make it another time? I figure she is canceling because she is nervous, so instead of
calling her back, I show up at her door at the prearranged time. She lives
in the top-floor flat of a pale green Victorian on Fourteenth near
Sanchez. There are large bay windows, a fake front, and ornamental
trim that circles large white stone pillars on the porch. I walk up the
steep flight of wooden steps and ring the bell. No one answers. I can
hear a television from an open window on the second floor. The opening song from *WKRP in Cincinnati* plays. I ring again. Still no answer. I
knock. I ring some more, once, twice, three times, until I hear footsteps.
I nervously run a hand through my hair to smooth it down. The door
opens and Mimi stands there wearing a silk burgundy dressing gown.
She looks tired, yet beautiful. Her deep brown eyes are soft and her
long brown wavy hair is tied into a braid in the back.

I smile. "Hi."

"Oh," she says. "I guess you didn't get my message."

"Well, actually I did."

She cocks her head to one side. "Oh?"

"But I decided to come on over anyway. I was hoping to convince you
to at least come out and have a coffee with me."

"I'm really beat." She pulls the sides of her gown tighter to emphasize
her point.

I try to look as cute as possible. "Please. Just one coffee. Come on, it'll
be fun."

"I don't know."

I put my hands together in front of me like I am praying. "Please."

She laughs and shakes her head. "Okay. Just one coffee. But wait here.
I've got to get dressed."

I go to step inside, but she closes the door, leaving me on the front
steps. I sit down to wait. Across the street is a corner grocery store. A pink
neon LIQUOR sign fills the front window. Jenny's Flowers takes up the
opposite corner. Five-gallon white pails sit outside the store on the sidewalk. They hold bunches of white and yellow daisies, orange birds-of-
paradise, white calla lilies, and pink carnations. A full-figured shaved and

tattooed dyke in a black leather jacket, blue jeans, and Doc Martens walks by. Running along beside her on a retractable leash is a fluffy, black, manicured French poodle. I smile at the woman.

"Come on, RuPaul," she says, tugging on the leash. The dog has found some dirt of interest around a small fig tree that sprouts out of a two-by-two square patch of earth cut into the cement.

Three teenage girls and a boy approach from the opposite direction. The boy holds a huge cassette player on his shoulder. Rap music blares from the speakers. The kids half dance, half walk their way down Fourteenth.

Twenty minutes later the door opens. Mimi appears, wearing tight black jeans, a red V-necked sweater, and a black leather jacket. She has let her hair out and it now hangs halfway down her back. She looks like a femme biker, or some big tough guy's girlfriend. I hold out my arm for her to take as we stroll down the street.

Over double lattes we talk. Her life sounds even crazier than mine. She has been involved for four years with a big old butch called Nat, although her real name is Teresa Maria. They haven't had sex in over three years.

"But the first six months were great," Mimi stresses.

She still calls Nat her partner even though they have officially broken up. She still cooks Nat's dinner and does her laundry. They split up nine months ago when Nat announced that she was a female-to-male transsexual and that she had entered the sex-change program at the University of California, San Francisco. For the last six months, Mimi has been seeing a bisexual woman named Wanda who also isn't having sex with her.

"I go over to her place and we watch videos. I come on to her and she says she's tired," says Mimi. "Every single time. I don't know what to do."

I haven't a stitch of advice to give. At this point, I can barely sort out my own life.

"More coffee?" I say, pushing my chair back to stand.

Against her earlier protests, she agrees to join me for steak-and-whole-bean burritos at La Paloma Blanca on Eighteenth and then at the Cafe for a nightcap. After two drinks she says she really has to go home.

"I'll walk you," I offer. She takes my arm and we leave the bar.

On the porch at her place, I wait while she opens the door.

She looks at me, reaches over and brushes hair out of my eyes. "Would you like to come in for a bit?"

"What about Nat?"

"She's not here. She's gone to visit her mother in Sacramento. She's going to tell her tonight."

"Tell her what?"

"About her sex-change operation."

"Wow."

"Come on in." She takes my hand. It is soft and warm. I squeeze gently. She leads me up a steep flight of stairs and into a large two-bedroom flat with ten-foot ceilings. She gets two bottles of cold Mexican beer out of the fridge and we sit on a couch in the living room. On the far wall is a huge entertainment center with a TV, VCR, and stereo. In a corner of the room, on the floor, sit various sizes of barbells. A bright yellow streetlight sends a harsh glare through the front window. A distant siren wails.

"So?" Mimi says.

"So," I say back.

She takes a sip of beer.

I do the same.

"How long did you say you and Sapphire were together?"

"I didn't." I look into her eyes with desire. She smiles. I move closer to her and take her hand.

"I'd like to kiss you," I say.

She looks nervous as she says, "Okay."

I lean forward and put my lips against hers. I kiss her, but she doesn't exactly kiss back. She just sits there while I do all the kissing. I pull away and look at her.

"Don't you want me to?"

She sighs. "I thought I did," she says. "You're very attractive." She leans forward and runs her fingers through my hair again. "It's just that I didn't realize until this moment that I'm still in love with Nat. It feels wrong to be with somebody else."

"But I thought you said you broke up?"

"We did."

"And she's a transsexual now, or whatever you call it."

"An FTM."

"She's going to become a man."

"I know."

"So how can you be in love with her?"

She folds her arms across her chest like she is getting mad at me. "I don't know. I just am."

"Well, Mimi." I don't know what to say, but I want to say something. This is ridiculous. "Well. As a friend — that is, if I were your friend — I'd say you're selling yourself short. I mean, you said yourself that you haven't had sex with her for three years, and the bisexual isn't having sex with you either."

"Yeah? So? What's your point?"

Uh oh, she is getting mad at me. "Uh..." I laugh, mostly from nerves. "Well, nothing, I guess. I guess I have no point. I guess I'll leave." I stand up, hoping she will grab my arm and say she is sorry, that she is being a fool, please stay. But she does not say anything. I put on my coat. "Well." I stick out my hand.

She takes it and shakes lamely.

"Good-bye," I say, there being nothing else left to say. I open the door and let myself out.

"Who says I'm depressed?" I say on the phone to my mother. I am back on Betty's couch with the quilt pulled up over my head like a tent. Betty is starting to look at me funny. She thinks I'm cracking up.

"Believe me, Nomi. A mother knows."

"Ma. That is so cliche." I pull the quilt up a few inches at the bottom to let in some air.

"Are you eating?"

"Yeah, Ma. Last night I ate a whole box of Oreos."

"You didn't."

"Okay. It was half a box."

Betty is trying to sew a button onto a black denim shirt. She is just about the worst sewer I've ever seen. She keeps jabbing her finger, or losing the needle, or sewing the shirt closed by accident.

"Give me that." I snatch it out of her hand and start sewing it properly.

"Why don't you come too? We're going to the G Spot. It'll be fun. Maybe you'll meet someone."

"No thanks. I'm through with dating. I'm no good at it." I twist the end of the thread into a knot and break it with my teeth.

Betty laughs. "You'll be fine. You just need more practice. Come on. I'll wait while you get ready."

I check the rest of the buttons on her shirt and find a loose one, which I begin to mend. "No. I'm going to stay in and watch *Moonstruck*."

"Again?"

I hand the shirt and the needle to her.

Betty takes a long time getting ready, trying on different clothes, gelling her hair, shining her shoes. When she finally goes, I settle down on the living room couch with a bowl of popcorn, a bottle of Dr. Pepper, and Betty's quilt. I slip *Moonstruck* into the VCR. Dean Martin begins to sing. The phone rings.

"Hello?"

There is silence on the other end.

"Hello? Hello? Who's there?"

"It's me," Sapphire says quietly.

There is silence.

"Hello? Nomi?"

"Yeah. I'm still here. What do you want?"

There is silence.

"I want to see you. Can I come over?"

"No."

"Nomi, please? I want to talk to you."

"Why?" My heart pounds in my chest. The sound of Sapphire's voice moves me deeply — more than I want it to. I put one hand over my rib cage.

"Can't I come over to Betty's? I want to talk in person."

"What happened? Did he dump you?"

There is silence.

I laugh cruelly. "He did, didn't he?" I wait for her to answer.

"Yes," she says quietly.

There is silence.

"So what do you want me to do about it?"

"I want to talk. I'm coming over."

"No! Don't bother." I hang up. Loudly.

Ten minutes later the doorbell rings. I open the door. Sapphire looks terrible, like she's been crying. I want to tell her to go to hell, but I can't. She looks sad, defeated, and lonely. I hold the door open wide. She walks past me and up the stairs. I follow her. She stands in the middle of the living room, hands at her sides. She looks at me, her eyes soft, full of emotion. I can't tell what it is. It might be love, but it could also be regret, or guilt.

"I made a mistake. Nomi. I don't know what else to say. It's over now. Please. I want you back."

I push past her, plop down on the couch, pick up my bowl of popcorn and hold it in my lap. "Are you crazy?"

Sapphire sits beside me on the couch. "Maybe I am. I don't know. I miss you."

I grab a handful of popcorn, shove it into my mouth and chew loudly. On the TV, Cher is fixing Ronny Cammareri a steak.

"Nomi..." Sapphire puts her hand on my arm. I turn to look at her. She is crying. "I'm sorry, Nomi. I love you."

I feel confused. My head feels big and detached, like a helium balloon that wants to float away. The familiar feel of her touch soothes and infuriates me at the same time. I don't know what to do. Nothing like this has ever happened to me before. I jump up and pace back and forth on the living room carpet.

"Let me get this straight, Sapphire. You met some guy, fell in love with him, got dumped, and now you want me back?"

She nods her head and grimaces.

I laugh and slap my hands against my sides. "That's great, Sapphire. That is truly twisted. How do you think I have felt all this time? What do you think this has been like for me? Do you have any idea? You think I can just forgive you? Just like that? And forget that you dumped our three-year relationship on account of some *guy*? Some straight guy?"

"He's bi."

"Oh great. Even better. I hope you used condoms."

"I know you're mad..."

"Mad!? Mad? Are you kidding? I'm furious. And hurt. And humiliated ... and lonely."

"Me too," she says. "I miss you."

I turn my back to her and face the television. Ronny Cammareri throws all of the dinner dishes onto the floor with one drastic sweep of his good arm. Dramatically, he crosses the room and grabs Cher. They kiss. The music swells to a crescendo. I look at Sapphire. I know her so well. I know everything about her.

"You didn't miss me so much last week. Did you?" I snap.

"Nomi. Please, don't do this." From the couch where she sits, Sapphire's head goes back and forth, following my moves as I begin to pace again. She looks like someone who is watching a tennis match. I throw her my best curveball.

"So? Was the sex good?"

"Nomi..."

I step closer to her so that I stand before her, towering over her. "Was it?"

She leaps up and goes to stand by the window, her back to me. The voices of two men talking and laughing in the street drift up through the open window.

"Work it, girlfriend," one of them says.

"Was it!?" I scream across the room at Sapphire.

She turns, glares at me, sighs. "Want do you want, Nomi?"

"Answer my question. Was it good?"

"It was..." She frowns and looks off to the side, almost like she is searching for the right words.

"What?"

"Different." She looks me in the eye. "It was different. Okay? That's all. Just different."

Some instant primal urge comes over me. A vibration starts in my toes and surges through my body at the speed of light. It is absolutely crazy, but I want her. From the street outside, we both hear the screech of car brakes, followed by the unmistakable crash of metal on metal. Then, a cacophony of horns honking. Neither one of us looks out the window. I stare at Sapphire, my eyes set, determined. Wordless, I cross the room. Sapphire gasps. Her hand flies involuntarily to her forehead. She looks like a Southern belle, dazed from the heat and too much gin.

Someone outside is yelling.

I grab Sapphire by the shoulders and bring her to me, my lips on hers, hard, frantic, reckless. She moans, kisses me back, throws her arms around my neck. Just like Ronny Cammareri, I bend over, pick her up under her knees, and carry her to the couch.

"Nomi?"

"Shhh."

I push her back against the cushions and lie on top of her. My hands on both sides of her face, I devour her lips. It feels like our first time and all the other times mixed up into one climactic moment. I reach for her breasts as she tears at my t-shirt. Our clothes drop away and we thrash around, skin against skin, hands wild, free, desperate, climbing, flying on angel-hair wings, to the skies, to the sea, *by the beautiful sea,*
*You and me, you and me, oh how happy we'd be.*
*When the moon hits your eye, like a big pizza pie, that's amore.*
*When the world seems to shine, like you've had too much wine, you're in love.*

My fingers are inside her. I know her body so well. I know just how she likes it. She moves on me, in circles, pushing, sliding. She is soft and wet. I bury my face in her breasts. I fall, sink into a slippery, warm, red liquid fire. Fierce, longing arms hold me, tight, tight, waves crash, break. We kiss. She moans. I feel her inside me, searching, hungry, reaching for my center, my heart, oh honey, oh baby, I miss you. I want you. My body and my heart explode all at once as I come.

"Yes, baby, yes!" I yell. Her hair is in my face, sweet scent of her everywhere, in the air, on my tongue, my fingers, in my mouth, her mouth, my face. Her tongue on my neck, in my ear. She bites my nipples, raw, hard, sweet, pain, pleasure, sliding in and out of me, her, reality, the living room, my life. We drift, float, bob on the sea, *on the sea, on the beautiful sea, you and me, you and me, oh how happy we'd be.*

She comes as fiercely as I, head arched back, eyes closed, spirit open. Her fingernails scratch the skin on my back, in a trail down to my ass, deep, deep, sharp, razor-thin strokes of passion. Longing. Desire. Home. *You and me, you and me, oh how happy we'd be.* Sirens wail in the distance, growing louder. We lie still. I hold her in my arms. A man is still yelling. The ambulance stops right outside the window. The glare of its flashing red light circles around the living room walls. We sweat and we breathe.

From the television in the background, I hear Ronny say, "Love isn't perfeck. Love ruins everything. Love breaks your heart," and I understand for the first time how true the words are. I love Sapphire. And everything is ruined. Our lives, our relationship, our home, my trust, our love. I softly stroke her sweaty forehead, my other arm tight around her. I realize I have no idea what I want to do. Part of me wants our old life back, but I know you can never go backward. The past is past. And everything is different now. Part of me wants to kick her out and make her suffer the way I did. Part of me wants to kiss her, make love with her again, loose myself in her heart, her body, her sweet salty kisses, the comfort of her familiar embrace.

A key turns in the lock. The apartment door opens and Betty walks in. She practically drops a chocolate milkshake she is carrying when she sees me and Sapphire naked and entwined on her couch. I smile meekly, slightly embarrassed. She gives me a look that says she can't wait to hear about this later, smiles, and heads for her bedroom. I squeeze Sapphire tighter to me. We watch the rest of the movie together in silence. I decide not to decide anything until morning.

# Nightlife: Some Kind of Submission

## by Judith P. Stelboum

On the drive back to the house, Veronica listened as her family talked about her sister's wedding. "My baby, my first baby." Her mother kept wiping at her eyes, clutching Veronica's hand, fearful that she, too, would soon leave her. She told Veronica she would save Marie's wedding bouquet for her; it would bring good luck. Aunts, uncles, cousins, friends were pulled apart and dissected: what *she* wore, what *he* said, who looked happy, who had put on weight. Her father chuckled as he reminisced about his favorite relatives, repeating the same stories Veronica had heard all her life. Terry, her younger brother, was a little drunk, moving his arms and humming one of the pop songs played earlier by the band. Hating herself for her inability to enter into the festive family mood and wishing the weekend were over so she could return to her own apartment and her own life, Veronica slouched deeper into her seat and remained silent.

It was past two a.m. before the Santini family calmed down enough to sleep and the bedroom doors were all shut.

Veronica sat on the edge of her bed trying to move her fingers through the sticky spray that plasticized her soft, fine hair. Mechanically, she stepped out of the pink satin dress, showered, washed her hair free from the spray, and scrubbed off the makeup. She put on her black leather jeans, black sweater, and leather jacket. Quietly, she walked down the stairs and out the back door, locking it behind her. She pushed her motorcycle into the darkened street and down to the middle of the block before starting it up; she didn't want the sound of the engine under their windows to wake any of her family.

There was little traffic in the streets so early in the morning, and Veronica could really let the bike out. With the wind blowing against her body, she knew she was riding farther and farther away from the girl who had so passively and politely endured hours of family wishes for her future wedding. *The only thing I have in common with her*, she thought, *is my name*. She wanted to shout out loud, in time with the pumping pistons of the motor-cycle, "I am the real Veronica Santini." She smiled broadly, letting the wind pummel her shoulders and sting her teeth and gums when she opened her mouth to hoop and yell. She roared through the Holland Tunnel with the zeal of a convert and the excitement of the born-again.

When she got to the bar, she circled her bike a few times, giving all the women hanging around outside a chance to look at her. As she turned off the ignition, she could hear the loud, pulsating blast of the music. She unzipped her leather jacket, removed her black helmet, and swung her blond hair free. Anxious with anticipation, she paid the cover charge, checked her helmet, and quickly walked through the smoke-filled, noisy room, to the bar. It had been some time since she had been here as a regular. Beer in hand, she turned, leaned both elbows back on the bar, and surveyed the scene. It was good to be here. The place was packed. She knew it would be on a Saturday night. Where else would they all go? She breathed deeply. The smoke made her eyes blink and burn, and the insistent beat of the music made her heart imitate the bass sounds of the speakers, yet she felt comfortable and began to relax. After a few minutes she noticed individual women, and she cruised the ones she found attractive, her eyes moving quickly along bodies, scanning breasts, asses, legs, arms, hair, and lastly, faces. They were all ages, but she wasn't that particular. She quickly glanced away from couples clinging together, and turned her attention to women who were alone or with friends.

She approached a young woman wearing a t-shirt and jeans and a studded black leather band on her upper arm. She seemed younger than Veronica, probably in her early twenties, with thick, black, curly hair to her shoulders. Her pale skin looked almost ghostlike in the flashing lights of the bar. She was standing with two women, both dressed in black leather jackets similar to Veronica's.

"Hi, do you want another drink?"

"Sure. Thanks." The woman smiled as she looked Veronica up and down. She put out her hand. "My name's Lindsay."

"Veronica." She held Lindsay's hand and squeezed it.

"Are you from New York?"

"No, no. You?"

"No, I came with some friends from Staten Island."

"Oh."

They could hardly hear each other over the music. Veronica suggested they go downstairs. Lindsay spoke to her friends and followed Veronica. The downstairs was quieter, and dimly lit. Five women, smoking cigarettes and holding cue sticks, were huddled over the pool table in the main room. The old carpeting kept in all of the musty mildew smells and Veronica remembered her first time here, when she was so turned off by the grunginess of the place she almost left. Now it didn't seem to matter. There were a few chairs around, and Veronica motioned Lindsay to two that faced each other in a corner.

"Why did you come to this particular bar, Lindsay?"

She had to make sure Lindsay knew what she was getting into.

Lindsay looked at her, shook her head, and laughed quietly. "I know what I'm doing here. Do you?"

Veronica let out a whistling sound from between her teeth, smiled, and held Lindsay firmly by the chin. They laughed together. She took Lindsay's beer and put it down on one of the tables. They got up and walked down the narrow corridor toward the smaller rooms underneath the main dance floor. Veronica could feel the vibration of the music from the walls and the floor. She stopped and turned to face Lindsay, then took her hand and patted it. Lindsay's eyes were wide and Veronica thought she seemed scared. Veronica pushed her gently against the wall and moved her hands up and down the sides of Lindsay's body, touching her nipples with her thumbs and squeezing her breasts gently. She put her face in Lindsay's neck, kissed her, and breathed in a scent of lavender.

"I love the way you smell, Lindsay, but my taste is for something more natural."

She reached down, spread Lindsay's legs, and rubbed her fingers along the seams of the jeans. She smiled to find that Lindsay was already giving off heat and was more than a little bit wet.

Lindsay raised Veronica's face to her own. They kissed and Veronica slipped her tongue into Lindsay's mouth, tasting her lips and pushing against her teeth. Lifting Lindsay's black hair, Veronica put her hand on the back of Lindsay's neck. They turned, looked at each other, and silently walked into one of the rooms.

The room was dark, but they knew they were not alone. They heard sounds coming from every corner. For Veronica, this was part of the excitement of the place. When their eyes adjusted to the dim light, they could discern other bodies. Veronica turned to Lindsay and began to lift off her t-shirt. When Lindsay's head was through, Veronica stopped pulling on the shirt and held Lindsay's hands pinned together over her head.

"Did you know this was what I wanted?" Veronica whispered to her.

"Yes." Lindsay's voice returned the whisper.

"Good."

Veronica pulled Lindsay to her, then caressed her face and kissed her. Lindsay moved her body closer to Veronica's and rubbed herself up and down the leather jacket, her arms still pinned above her head. Veronica ran her hands over Lindsay's exposed breasts, becoming excited by the feel of the smooth, thin skin that covered her rib cage and waist. She pushed her thumb into Lindsay's navel and pressed down. Lindsay raised her fettered arms and encircled Veronica's neck, the cotton fabric of the t-shirt handcuffing her wrists. Veronica's arms tightened in a viselike grip and her mouth hardened as she pulled Lindsay's naked torso tightly against her, knowing that the zippers and buckles of her jacket and pants would mark and cut Lindsay's delicate skin.

Veronica placed one leg behind the pinioned Lindsay, causing her knees to fold, then lowered her, backward, to the floor mat. She opened Lindsay's jeans and began to pull them down over her legs. Lindsay was still caught up in the t-shirt, which forced her arms to be stretched out over her head. Veronica knew that she must be uncomfortable. That's the way she wanted her to be. Lindsay said nothing. Veronica removed all of her own clothes and lay down on top of Lindsay.

"Do you need some help here?" A large, dark-haired woman came over and kneeled down above Lindsay's head, looking straight at Veronica.

Veronica looked down at Lindsay. Her lips turned up at the corners into what was almost a smile. "Do I need help with you?"

"Yes, maybe you should have someone. I ... I would like..." Lindsay looked up at both of them with half-opened eyes and moved her tongue over her open lips.

Veronica turned to the bigger woman. "Okay. Just hold her arms there like that. Make sure she doesn't move."

Veronica moved down Lindsay's body. Her hands fondled Lindsay's ass and she pulled herself up, resting between Lindsay's legs.

The large woman held Lindsay's slender arms out straight in one hand, and with the other began to stroke her exposed breasts.

Veronica was moving her fingers between Lindsay's legs. Lindsay was moaning from the massage on her breasts and from Veronica's soft hands moving up her legs.

Veronica felt the heat between Lindsay's legs. She stroked her clit and moved her fingers to feel the wetness dripping out of her. Then she took the rubber glove from her back pocket and slipped it over her hand, letting the latex slap against her wrist. Lindsay opened her eyes briefly and smiled at Veronica. She rocked her hips slowly from side to side and closed her eyes.

"Lindsay," Veronica breathed, in a low, husky voice, "I'm going to fuck you, so slowly and so long, and there's nothing you can do to stop me. I don't care what you want or how you want it. You'll do what I want now." She softly kissed Lindsay's neck and moved to her throat and mouth, slowly moving her tongue over Lindsay's lips but never going inside her mouth. Lindsay tried to move her head up off the floor to meet Veronica's mouth, but she was being held firmly by her arms and was helpless.

Veronica spread Lindsay's legs as far as they would go, forcing Lindsay to raise her knees off the floor. Even though Lindsay was so wet that she didn't need much lube, Veronica slowly rubbed a generous amount on her glove. First her overlapping fingers entered Lindsay, then her thumb, folded inside her palm. Moving slowly in and out, deeper with each thrust, she pressed into her, past the widest part of her hand. Pushing inside her, intent on the rhythmic ebb and flow, she felt Lindsay open up to take her all in. Inside her now, her hand curled to fit and fill the shape of Lindsay. Her hand would be what Lindsay needed.

Lindsay was shaking her head and starting to gasp, but the woman over her removed her hand from Lindsay's breast and clamped it over her mouth so that Lindsay could not scream. Veronica gave her the nod when she stopped moving her arm, and the woman released Lindsay's mouth and went back to her breasts. She rubbed Lindsay's nipples and squeezed her breasts. Then she bent down and took Lindsay's small tit into her mouth to bite on. Veronica knew Lindsay would have some bruises, but hoped she would have good memories to go with them. She concentrated now on the feeling of being inside this woman, of stretching her wide and pushing into her so deep. She was in past her wrist. Lindsay was breathing hard and fast.

"Lindsay. Lindsay," Veronica called to her.

Veronica began to open her hand just a little bit. She felt Lindsay contract and try to move away. Veronica would not let her escape. She pulled Lindsay's hips forward, toward the arm that was planted inside of her, and sat looking at Lindsay's face.

"What do you think?" asked the woman at Lindsay's head. "Want something for this little one's butt?" She called to another woman who was leaning against the wall watching, her hands between her naked legs.

"Hey, can you get us some equipment from the closet over there?" She motioned with her head, not wanting to remove her hands from Lindsay's breasts.

The woman nodded and returned with a large dildo, a butt plug, and a condom.

"You can use this harness when you want." She placed all of the items next to Veronica.

Veronica glanced down at the pink dildo and black leather harness. She was engrossed in being deep inside Lindsay and didn't want to think about other possibilities.

*I don't even know her,* she thought. *Probably Lindsay is not even her real name. But, at this moment, I know her better than anyone in the world, and she knows me. She trusts me not to hurt her.*

Slowly, she began to move her arm and spread her fingers inside Lindsay. The woman at Lindsay's head continued to hold Lindsay and squeeze her breasts, pulling hard and twisting each of her nipples.

Veronica was very excited. She knew she must control herself. Each thrust and opening of her fist brought her closer to orgasm, and she knew she was just waiting for Lindsay so her own orgasm would be intensified. She placed her head and shoulder on Lindsay's belly and began to talk to her. Urging her on, Veronica whispered how good she felt inside and how open she was. She told her she wanted to come together with her.

Lindsay came while the woman above her had her tongue inside Lindsay's mouth. Veronica could feel the contractions deep inside Lindsay's body and, in unison, she felt those same contractions start deep inside herself. Everything seemed to stop: the movement, the noise, the throb of the music, the moans from Lindsay. The room was removed from the world. They were floating, swimming, flying together, no longer tied here to this earth by their disembodied bodies. The two of them were flying high, looking down, joined together in their most intimate parts, never to separate. Never to let this feeling go. Infinite and finite together. Veronica kept still inside Lindsay for a long time, then slowly removed her hand.

Sweat covered Lindsay's body, and Veronica motioned for the woman above Lindsay's head to release her. Veronica gently pulled the t-shirt off, lowered Lindsay's arms to her sides, and began to wipe the sweat off her face, neck, and breasts. She moved up to Lindsay's side. "Lie still. Don't tense the muscles in your stomach. Just relax. You'll be fine."

"Yeah, I know. I feel just fine already." She smiled. "More than fine. Great." Lindsay reached for Veronica's hand and held it to her mouth.

"Yes," Veronica said, smiling back. "I know what you mean."

Veronica leaned back against the wall, held Lindsay in her lap, and let out a long sigh. At last her body slumped and she closed her eyes.

The sun was already up when Veronica turned her motorcycle into the driveway of her parents' home.

Veronica was surprised to find her mother sitting at the kitchen table so early in the morning. She had planned to quietly slip back into her room and into bed before anyone had seen her.

"Veronica, I thought you were still sleeping."

Her mother was staring at her. She tried to act nonchalant and tucked her helmet under her arm, but she knew that the boots, black leather jacket, and dark, mirrored aviator glasses were too much of a contrast to the Veronica who had so pleased her mother just a few hours ago.

*Well tough,* she thought. *This is the real me.*

"Mom, I ... I just couldn't sleep. All the excitement of the wedding. So I thought I would just take a little ride for a while."

"I hate that motorcycle. You and Terry fooling around with those ... bikes, you call them. It's dangerous. Every time you come down from Connecticut on your motorcycle, I worry."

Both of them avoided talking about the real problem.

"I'm always careful. You shouldn't worry so much. You know I don't ride in the winter, or when it's wet outside. It's okay, really."

She walked over to her mother and kissed her on the cheek. "I'm really tired, Mom. Think I'll just sleep for a little bit this morning."

Alone in her room, sitting on her bed, Veronica was conscious of having to reinforce her identity all the time. Sometimes the markers of her self took strange expressions. She knew that. It didn't matter and she didn't care. She was in new territory and she wasn't afraid. She was excited about the possibilities. She could create the world if she had to, in order to keep who she wanted to be alive and intact. But most of the time, it took all of her energies to create her self in so many different ways. Everyone and everything tried to force her into those selves already known. She knew what she didn't want. It wasn't as clear what she did want.

She sat down on the bed and wondered if she would ever be in a place where she felt secure, where she wouldn't have to push herself, test herself, reinvent herself again and again. Who would she be then? What would she be? She didn't know and was too drained and tired to think anymore. Right now the end was not in sight. Right now, the road was all in front of her. With her right hand lightly covering her face, each inhalation of Lindsay softened her hard, tense body into sleep.

# Shoe Stop

## by Carolyn L. King

Dacia had changed six times and had spent the last twenty minutes trying to find the right shoes for an outfit she wasn't sure she wanted to wear.

Karen, her lover of eleven months, was ready save for her shoes, which were buried under the pile Dacia had created.

The last three times Dacia had visited Atlanta, she had dodged meeting Karen's mother. Finally Karen caught on to the scam, and on this go round had made up her mind that the jig was up. Dacia would meet her mother ... today!!

Dacia knew she had no way out, but there was no rule that she could not procrastinate for as long as possible.

She was working on prolonging the inevitable into a fine art when Karen opened her mouth and broke the spell. "You can't avoid this again, baby. You're going to meet my mother today." Dacia continued to stare into the pile of shoes as Karen spoke. "We've put her off too many times already."

"Oh, I-I know! I just wanna find the right shoes," Dacia mumbled softly.

"She's not going to look at your shoes."

"Oh, I know. I just wanna be comfortable. Plus, I'm not sure I wanna wear this outfit."

Karen was getting annoyed. "What you're wearing is fine."

"I-I know. I just wanna be comfortable," she repeated. "Look at you. You're comfortable. Why shouldn't I be?"

"I know you're nervous, but trust me, baby, you really don't need to be this way."

"Be what way?" Now Dacia was annoyed.

"Nervous!" Karen challenged her lover's denial.

"Nervous?! Nervous?!" Dacia slipped into grande diva for this show-down. Her neck started to roll, a hand went up on a hip, and a singular finger was waving in the air. "Excuse me, Miss Thing, but I am *not* nervous. You *know* when I'm nervous. I talk a lot and my throat gets dry. My throat is not dry and I do believe I was in a quiet mood until *you* accused me of being nervous! Thank you *very* much!"

To punctuate the end of her speech, Dacia rolled her head back into its original start position (with assistance from invisible ball bearings) and placed her finger-weapon back into the invisible holster at her other hip. Despite this performance, she was startled by the look in Karen's eyes. It was that I'm-about-to-say-something-about-all-of-this-and-I-want-you-to-be-prepared-'cause-it-ain't-gonna-be-pretty-and-I-might-hurt-your-feelings-so-you-need-to-brace-yourself look.

Instead, Karen uttered between clenched teeth, "You're nervous."

"Think what cha wanna think. I don't care." Dacia's voice had taken on a bit of a sarcastic edge in preparation for round two. "We're just meeting your mother, who just happens to be a minister in the church you grew up in all your life. It's not a big deal. This happens to me all the time."

"I told you a long time ago. My mother has always known about me. Yeah, she may not approve of my lifestyle, but she also knows she can't change me. She loves me and wants me to be happy. She knows I'm happy with you and that makes us both happy."

Karen stood up and moved closer to Dacia and the pile of shoes. "Look. She *wants* to meet you. Once she figured out that the distance created between us when I tell her nothing about my life is worse than the few minutes of discomfort she experiences just talking about it, she was okay. She has already lost one child to drugs. She doesn't want to lose another to intolerance."

Karen stretched her arms out to embrace Dacia, who offered a bit of resistance but soon melted into her lover's arms.

Before Dacia could react, Karen was behind her, sliding her arms around Dacia's waist and cupping her breasts tightly. She talked softly into Dacia's shoulder and rocked her gently from side to side.

"You're nervous and we both know it. You're full of excess energy and you really need to release it." She laughed that naughty laugh that always gave Dacia goose bumps when they had phone sex. "I'm going to help you ... release."

Karen slipped her hands from Dacia's breasts to her rounded belly, then to her pants. Dacia melted further into her lover's chest as her belt was unbuckled, her zipper unzipped, and her button undone. Her loose-fitting slacks fell to her ankles and joined the pile of shoes.

Karen started to hum that bump-and-grind song as she continued to rock her lover. On the chorus, she sang the words softly into Dacia's ear, sending those familiar goose bumps all over Dacia's body again. Dacia's nipples responded accordingly.

Karen ran her hands slowly over Dacia's belly, hips, and breasts. She ground her hips into Dacia in a circular fashion that matched the tempo of her humming. Dacia pressed her ass back at Karen to catch a ride on the wave of her lover's motions.

"Turn around ... slowly," Karen whispered into Dacia's ear.

Dacia began to turn, reluctant to disconnect from the movement behind her and hindered slightly by the pants around her ankles. She stared her lover in the eye, noticing that sexy half-mast look that always meant *oh chil' things 'bout to get good.* Dacia closed her eyes, letting whatever was to happen, happen.

With a blink of an eye, Karen whisked Dacia's panties down to her ankles. Dacia stepped out of them and her slacks willingly. Karen was still humming that song. Dacia's breath caught in her chest when she felt warm breath and little wet licks on her belly button. Oh, how she loved having her belly button licked. The sensation shot straight to her cunt, making her knees weak and her thighs quake. Karen always contended that she could make Dacia come by simply licking her belly button, though, to date, she has not followed through on that promise.

She was still humming that song.

Dacia's eyes remained closed. She didn't want to ruin the mood by remembering that they were in Karen's small apartment and not on a magic carpet riding high above Egypt or Nairobi or some other exotic destination. For now, she and her baby were above the clouds, ridin' high.

Karen's tongue progressed downward along Dacia's treasure trail, that fine line of hair that always led to paradise, as far as she was concerned. Dacia's breathing was more rapid, but she was quiet, riding in her mind with her baby.

She returned home for just a moment to part her thick thighs for Karen, then she was off again. Karen dragged her tongue slowly from the bottom to the top of Dacia's wet lips. The taste was a combination of cum, sweat, and a strange sweet. Karen adored how her lover tasted. She had to hold herself back from mashing her face into Dacia's cunt and making her come too soon.

Dacia began gently pumping her hips toward Karen's mouth. Karen firmly held on to her girlfriend's sexy honey-colored hips. She knew what would follow the gentle rhythmic hip action.

Karen was getting high from the smell, the taste, and the movement of her lover. Her own eyes were closed, but she knew exactly where she was going. Her tongue hit the target! She took short little licks at first, then edged into long, flat-tongued licks. Dacia's hips moved faster now, urging that tongue to lick deeper, lick longer. Karen's nose and chin were getting wet.

She dragged her tongue slowly to the opening, which was spilling out copious amounts of what she affectionately called fruit juice. Karen liked fruit juice ... a lot! She cupped her tongue and collected a spoonful to drink and savor. The smooth liquid coated her entire tongue, and Karen tasted every aspect of its peculiar flavor. Sweet. Salty. Bitter. She liked it all. Karen liked fruit juice ... a lot!

With the increase in hip gyrations, Karen knew it was time to bring her baby home. Time to put that magic carpet into overdrive and do a couple of wheelies! She swirled her tongue frantically around Dacia's clit. She used her lips and teeth until she felt trembling in the soft hips she held. She could hear increased breathing overhead, but no words.

"Twizzle, twazzle, twizzle, twome. Time for this one to come home." Being the cartoon fanatic that she was, Karen never missed an opportunity to use a line from one of her favorite characters, Mr. Wizard.

She mashed her nose farther into Dacia's cunt to bring her lover home sweet home. Karen licked and sucked Dacia's cunt from top to bottom, using her tongue to touch and taste every inch of her lover. Dacia was rapidly moving back and forth over Karen's mouth and tongue, lost in what was building and moving fiercely through her body. Ka-blam!!!

Once she released Karen's hair, where her fingers were unconsciously tangled, Dacia allowed her body to crumble to the floor, joining the pile of shoes. She breathed in deep the smell of old leather and sweat, then drifted into an afterglow nap.

She was awakened by a gentle hand stroking her high-top fade. Karen was trying not to laugh as she stared into Dacia's sleepy eyes. "I just called my mother, to let her know we would be a little late. She said not to rush. She said she was having trouble deciding which shoes to wear."

They both screamed and bellowed out riotous laughter. Dacia pulled Karen down to join her among the shoes. She planted one of her okay-baby-pack-a-lunch-'cause-this-is-going-to-be-a-good-long-ride kisses on her lover's lips. Ladies, start your engines! The checkered flag was dropped and they were off. Karen was behind the wheel of a classic 1967 red convertible Ford Mustang, with four on the floor and plenty of petro. Dacia gently eased into first, then slammed into third. Karen's head was resting on the plush headrest, which doubled as a pair of Air Jordan's. She relaxed her body into the seat and let Dacia navigate her to the finish line.

# I Learned My Lesson

## by Paula K. Bodenstein

I guess you could've called me rebellious in high school, though I was not really a troublemaker. I merely detested stupid rules and forms that existed only to perpetuate the status quo. I did, however, like to push the boundaries of convention at times, for the world seemed a safer place if I knew where the edges were. And, with the exception of the head girls' gym coach, I was generally respectful of those edges. Something about her made me step over the brink even when it meant I'd be hanging over a chasm by my fingertips.

Miss Julrian and I had developed a sparring relationship fairly early on in my freshman year. I'd try to fly in the face of just about everything she did, and she'd try to catch me at it every single time. She'd make us run around the track twenty times; I'd try to get away with eighteen and end up doing forty. She'd pair me up with the most hopeless teammate in the class; I'd turn the girl into an athlete. It was about defiance, about power. She had the upper hand, and we both knew it. *But, after all...,* I'd think, *what can she really do to me, anyway?*

One day in my junior year, it was snowing hard so we took gym inside. Having gone without breakfast, I was hungry and tired. My blood sugar level was probably off the charts. I had spent my small reserve of energy getting dressed into the stupid uniform. We played volleyball. Everyone played so pitifully that the ball barely ever so much as grazed the net. At any rate, I certainly never came close to breaking a sweat. So when we finally broke for lunch, I decided to forgo the showers in order to get a jump on the cafeteria line.

This took a little scheming. Skipping the shower was close to a cardinal sin in this school. I never could get what the big deal was. Anyway, I got caught. Just as I was about to happily slip through those musty portals and skip into the path of steamy, buttery kitchen aromas, I heard my name being screamed from the back of the locker room: "Turner, get back here!" I decided to pretend I hadn't heard, and scurried onward like a mouse that had just felt the wind of a snapped trap on the tip of its tail.

But it was not to be. A classmate drifted up limply behind me, carrying the message like an automaton, and said in a dispassionate monotone, "Carlee, Miss Julrian's calling you." I was only a few feet from the end of the lunch line, but saw that I couldn't just keep going. I eyed the classmate with contempt. Such a mindless puppet!

I figured it was just out of meanness that Miss Julrian waited until everyone had filed out before she addressed me. "Turner, you didn't shower," she sang.

"I didn't need to," I returned.

"It doesn't matter if you need to or not. Rule is that everyone showers."

"But it's stupid. I never even broke a sweat!"

"Sorry ... After school."

"What?!"

"I said you'll see me after school. You don't have time for a shower now, so you'll take one then."

"Are you serious?" I jeered. "I ain't takin' no shower after school!"

"Yes, you are, or you'll find yourself suspended." Her voice was so calm and self-assured. She folded her husky arms in front of her, and raised her eyebrows and dropped her jaw, sucking in her cheeks and eyeing me as if she could care less one way or the other. I spun on my heel and stormed out, throwing the heavy door open as far as it'd reach. Just before it burped shut I heard her laugh and say, "Don't cross me, Turner. I have all the guns!"

By the time school let out, I had calmed down a bit. It was still snowing hard. The thought of walking over three miles home after taking a shower spurred me to hurry. The buses were moving slowly in the piling drifts, and I figured there was an outside chance that I could even catch one if I got done quickly.

One look at Julrian's face, and I knew I didn't have an ice cube's chance in hell. This was doomed to be an ordeal. We were alone in the locker room. The other coaches had the good sense to get out while they could still navigate the parking lot. A table stood outside her office. She motioned for me to drop my books on it and told me to get undressed.

"Right here?" I bid incredulously.

"Right here," she confirmed.

I'm thinking, *oh shit, this is for real. She's gonna make me squirm. She must be pissed.* I could feel my chest cave in like a shrinking tire, my confidence seeping through the crack. I undressed in a flash. Her eyes didn't leave me once. I could feel them wherever they landed, even when I turned away to slip out of my panties. I remembered hearing girls call her a "lezzie" or a "dyke," but I had always walked away when they started up on her. I'd feel a kind of creeping heat crawl up my neck, and my entire scalp would scrunch up as if it were being pulled by a thousand tiny stitched-in threads. Back then, I didn't know why.

Now, while I stood there, opened to her scrutiny like one of those poor frogs pinned down on a biology tray, that creeping heat surprised me. This time it started lower, in my belly. She seemed to register my confusion, and handing me the shampoo and an open, new bar of soap, motioned me to the stalls.

"I have to shampoo, too?!" I bellowed. She gave no reply, just herded me with her sheer bulk to the far end. She tossed a towel over her shoulder and grabbed the other end from behind her neck. I started the water. There were no curtains to fool with, but I could partially duck into a corner while I adjusted the temperature. I glanced her way. She stood directly in front of the opening, her feet spread wide apart, evenly, her two hands grasping the towel ends at breast height.

"Reach up and grab that nozzle so I can be sure you wet down all the way," she ordered. I did it. The warm water felt good as it ran from the crown of my head down over my shoulders. I adjusted the temperature higher. Then I poured some shampoo and lathered up. It struck me why she had made me wash my hair when it wasn't normally required: it'd take a lot longer, especially with hair as long and thick as mine.

When I rinsed, big soft rafts of suds floated down my body and snagged at various junctions until a giant wash of water would send them on. I kept my eyes closed, knowing hers were probably like saucers. "Get under your armpits, too," she barked. I looked at her. Being one of the first women's libbers, my soft underarm hair grew as wild and free as moss. She watched approvingly while I soaped it to a froth.

Shoulders, neck, arms ... I spent too long on my arms, turning sideways to her and soaping them over and over. Bared as they normally are to the mundane world, I thought my arms would assuage her ardor and I flushed when I realized that, to the contrary, they suddenly exuded a lithesome sensuality that I had never noticed before. There was desire in their folds, beckoning in every screaming cell. I began to realize that I had some power here, as well. I could freak old Julrian out. I could play the game better than she would dare. The shame I felt about my own oozing sexuality began to recede like a tide, and an unfamiliar boldness washed in.

I let my hands graze my breasts and tease my nipples, which rose to a point — probably more from what I was thinking than from the touch. I threw my head back and caressed my neck from the ridge of my jawline down my open throat to my clavicle. I smoothed the soap along my neck, under my ears, down my shoulders, and across my chest, making my forearm crush my breasts. When I released my arm, my breasts bounced back and a gush of suds ran down my body. I saw her shift. It was working.

Gliding the bar of Palmolive down my belly, I started soaping in circles. I was thin, but not skinny. My stomach caved in slightly from my long sloped hipbones. The suds collected when I turned away from the spray and formed a shelf of foam along the top of my pubic hairline. I could see that this was driving her mad. She swallowed, pretending not to notice. The shower echoed in the empty stalls, a constant and deafening barrage to our ears that created a container around us. We were held together by the thundering and the steam, she and I. And it seemed to barricade us from the outside world, a wall of sound that locked us in the closeness of the present. Nothing outside of this moment existed.

I twirled the bar in my hands about ten times and set it in the dish. Then, with my back to the water, I began to lather my pubic hair with my hands. I spread my legs slightly and let my hands wander to my inner thighs as well. But the water over my shoulder kept rinsing the suds away. In a spurt of audacity that surprised even me, I reached for the big bar of soap and slowly pushed it between my legs. From her vantage point, it must've looked as though I'd swallowed the creamy green bar up into my nether mouth. It slid like shiny wax knuckles along the folds of my lips, the hard rounded edge of it glancing my clitoris deliciously. I caught her thwarted glare and had to squelch a sigh and a snicker at the same time.

"All right, all right!" Julrian tore in. "Hurry up and rinse off." She turned sideways to me, folding her arms over her chest. I could see that her nipples were as hard as trigonometry. I had won a small victory. I aimed the spray at my mound and rinsed away. Then I turned my back to her and shut off the water with one hand. With the other, I squeezed the water from my clean hair, sending a torrent down my back. I could feel the water funnel in a V from the soft upper round of my hips down into a rivulet at the crack of my ass. It felt good.

When the noise stopped, the quiet expanse of the cement walls and the utter silence were like a splash of cold water. The dripping faucet echoed eerily. She handed me the towel and I wrapped myself in it and ran gracelessly, teetering on the sides of my feet in an attempt to keep them off the freezing floor. I dried in a flash and started to dress. Julrian went into the glassed-in cubicle of her office. She could've watched me from in there, but she didn't. I started to think about what I'd just done. Quickening my pace even more, I jumped into the lavatory and plugged in the spare hairdryer. The counter along the mirror was littered with bobbypins, brushes, and discarded makeup. Bending at the waist, I threw my hair forward and began to apply the hot wind of the dryer. On the tile under the counter, someone had written in lipstick, "Julrian eats pussy." My hair seemed to take forever to dry.

Coat and books in hand, I walked to her door and stopped. I knew I should. "You'll catch your death out there," she said softly. "I'd better give you a lift home." I felt the respect in her demeanor and knew I had nothing to fear.

"No, thanks anyway," I replied. "I think I'd prefer to walk." I strolled out.

The snow was drifting down in big, luscious flakes that billowed and gathered soundlessly. The world was deep blue and silent. I felt the warm moisture of my skin welcome the sobering cold. Inside, a heat arose in me. This time, it started between my ears and flushed downward. It was my opening, my awakening.

# Special Delivery

## by Kitty Tsui

It was a foggy Sunday afternoon at the height of the San Francisco summer. Cassidy had already finished reading both the *Sunday Chronicle* and the *New York Times*, done three loads of laundry, paid overdue bills, and washed and waxed her car. She had planned to take a hike along the Point Reyes shoreline with her dog, Jessie, but somehow it was already the middle of the afternoon and too late to take a long drive.

Cassidy was a single girl. Had been for some months. Her last relationship had lasted two years, a record for her. But the ex-lover had been dependent and domineering, and Cassidy had vowed not to have another repeat. Not for a long time.

It had been months since she had been with anyone. She was horny as hell. Heck, it had been months since she had even *thought* of sex. But she was thinking about it now.

Her first time with Lena. Dusk at Baker Beach. Two lone fishermen wading in the waves, their lines silver arcs in the air. She and Lena huddled behind a sand dune. The roar of the ocean matched the cadence of her heartbeat. The moon rose, a brilliant white in the indigo sky. She stared for so long that the image burned into her retinas.

At first their kisses had been shy, tentative. Then the months of pent-up energy were released. The tsunami hit them full force. One minute they had been kissing awkwardly. Teeth hitting. Embarrassed laughter. The next thing she knew, she was on her stomach, her face in the sand, the taste of the sea in her mouth. The air was startling, like cold water from a shower turned on full force. Somehow her jeans were halfway down her legs and Lena was on top of her, her fingers working their way expertly, exquisitely, inside.

She groaned, her mouth gritty with sand.

"Yes, yes. Oh, that feels so good."

She was so wet she couldn't believe it. Had the ocean somehow defied the laws of nature and traveled uphill, soaking her while she had been pre-occupied? But no, it was a wet warmth, familiar and pleasing, like hot cocoa. Lena was rocking on top of her. The weight of her body felt solid, comforting. Lena's fingers, slick with her juices, slipped out of her and slowly traced the line of her crack. She stiffened.

"You okay?" Lena whispered. Her fingers stopped, lingered.

Yes, she was okay. She did not want the feeling to end.

"Don't stop. Oh, baby, don't stop, please don't!"

She lay very still then, pressed to the cold sand, her every pore open. Goose bumps spread across her body like wildfire. Lena's mouth was bit-ing her neck, her shoulders. Savage bites, followed by long sucking caresses. Lena's fingers were coaxing her flesh to sing. She was burning down there. Burning. Hot. Cold. Nails of ice piercing her flesh. Silken strands caressing her skin. She was afraid. She had never felt like this before. She wanted it. Oh, yes, she wanted to be fucked.

When Lena entered her, she thought she would die from sheer plea-sure. Her cries tore the thick quilt of night. Lena held her tight, stayed inside her, unmoving. The pleasure gathered deep inside, where Lena's fingers were. But she could restrain herself no longer. Her muscles gripped and strained, moving with their own power.

Finally, she could stand it no longer.

The words, "Fuck me, please, fuck me," burst from her lips.

Lena happily complied.

Later, under the moonlight, Cassidy had admired Lena's forearm, pumped with blood and pulsing with power.

"Thanks for the workout," Cassidy had grinned.

"My pleasure," Lena grinned back.

What a night that had been! Cassidy smiled at the memory. It had been months since she had been with anyone and she was ripe for picking and ready for anything.

As she was newly clean and sober, the thought of going to a bar and cruising nauseated her. She thought about going to some political event but felt uneasy about pursuing her real agenda in those oh-so-correct sit-uations. At times like these, she was jealous of gay men in the carefree seventies, with their bathhouses and back rooms for anonymous sex.

Cassidy tried to think of other things to do: work out at the gym, jog in Golden Gate Park with Jessie, have coffee in the Castro, cruise at the

Museum of Modern Art, go shopping for things she didn't need and put them on plastic. Or order a pizza with everything on it.

Cassidy decided the latter was her safest bet. Pizza with extra everything. Still there were so many choices; it was not as simple as sausage or pepperoni, onions or mushrooms anymore. There was feta and cilantro, eggplant and Gruyère, garlic and sundried tomato. Regular, whole wheat, thin crust, deep dish.

She decided on garlic and baby clams and ordered a large with extra cheese. It wouldn't matter if she couldn't finish it, she could have cold pizza with coffee for breakfast. Best of all, her Jessie didn't mind garlic breath, and she got to eat pizza too.

The pizza place was true to its ad: the doorbell rang in fifty minutes. Jessie jumped up and ran to the door barking as the delivery person approached, cloaked with the heady aroma of pizza. Jessie loved anyone bearing food, even if it was not meant for her. But that didn't matter; she always got something.

It wasn't until Cassidy pulled money out of her wallet and handed it to the deliveryman that she realized that he was actually a she. Tall, broad-shouldered, with square, brown hands. And good-looking to boot.

Got to be a dyke, she said half out loud.

"Excuse me?" The woman grinned, showing white, even teeth.

"Uh, nothing." Cassidy turned as red as a beet.

She took the pizza and shut the door in a hurry.

"Did ya get a look at her, Jessie? Woulda liked to have asked her in to eat! Woulda liked to eat her! What would you have done, huh, girl?"

Jessie licked her chops, her tail wagging a mile a minute at the prospect of food.

"I swear, girl, you have no shame. Jessie, I'm talking to you about serious stuff and all you're interested in is food. Okay, hold on, you can have a piece too."

Between the two of them, they finished the pizza easily.

"Damn, that was good. I'm stuffed. Are you?"

Jessie wagged her tail and whined for more.

"That's it, girl. All gone. Okay, you want more, you call the pizza place and request the same delivery person and I'll spring for another, okay?"

Jessie looked at her mistress and wagged her tail happily.

"Forget it, girl. I know you want more. But I've had enough. Or have I?"

The next day at work Cassidy couldn't stop thinking about the delivery person. When she got home there were no messages on her machine, something that always made her feel forlorn. After she took Jessie for a romp in the park, she contemplated her choices for dinner. The worst part of living alone was cooking for herself. And damn, she couldn't stop thinking about the delivery person.

"No way am I going to eat pizza two nights in a row," she said to Jessie.

*Pizza's great every night, Mom,* Jessie replied.

She scanned a stack of take-out menus lazily, as if to trick her true intentions. There was Chinese, barbecue, Italian, Thai, or sushi.

*Pizza, Mom, pizza,* urged Jessie, wagging her tail.

"Okay, you've convinced me. What shall we have on it tonight? I know, anything with meat, right?"

*You got it, Mom! Oh, and don't forget extra cheese. Skip the garlic though, just in case.*

Cassidy remembered that a two-dollar-off coupon had been attached to her bill the previous evening. That was it. A sure sign that she was to order out. She called the pizza place and was put on hold for what seemed like forever. Then she got disconnected.

"I'm not supposed to be doing this. What if it's her night off? What if she has a different route tonight?"

Jessie fixed her with her liquid brown eyes.

*Mo-ther!*

"Okay, okay. One more try."

This time she was successful in placing her order. Before she hung up she added, "Um, the woman who delivered last night, is she working this evening? Oh, okay. Thanks."

Jessie looked up at her mother's crestfallen face.

"Tough luck, kiddo, she's doing special deliveries. Oh, well, it's just you and me, girl. Better luck next time, huh?"

When the doorbell rang, Jessie sprang off her bed, barking.

"Hold on," Cassidy shouted as she went to find her wallet. She was in no hurry. The doorbell rang again.

"Okay, already. You want to be paid or not?"

She opened the door. Jessie ran out between her legs, tail wagging furiously.

"Jessie, get in here. Jessie! What do I owe you?"

She started to count out dollar bills. Jessie bumped into her excitedly, and the money fell from her hand. She bent to pick it up. As she stood, she noticed a suspicious bulge in the crotch of the deliveryman's jeans.

*Oh, great,* she thought, *just great. A young jock with a hard-on.*

Her eyes went from his crotch to his hands. They were brown and very square. She looked at his face, partially hidden under a baseball cap. The delivery person had a grin the size of a watermelon.

"Sausage with extra cheese. Skip the garlic. Special delivery."

*Oh, yes,* Cassidy purred, *I love a woman who packs.*

"Come on in," she invited, "come in and help me eat."

# Life with B: Erotica in G Major Opus 33

## by Lindsay Taylor

*A*DAGIO *(slow tempo), with moments of RITENUTO (holding back):* March 4, 1992. Your office, overlooking the Brooklyn Bridge. Six-thirty p.m. The other attorneys have gone home. I am resolved to bring a sexual harassment suit against my supervisor. Your legal advice is business as usual. Seven months later you will tell me how that night you had to fight the other feelings.

*March 18.* You phone me at my office to further clarify my options. You leave out the one I hoped you would include.

*March 30.* I learn from the mutual friend who referred you that you are an odd assortment. Your now-divorced parents brought you into this world as a red-diaper baby and sang you to sleep with labor songs. You were bred in San Francisco, with all the makings of a lefty. In the late sixties you and your then-fiancé, a hippie trapped in a business suit, demonstrated at events that history now calls the Free Speech Movement. The eighties found you, like so many of your fellow baby boomers, leaving San Francisco, and the world of protest, far behind. You became a lawyer and bought a Beamer.

You soon learn from the same mutual friend that my checkerboard past began in New England, many years later. You learn that I exude upper-middle-class values through my knowledge of fine art and music, but lived my childhood in impoverished gentry. You typecast me as the quintessential New York dyke who wears too much black, knows all the good Chinese restaurants from midtown to Canal Street, recites the underground club scene from A to Z, and subscribes to *Out, Deneuve, Ten Percent,* and *Girljock*. You learn that in 1985 I fled from New England and planted my one suitcase in SoHo, sight unseen. You are impressed that someone in her twenties has so quickly moved up the ranks in the recording industry, though you are quick to remember that, with my pending sexual harassment case, this soon may topple.

*April 4*. I confess to my lover of three years, who also wears too much black, that I have a crush on you. She accuses me of being infatuated with an authority figure. To console myself, I write.

*I can't believe I've been thinking what I've been thinking. It started soon after I met you. It's only gotten worse-better. I think of how I would make love to you. About three times every hour. Thinking the thought. And making love. I imagine how you sound when you reach a climax inside yourself. I want to know how this sounds.*

*I hold my lips slightly apart and imagine yours brushing over them. I picture myself slowly lying you down on your bed. You have fresh white cotton sheets. But not for long.*

*I feel myself descend upon your welcoming naked body. You take me in. I move slowly over you, touching you lightly. You move with me, guiding me. Your well-defined biceps lead me to speculate that, customarily, you have to be coaxed into being a bottom.*

*I ask you how you like to be made love to, and how you want me to begin touching you now. You playfully tell me that you want me to find out for myself.*

*We share eye contact that doesn't make us turn away. Your warm, blue-gray eyes make my insides drop. I brush your golden brown hair back, revealing a hint of gray underneath, and lean on my elbows to look at you. You grin as you reach out to touch my blond hair, remarking that my eyes are growing greener. You let me into your mouth, deep. You murmur, and it seems to come from your whole body. You wrap your arms around me and pull me in. Our bodies become moist. I stay in your mouth.*

*With my thigh I make light, circular motions over your clitoris. Your short, irregular breaths tell me that you like this. I give you one more deep kiss before I descend upon the insides of your legs. You spread them for me, telling me that I am well on my way to finding out what you like.*

*My tongue barely brushes inside you, the sensation of mango forming around my mouth, before your body jerks up and arcs like a small wave. You spread your fingers wide and flat before settling back onto the semifresh white cotton sheets. You pull on my shoulder and ask me to come up to your face. You whisper that you want to come again. I quickly cover your mouth with mine and insert two fingers. You inhale quickly, as if you have been caught by surprise. I place your middle finger on your clitoris and begin a soft, circular motion. You flutter, unsure as to whether you should feel pleased by, or exposed from, touching yourself in front of me. I keep my mouth over yours.*

*Together we move inside you. Within moments your body arcs again. You sigh inside my mouth. I do not take mine away. Seconds pass. You suddenly roll us over and we flip positions. I barely catch my breath as you straddle yourself over me. You turn me over on my stomach and press down hard on my upper arms. You begin to laugh mischievously. You take the back of my neck in your teeth and begin spreading my legs from behind.*

*I can't believe I've been thinking what I've been thinking. I can't believe I met you filing a sexual harassment suit.*

*May 26.* At your suggestion, my lover, your on-again off-again lover, you, and I have dinner at the Russian Tea Room prior to the one-night-only appearance of the San Francisco Gay and Lesbian Chorus. Your profile. Your smile. Your gestures. Your laugh. Do not go unnoticed. Part of me wants you to notice that I am noticing.

*June 1.* Business as usual. The opposing counsel drags its feet responding to my claim. The subsequent days and weeks and months are spent responding to false counter accusations and overcoming ploys to make me resign out of exhaustion. Your lawyerly persona is frustrating.

*July 4.* Independence Day. My lover and I call it quits, each of us knowing that a separation was coming for the last two years. I cannot stop the tears in a crowded restaurant, but in the back of my mind I wonder if this new development will bring me closer to you.

*July 25.* The notion that "One must give up to get" is not playing itself out. To console myself, I write.

*Pain, that place we find ourselves from time to time. We feel the gouge and we must fill it. Somehow, and quickly.*

*My attorney has become this gouge: a long, steep series of stairs, walls smeared brown-red, a room that has gone damp.*

*She told me she was on her way to beginning something with her, a new her, in fact, someone with whom she'd been playing squash last fall. The news about my lover and me had not made a difference. Her shift in energy made it painfully apparent that they had made love. They plan to go to Nice together in late summer.*

*I teetered above those long, steep stairs. A rusty piece of steel dragged up through my throat. I tried not to show any emotion. She had put the matter to bed, though differently than I would have. How strange it feels to have her leave me before she was ever there to let go. I hate her. Love her. Wish her the best. Still want more.*

*I took the subway to my ex-lover's apartment to feel wanted, maybe even needed, knowing the truth about you both yet still needing the fantasy from each of you.*

*I stood on the stoop. Was it my attorney who opened the door, light shining behind her? Was it she who invited me in, to enter that place of pain we find ourselves from time to time? To feel the gouge and fill it, somehow and quickly?*

*I greeted my ex-lover, thinking to myself that you will become a short story. I will relegate to fiction my unmet fantasies of you, especially the one on your kitchen floor minutes before your guests arrive and the one in the stalled elevator, for safer keeping. Knowing all the while that you will never completely go away.*

August 20. A postcard from Nice. I am relieved that you have written.

Behind your words, "Nice is delightful," I can read that the itinerary is not going as planned. I pray it gets worse.

August 30. You are back in your office feeling like you never left. I try to offer solace, but am aware of my own agenda.

*ADAGIETTO (tempo slightly faster):*

September 1. Your phone message consists of inviting me to have dinner with friends before *Mefistofele* at the Met and informing me that my employer wants to settle. My insides move up and down and sideways as I listen to your message. Playing it back several times, I am unable to decide which makes me more ecstatic: the case drawing to a close or your invitation. Your voice is lighter. I sense progress. To control myself, I write.

*RealFantasy: I stretch out on the sofa. It is warm and welcoming, having been in the afternoon sun for hours. I lay back my head and sink a few inches. I breathe in deeply, letting myself feel like liquid settling into place. I unbutton my white oxford shirt and open it to either side. I snicker to myself, thinking how conservative I like to look. I spread my shirt wider, revealing my chest and breasts. Yours come into view.*

*As I touch myself I begin touching you. I make light strokes around your nipples. Mine become erect. Liquid emerges from between my legs. I remain still, with my eyes tightly shut, making you last as long as I can.*

October 2. A respectable dinner at Deco on Amsterdam. I am the last to arrive at our table of seven. The seat next to you is vacant.

October 7. Anniversary week of the Hill-Thomas hearings. My case officially settles. Undercurrents rise to the level where business as usual had been.

*ACCELERANDO (speed quickening):*

October 9. I convince you (and me) that I can ride one hundred miles on my bicycle. White lie number one. Convincing you (and me) allows me to join you in Cape Cod for a bike trip that you had planned with your now ex-her. I offer to make the hotel reservation.

October 16. When we arrive at the hotel room I explain that they only had double beds available. White lie number two.

October 17. We manage seventy-five miles and cover a seemingly equal amount in our personal lives. At the finish line, eight hours later, I confess that I have never ridden more than twenty miles in my life.

Later that night, back in New York, I confess again. This time, it is that I want you to stay the night. Nearly an hour goes by before you agree to come in.

You tell me that you have reservations about getting involved with me (to say nothing of letting me handle future lodging needs) because you are my attorney and older. You think it best we be just friends. I lower my eyes and remind you that you no longer are my attorney, but concede to my inability to change my age. In your silence, and in the way that you hold me, I sense progress.

You park your bicycle in my living room. We shower together. You soap me from the waist up. We kiss on the lips. We hold each other's wet, warm skin. We volley thoughts and feelings about what this all means until five o'clock in the morning.

*ALLEGRO (fast), with instances of ALLEGRETTO (moderate speed):*

October 21. Your apartment. You smile playfully as you let the tie to your robe drop gently onto the bed.

October 22. I ask you to undress me, and you comply. I ask you to hold me tightly, and you comply. I ask you to kiss me deeply, and you comply. I ask you to lay me down slowly, and you comply. I ask you to get on top of me, and you comply. I ask you to make love to me, and you comply. With you, I unleash the unbearable power of passivity.

October 23. I suggest we fly to Paris. Just drop everything and go. You think the Keys are better, explaining that there is less pressure to sightsee and, therefore, leave the room. We book a flight the next morning.

November 1. In eighty-five degree weather we make love morning, noon, and night. By shimmering candlelight and music by Vangelis I confess again, knowing three is a charm, that I could easily fall in love with you.

November 9. Your apartment. We each speak The Three Words that had been on our lips in Florida but we dared not speak. We exchange apartment keys. You give me a going-steady ring. I wear it on my index finger to keep it from falling off.

*November* 30. I am alone in my apartment missing you. To console myself, I write.

*What makes you erotic? When I find the back to your earring on my kitchen floor. When you turn your head sideways on my pillow, accentuating your neck muscles. When we first catch sight of one another in public and you half shut your eyes, look down and grin. When you force yourself to gain composure when I say something suggestive to you over the phone. When you are at the office. With your assistants hurrying in and out. When you walk with calm self-possession. When I discovered you were a femme and a butch. When your lawyerly persona melts away.*

*When your soft, moist lips find mine. When your tongue scoops me up into you. When you lie on top of me. When you place my arms above my head. And hold them there. When I tell you that I can't wait any longer. When you tell me to get on my stomach. When you insert two fingers. And remove them just as fast. When you stay on top of me clothed. When I am not.*

*December* 20. Holiday season. Time to meet the in-laws. I am not what your mother had in mind. In a roomful of family and extended family, including your ex-lover of ten years, your mother rushes past me to embrace your ex.

*December* 27. Sitting on your living room floor, a fire crackling beside us, I give you a tiny box containing a gold ring. It is the first time that I see Ms. Calm, Cool, Collected uncalm, uncool, uncollected.

*December* 30. All I replay in my mind is you holding my arms down, my legs spread and neck straining, and me pleading with you not to stop.

*January* 3, *1993.* Sunday, six-thirty p.m. We make love before you go back to the office. In the midst of preparing for trial, you are working seven days a week. I feel widowed. To console myself, I write.

*Nothing feels as good as you and me gaining rhythm, in sync. Nothing looks as good as your breasts illuminated by the streetlight. Nothing seems as right as me sliding down the front of you and slowly spreading your legs.*

*When you telephoned, moments after you left, I didn't know what to say. Writing about you and me and us will be my only salvation.*

*February* 13. I am unable to fully put into word, phrase, or sentence the impact that you have on me. With you, I have begun to understand the unspoken sense of emotions speaking louder than words.

*March* 5. You, lying there, your arms encircling your head turned sideways, halo-like. I know better. Your alternating expressions translate a fine line between peaceful *Ophelia* and Edvard Munch's ecstatic

*Madonna.* Stay open to me. Let me in further and further. Farther and farther. There must be one hundred ways to love and please you. I want to know them all.

*April 20.* Touching your slightly clenched hand as you sleep, I look at your fingers and think of how they go inside me. Leaning toward you, I brush your soft hair and let it fall back onto my hand. May I always feel these things? May I always feel these things.

*May 15.* You have said from time to time that your most outlandish (or, in your lawyerly words, your occasional but most compelling) fantasy is to sexually dominate me.

I have given you permission from time to time; who, then, is dominating whom?

*May 23.* We stand at the edge of the bed. You turn off the lamp and the candles take effect. In the changing light all that can be heard is your pinkie ring circling to a halt on the table. I know what you have in mind.

*May 30.* We wake up and enter the world. Each of the three roses that you gave me the night before, the red, the yellow, the rose, has a different scent. You are smiling, your eyes warm and soft, open to me. You welcome me into you. I feel this instantly in my soul. We embrace, not uttering a word, yet the room is filled with voices. With you, I have begun to understand that feelings are words spoken.

*June 15.* A quiet weekend on Fire Island. Except for us.

The first evening you find your way on top. I spread my legs wide. They ache. I want all of you. I get all of you.

The second evening you find your way up there again. I feel several soft waves. Yours come harder. And again.

The third evening I find my way on top. And never want to leave. Our mouths bury themselves on each other's neck's and around each other's tongue's until we gasp for air. I cry out that I want all of you. The room disappears. We are lost, never wanting to come back. Fire Island feels the same way about us.

*June 21.* Twelve-thirty on a Saturday night. A dimly lit street on the outskirts of Brooklyn Heights. We leave the party and return to your car. As we lock the doors you tell me how uncomfortable you felt when he kept eyeing me over the hors d'oeuvres. You hesitate, explaining that you don't want to seem protective, most of all, possessive. I clench the hair on the back of your head and make a fist. The magic word. I whisper that you have permission to possess me.

Silence.
You say my words cut deep. You smother me with long, wet kisses, leaving me to take only erratic, short breaths. You bury your tongue in my mouth. You saddle yourself over me. I unzip my pants and unlatch my belt. You arch your head back, take a long, deep breath, and hold me tight. I spread my legs for you to enter. You moved forcefully inside. I spread them farther until my knees press underneath the dashboard. I desperately maneuver my body between the seat, the steering wheel, and you.

You pump hard and tell me to be quiet. You kiss me deep and keep watch. I spread my legs farther, stretching my arms and pressing my hands down on the seat. I plead with you not to stop. I kiss and breathe and moan into your mouth before settling back onto the seat. You hold me tight.

Later that night I play Liszt's *Sposalizio* for you. The frenetic first movement of that piece tells it all.

*July 7*. We'd seen the advertisement for The Portman Perfect Weekend several weeks ago: A five-star hotel in midtown. So close to where we both live and work. So far from where we both live and work.

A Saturday afternoon. Destination unknown. We drive through the city streets, your sunroof open and music playing. The world is ours. You say you need a new suit, the upcoming trial and all, and I have no reason not to believe you.

You move into the right lane when I know, and you know, that you need the left lane for a new suit. You veer into the Portman valet, jerk the car into park, and say, "We're checking in."

Three o'clock on a sunny afternoon. Overlooking Manhattan and beyond from the thirty-first floor. So close to where we both live and work. So far from where we both live and work. We have three hours to make love before our dinner reservation at the Russian Tea Room, where it all began last May.

I whisper that I want to undress you. You let me, never uttering a word. The room is filled with warm light as you and I descend upon the bed. And each other. From behind I insert two fingers, then turn you over on your back to insert them again. My mouth and tongue join my fingers, knowing that this will put you over that edge we love to travel. Within moments, those familiar short breaths come from your lips as I move faster inside. When you hold my shoulders I know that we are close. Your body stiffens and jerks before settling back into place. Stopping momentarily, I know, and you know, that we can go back to that place one more time. You hold me tightly as I begin. Within moments you surprise us both by jumping off that cliff twice more. We awaken ten minutes before our reservation.

The Russian Tea Room, where we enjoyed dinner and undercurrents last spring. I hardly remembered how to speak that night. I studied you, taking you in, hoping you wouldn't notice. Hoping you would. That night I ordered the same dish that your then-lover ordered, knowing how much I wanted what she still had.

We return to the room. The sun is setting. You suggest a hot bath. You are already in the tub when I begin undressing in the candlelight. The sound of you swishing in the water brings me to my knees by the edge of the tub. I slip my left leg beside you and hold you tight. I immerse my whole body in the water. And onto you.

My lips brush over a thin layer of warm water to caress your soft, wet skin. I run my hands down the length of you, feeling you move with me. I cup your breasts and slide down your legs to that wonderful place in between. Weightless, we take flight.

We towel-dry and put on fresh robes, only to have you throw off yours by the side of the bed and glide on top of me. I pull you in. You bring me to the edge of the bed and wrap my legs around your neck. You lap me up and insert two fingers, bringing me to you as you always do. You lie on top of me and hold me tight. You lean over on one side and insert your fingers again, moving hard and steady. My voice releases a groan when you enter me so suddenly. You bury your mouth over mine. You hold me tighter, trying to contain my sounds. You take me again, completely by surprise. We fall asleep, the bed lamp growing hot and Chopin's *Etudes* filling the room.

Morning comes and so do you, with my mouth and fingers. I, too, from behind, my face buried in the pillow. Morning came and went. So did checkout time.

*August 8.* Sensations of you. On me. In me. Moving me. Holding me. You exhaling hard. Me gasping in. You tasting my nipples. Me capturing your tongue.

In the morning, the mango that we share turns night and day into one and the other.

*August 9.* A dignified concert at Saint Peters Episcopal on West Twentieth. I discover dried lubrication in between my fingers. The scent takes me back to when you started in me from behind and finished me off on my back. I cried out your name as soft, even ripples flowed up from my legs.

When it came time to lay you down, I used my tongue to make soft, circular motions over and around your clitoris before slipping in one finger at a time. When you teetered over that edge, ready to jump off and take me with you, you begged me to move harder.

You pulled tightly on my hair, bringing me up to your face. You grabbed my shoulders, my hand still inside you, and told me to look into your eyes and keep moving my hand. I bore into your eyes, the intimacy nearly too much. I thrust deeper and faster, making hard circular motions, your wetness trailing my every move. You inhaled a sliver of breath before clutching me tightly and remaining silent.

*ANDANTE (smooth, moderate speed):*

*August 13.* It is reaffirming to me that we are meant to be together when the absolute moment I finish coming, alone, thinking of you, the phone rings. Your upbeat, seductive voice permeates the receiver.

*September 27.* All I replay in my mind is you looking up from your stack of papers, over the top of your lawyerly horn-rims, and saying, "I love you intensely."

*September 30.* Moments before we begin dinner you slide a tiny box, containing a gold band, toward my plate. I feel deep within me just how much I want to be kept by you.

*October 1.* Lying on our backs, trying to catch our breath, I think of how we each have just experienced every letter of the word *passion.* I replay our lovemaking in my mind for hours. But as time draws me farther from these moments, I am led unwillingly from their view.

*October 3.* Sitting on your sofa, eating Cajun chips and barbecue, makes the world seem mighty right. That is, until the video is over. Then the world becomes really right.

I unbutton my shirt while you're still talking about the film. As always, you notice immediately and put your lips between my breasts. As the credits roll, your hand slips into my already unzipped pants as you guide my hand along the rough fabric of your jeans.

Thankfully, we had the foresight not to order a double feature.

*October 5.* You hold me tight, bite my nipple just hard enough, rub your finger tip around my wet clitoris just fast enough, as I repeat your name over and over.

*RONDO (final movement), with REPRISE (recapitulation):*

*October 9.* You tell me how attractive I am, and that you've been attracted to me from the minute you laid eyes on me. I reach for your hand.

*October 15.* Almost a year, my love. I travel in my mind to the Rainbow Room, where last October you told our waiter that we were beginning a relationship. Onlookers were gracious. I travel to Florida, where we lost any semblance of a tan. To Washington D.C., where we marched with one million of us. To the first five minutes any time we arrive at a hotel room.

# The Perfect Fit

## by Katya Andreevna

It was one of those days. I spilled coffee all over my desk. The copy machine broke down. While I was receiving a twenty-three-page fax, the paper kept jamming and the machine printed the same page over and over. As soon as the church bells next door struck six, I was out the door and headed, where else, but to Macy's, the largest department store in the world.

My feet slapped against the pavement as I overtook slow-moving commuters. I dipped into the street to cut around a pack of them, all smoking, and slipped into a moving revolving door. Inside, the cool air and the perfume enveloped me. I charged past some dazed tourists to the escalator and jogged by several women with shopping bags and a kid drooling on the handrail.

I hit the designer shoe section and, slowing, breathed deeply. I started cruising at the far end, keeping the truly expensive shoes for my climax.

A pair of oxblood pumps drew me. Too preppy, I thought, but the warm color of the leather made me stroke them and hold them close to my face so I could take in their rich scent. Then a pair of blue suede loafers caught my eye. I checked to see that no other shopper's were looking and rubbed their soft skin against my face. The delicate perfume filled my head. I closed my eyes and drank in the leather-laden air.

I felt someone looking at me, but I didn't turn to confront the eyes at my back. *Probably just some store detective,* I thought, and kept moving toward the even more expensive footwear.

Then I saw them. The heel was probably higher than I could comfortably wear, but it was exquisitely crafted. Chunky and solid, yet elegant, the heel, which arched toward the instep just slightly, would leave a half-moon print behind the delicately pointed toe. The rich burgundy leather called out for my touch.

I approached slowly, studying the play of light on the subtle sheen that complemented this pair. I leaned toward them as if greeting a dog that I didn't know, hands at my sides, ready for rejection. I could feel my heart beating in my sex as I moved a hand to meet them. I caressed the heel with one finger and gasped. The leather felt as smooth as fifty-year-old port, as soft as a wet labia. My hand closed around the heel gently. Realizing I was still being watched, I lifted one shoe, as if to read its designer label, and inhaled deeply.

"What size would you like to see, ma'am?" a husky, female voice asked me from behind.

"Seven, please." I smiled at the salesgirl, a tall brunette. Her eyes pried into me, but she acted cool.

"Would you like to see anything else? You know, we're closing soon." Her dark eyes held mine. I shook my head, still clutching the curve of heel.

The salesgirl was back before I knew it with a glint in her eye. She directed me to a seat and opened the box with a flourish. Slightly larger than the display pair, the shoes looked bolder and more powerful. I slipped out of my flats.

The salesgirl lifted one burgundy shoe out of the box and, with her other hand, took my arch. The firmness of her fingers made the pulse between my legs grow stronger. She slid my toes inside and smoothed the shoe over my heel, allowing her cool fingers to linger briefly at my ankle.

I gazed at the perfect shoe on my left foot. The salesgirl stepped back, wiping curly hair from her forehead. I followed her lead to the mirror near the cash register. She held the other shoe out to me. As I reached for it, she pulled away. A slight smile played across her chestnut-colored lips. Again I reached. And again she withdrew.

"Tsk, tsk," she said, holding the shoe out. "Patience." I stood my ground. She moved closer. My eyes focused on the shoe, but I saw her high breasts rise and fall with her breath. My bare foot on the carpet seemed glued to the spot. My eyes climbed, cautiously. Her face was utterly still, but I detected movement behind her deep eyes.

Slowly, she directed the shoe at me. She touched the tip of my breast with the toe and began to circle around my nipple. I closed my eyes as my nipple hardened and poked through my silk top. She pinched it firmly through my shirt and led me into the storage area. I was surrounded

by shoes, boxes and boxes of them emitting their opium. She applied the
toe of the shoe to my other breast.

Air rasped through my lungs. I clutched a metal shelf, my knees were
so weak. Where had this woman been all my other visits? I kept my eyes
closed for fear she would stop. I heard a register across the floor beginning to cash out.

I reached down and took the shoe from my left foot. I cradled it to my
face, pressed it against my cheek. This leather had an unusually sweet
bouquet that went right to my head. The salesgirl's cold fingers covered
my hand, loosening my grip from the burgundy prize. All the while she
held my right nipple firm.

"No. I want it," I whined as she dragged the shoe from my cheek.

"Show us how much," she said.

She held the shoe around the middle, just in front of my mouth. I
leaned forward and kissed the delicate leather, then unleashed my eager
tongue. I licked the toe as she moved her hand downward. I ran my
tongue along the side and dipped it into the crack where the upper meets
the sole.

"Yes, baby," she hissed through closed teeth as I squatted to the floor. I
lay down on my stomach and thoroughly explored that crack, tracing it
with my tongue from the point of the toe to the back of the heel. Her
breathing grew deeper and more rapid above me.

Kneeling in her short skirt, she rubbed the crescent of the heel
along my bottom lip. Momentarily I wondered if another salesperson
might see us, but then the shoe in front of me absorbed my attention.
At first I caressed delicately with just my lips, but soon I began swirling
my tongue around the heel, pondering the slight metallic flavor of
the inner part of the heel and its contrast with the rich burgundy
leather that wrapped its curved back. She moved the heel deeper
into my mouth, then drew it away so my lips could barely reach
its tip.

"Down," she said as I turned over and moved to sit up. She moved my
hand from where it had drifted between my own legs. "Lie still," she commanded.

My cunt absorbed her words and burned with them. I lay flat on my
back and closed my eyes. All was quiet for a moment, so still, in fact, that
I wondered if she had disappeared from my side. I held myself down on
the floor, my mind racing, anticipating what was to come.

She laughed slightly, a rich, throaty sound. The heel caressed under the arch of my foot and across my instep. I felt my toes parted. She ran the heel between my first and second toes, back and forth, and I gasped.

"Sh-sh," she replied and began to trace the bones around my ankle with that heel. She moved up my calf slowly, then teased at the back of my knee. I twitched on the floor, trying to keep my body still, as she had commanded.

"You want it, don't you?" she asked in a low, steady voice.

I moaned. "Y-yes," I stammered. My heart beat fiercely in the damp space between my legs.

Abruptly she pulled up my skirt. She played the heel over my knee then moved up, stroking my inner thigh. She rubbed my groin with the whole shoe and my hips rose involuntarily. She passed the shoe across my belly, along the bikini line. I was afraid to look at what she was doing; afraid if I did she would stop.

I moaned loudly as she dipped the heel under the waist of my panties. She brushed my bush hairs one way, and then the other. She slid the heel slowly down till it was just at the edge of my slit. I shifted my hips so I could feel its slight pressure on my clit.

"Please," I whispered hoarsely, looking up at her. My face was flushed and I felt sweat breaking out all over my body. I had never been so excited. "Please," I repeated.

She pushed on the heel a bit, making my clit, and my whole being, jump. She ripped down my panties. The sole grazed my bush, exciting every hair follicle. She ran the delicious shoe between my thigh and outer lip. The soft leather felt perfect against my delicate skin. I thought I would either come right then or die from arousal.

"Yes, now," I pleaded. My burning inner lips parted. The crescent heel slipped between the folds of my waiting flesh. Then withdrew.

"Do it. Do it now," I croaked. I couldn't stand any more teasing.

"Certainly, madam." She laughed again. And then it was inside of me, that perfect leather-covered heel. Something in my chest loosed and my limbs flopped on the floor as if a spring that had held me together had finally come undone.

She pumped the heel into me. My head rocked from side to side. She placed the shoe's mate in my hand and I held it against my cheek.

"Deeper," I cried, and she plunged. The sole of the shoe massaged my clit, while the heel pressed ever inward.

The words "yes yes yes" poured from my lips as I sucked in the scent of the shoe's mate. This time, as she slid the heel deep inside me, she twisted the shoe and pressed it hard against my G-spot.

"Harder," I whispered.

She rammed the heel inside me, holding at the top of the upswing. Her speed and force increased and all I knew was my smell, the pulsing between my legs, and the shoe, the perfect shoe inside of me where it fit so well.

My body had begun to tense and tremble. The air entering my lungs came in short gasps. I raised my head slightly, gazed at the salesgirl's face, intent on her work. Beyond her a mirror held the scene: I lay, legs parted, the heel of the perfect shoe disappearing into me. I watched the heel slide out and then plunge. All my muscles jerked, my spine arched up, my head fell back.

The heel still inside me, I drooped against the floor, turning my flushed face to the other shoe. My ears began to ring.

She slowly pulled the shoe from between my legs. Patting my bush with one hand, she placed the shoe next to its mate on the floor. She stood, and towering over me, smoothed her skirt and straightened her employee name tag.

"They're a perfect fit," she said.

"Yes," I croaked, scrambling up from the floor. "The heel's not too high?"

"They look great...," she paused, "on. They suit you."

"Yes," I said, smiling and pulling out my credit card. "Yes, they do."

# Briefly

## by Carmela F. Alfonso

The airport was quiet, not yet filled with early morning travelers. My flight would be the first off the ground into the bright sunshine. But that wasn't for an hour yet, and I was hungry. There was only one restaurant that I knew would be open, so I headed in that direction.

She stood behind the counter. I sat at a nearby table. She was pretty, with light blue eyes veiled in a haze. She looked as though she were lost, lost in a slow-motion world that was not treating her very well. I watched her move through the small dining room, table to table, watched her force a smile to her lips.

Catching her glance briefly, I began to feel uncomfortable. She kept looking at me over her shoulder, brushing her light brown hair from her eyes. Again our eyes met.

She stopped beside my table, with her weight resting on one foot and her hand on her hip. Using her order pad, she brushed her hair from her eyes again. The smile I got from her was genuine. I couldn't help but lean back in my chair and smile right back at her.

Diving into her light blue eyes, I said, "Good morning."

She shifted her weight from one foot to the other, but her eyes never left mine.

"Morning. Can I get you some coffee or tea or...," now she lowered her eyes, again shifted her weight to the other foot, and finished her offer, "...juice?"

This time what I saw was unmistakable.

"I'll have coffee. And definitely juice. Do you have pineapple? I like it very sweet."

Leaving my question unanswered, she smiled and went back to the counter. I watched her move between the two other occupied tables in the dining room, this time serving coffee and delivering eggs and toast. Each time she refilled coffee cups, she deliberately passed my table. But when she leaned over my shoulder to refill my cup, I got exactly what I ordered. As she poured coffee into my mug, her tongue moistened her lips and she "accidentally" touched my shoulder with her breast.

"I need help with your juice. And it's very sweet."

She moved past my table and into the ladies room. I could smell her perfume. I felt a rush of heat and I was no longer uncomfortable. I followed her quickly.

As the door to the tiny rest room closed behind us, I felt her hands at the back of my neck.

With a voice as sweet as caramel, she said, "I've seen you come through here before. But never this early."

"I don't remember ever seeing you. If I had, I'd remember."

Her hands snaked under my arms and gently massaged my back. With my hands against the counter beside her hips, I suspended myself above her, my weight evenly distributed.

"This time," she said, "you'll remember the taste of my juice."

I let myself melt into her body, pressing my full length against her. She responded with an insistent pressure.

My hands slid down her back to her buttocks and I pulled her closer. Her hungry mouth found mine and she greedily sucked in my tongue. As my tiny pleasure button began to tingle, I could feel my desire mount. My left leg slipped between hers as my right one gripped her left. That put her into high gear.

With her skirt hiked up around her waist, she humped my leg in a frenzy. Her hips moved her pleasure into the no-return zone. I could feel her wetness seeping through the leg of my jeans.

By this time my own hips were in rhythm with hers. I had one hand under her skirt and the other in her blouse, kneading her breasts. We were on the edge, but I couldn't let it end just yet, not without a taste of her sweet juice.

I pushed her back and in one swift movement had her sitting on the sink. Her eyes caught mine and I could see her desire, her need for an end. She ran her tongue over her lips as she pushed my head down. She knew where I wanted to be and I knew what she wanted.

Her deep sigh threw me into high gear. As she gasped for air, my tongue flicked her swollen clit. I sucked its tenderness between my lips and gently bit it until she grabbed my head. I slid my tongue through her juices and began to slowly take her. Her rhythmic moans and thrusts against my face were sending me into ecstasy. I couldn't help pushing myself against the edge of the cabinet. The more sounds she made and the tighter she held my head, the higher she took me.

When she started moaning louder, I knew it was time. I darted my tongue back to her button and began my lightning-quick specialty. I sucked hard and flicked my tongue in quick pace with her hips. Each time she came forward to meet my tongue, I unconsciously thrust my hips into the cabinet. In my mind I was fucking the hell out of her, thrust for thrust. I heard her voice deep inside my head telling me, "Now, please, now."

We raced to orgasm, together gasping for air, both in different worlds. As the thunder and waves subsided slightly, she pulled my head up and sucked my tongue into her mouth, tasting her own juices. I slid my hip between her legs and pulled her toward me. She immediately grabbed me and started grinding her wetness against my rough jeans.

She held me to her with one arm wrapped around my hips. Her other hand was inside my jeans, flicking insistently at my supercharged button. This time she had *me* in hand, and I didn't miss a stroke. Until we heard voices just outside the bathroom door.

"No, sir, I don't know where she is. Maybe she went to the ladies' room."

"Well, find her, damnit. I'm not paying her to disappear."

The closeness of the loud, male voice startled us, and the danger of discovery threw us into a frenzy of frantic movements. She grabbed my head and pulled my ear to her lips. She hoarsely whispered, "Hurry. Finish me."

I tightened my grip on her hips and we rocked even more rapidly against each other. Someone tried to turn the locked doorknob, and I stopped only long enough to get my hand under her skirt and my fingers into her slit. I jammed myself against her hip in rhythm with my fingers, sliding in and out of her juice. Again we peaked together and it was over.

Both spent, we quickly caught our breath. She went back into the dining room, her eyes bright with afterglow. I heard my flight announced a minute later, and I raced for my gate, just slightly self-conscious of the dark, wet spot on the hip of my jeans.

# Rough Crossing

## by Jane Futcher

On the New York State Thruway, the trees, naked in the snow, reminded Lee of what she and her father were trying to forget: the thin bones, the frightened eyes, the frozen hillside where they had buried her mother two days before, on the coldest day since 1913, which just happened to be the year of her mother's birth.

*It's gray from here to Canada,* Lee thought, tuning the dial to the golden oldies on WABC, the only station her father's AM radio could pick up. To the north and west, the Catskill Mountains rose abruptly; to the east stretched the sturdy hills of the Hudson River Valley. Lee glanced over to see if the Marvelettes were bothering her father and was relieved to discover that he'd fallen asleep, newspaper in hand, reading glasses perched on his nose, tweed cap pushed back on his head.

"I'm a mess," her mother had said last week in Philadelphia, staring hopelessly at the plastic bag that had replaced her colon and rectum. That day Lee had been bathing her mother with a warm washrag, holding her breath as she wiped the skin near the purple stoma, the part of her mother's gut that popped out through her side and attached to the bag. "You're heavenly good to me," her mother said softly, her gray-blue eyes reaching for Lee, who was patting her down with a towel, rubbing the dry skin of her legs with Keri lotion from the hospital.

"I love you, Mom." Lee kissed her mother's cool, familiar knuckles. "I'm sorry you feel rotten."

*Stop thinking about it,* Lee told herself. *You did what you could. Think of Judith and Maggie. In an hour, you'll be with your best friends, and you can relax.*

"You and your father need to get away," Judith had said at the funeral. She and Maggie had driven all night to get there. "Come stay with us."

"But what will you do with us? We'll get in your way."

"Don't be silly. We wouldn't ask you if we didn't want you. Think about it."

Lee hadn't thought long. She felt more comfortable with Judith than any person in the world. With Judith, she could be sad and pale and insecure. Her eyes could be swollen, her hair ragged, and Judith would still love her, still laugh at her jokes. Judith would make the coffee twice as strong as she and Maggie drank it, because that's the way Lee liked it. Besides, Lee and her father needed to escape, couldn't bear to look anymore at the oxygen compressor and the portable toilet and the wedding pictures from 1943.

Lee's father agreed immediately. Judith, Lee knew, felt safe to her father, felt like his other, missing daughter, the one who'd refused to come to her mother's funeral. Pop had known Judith for twelve years, since the day Lee and Judith had taken Amtrak from New York to tell her parents that they were lovers. Long after they had broken up, miles away in California, Judith had sent Lee's parents birthday cards and Christmas gifts and stayed with them when she visited Philadelphia. Judith's loyalty, her kindness to Lee's parents, touched them deeply. "Judith is," her mother had said many times, "by far the most decent, kindest lover you've ever had. It's too bad you let her go."

"I haven't let her go," Lee said softly. "She's my best friend."

Since her mother's diagnosis a year and a half ago, Lee had felt rootless and bereft. In California, she missed Judith terribly. After all, they had moved to San Francisco together, had vowed to grow old in matching rockers on the same front porch. Then Lee had exploded the dream by falling in love with Emily, and not long after, Judith met Maggie and moved back East, where she and Maggie both had family and could afford to buy a house. Lee had remained in California. She had seen Judith only three times, on trips back East to visit her mother.

Judith and Maggie were waiting at their house, a white New England clapboard on Main Street, when Lee and her father arrived. The house, which was just a few blocks from the Hudson River, had a little barn and garage in the back, a yard where the cat and dogs could run, and a porch with two bentwood rockers. The cat was curled on the radiator in the kitchen, and the dogs yelped and leaped when Lee and her father brought their suitcases inside. The warmth of the house, the depth of the two women's welcome, made Lee sob.

Judith fixed chicken and asparagus for dinner. They ate that night at the oak table that Lee and Judith had bought on Fourteenth Street in Oakland. *How frequently death works its way into conversation,* Lee noted, as they talked of a deer killed on the freeway and the fatal crash of a heavyweight boxing champ who had once trained in this town. Maggie and Judith used to see the boxer occasionally, they said — an odd, lonely figure driving down Main Street in his blue Rolls Royce, shaking hands with the teenagers who ogled his car.

Lee's father, who usually lectured good-naturedly at meals, said almost nothing. After dinner, he went upstairs to bed. As the three women sat talking by the fire, Lee noticed the sound of his heavy feet thudding across the floor above. He was unpacking his pajamas and woolen socks.

Judith gave Lee a quilt and the cat to hold. "I met someone," Lee said, relaxed at last.

"That's great," Maggie smiled. "Tell us everything."


Lee closed her eyes and tried to think where to start.

Pip was petite and funny and smart and a friend of Solomon's, Lee's closest friend in Philadelphia. Everything Pip owned was tiny. Her apartment was tiny, her feet were tiny, her little Maltese dog was tiny. Even the pony bottles of Rolling Rock beer that she drank while she chain-smoked were tiny. Pip's father had committed suicide when she was twelve. She was a bookkeeper for an arts organization in the day; at night, she taught at an Arthur Murray Dance Studio.

Last week, the night before her mother died, Lee and Pip and Marcia, Pip's lover, planned to go dancing. At eight, Lee stopped at Pip's to pick them up. It was very cold, but Pip wore a miniskirt and tiny red shoes. Marcia, she said, would not be coming.

"Why not?" Lee asked. Solomon had told her that Marcia, who worked at her parents' dry cleaning shop and had a daughter named Rebecca, was mean to Pip sometimes.

"She says the bar's too smoky."

They drove to Sneakers, on Second Street, just north of Market, and parked. Pip drank beer and Lee drank 7-Up. When they went downstairs to dance, Lee felt way too sober. "Marcia was right," she shouted over the music.

Pip raised her eyebrows. "About what?"

"It *is* smoky."

Pip shrugged and lit a cigarette. They stared at the bodies moving under the strobe lights. Lee was happy to be with Pip, to look at her alert brown eyes and smile that brightened Lee's mood. Still, when they stood up and danced, Lee felt like the Tin Woodsman, her joints thirsty for oil. Pip vogued and posed and moved so strikingly on the floor that many of the dancers stopped to watch her. Lee started to think about going home. After all, her mother was...

When the music slowed, Pip took her hand. "Hey," Pip smiled. She placed Lee's hands on her own small waist and moved so close Lee could feel a jolt of hot pink neon dance between their bodies.

"Wow." She had not felt anything like that in months, or perhaps it had been years.

The music changed to a slow tune: Gladys Knight and the Pips, steamy and urgent, singing "You're the Best Thing That Ever Happened to Me." Pip's hands closed on Lee's waist. "You follow. I'll lead."

Lee could feel Pip's fingers moving down the small of her back, then stopping at Lee's butt, pressing their bodies. Lee could see Pip's breasts beneath her white blouse, could taste the sweat in Pip's baby-blond hair, which was drenched, as if she'd been swimming. "You feel so good." Lust had reduced Lee to cliches.

Pip looked up. "Are you surprised?"

Lee swallowed. "Yes, I guess. Not that you feel good, but that *I* feel so good." Pip's breath on the side of Lee's neck made her shiver. "I've been..."

"Don't explain." Pip rested her head against Lee's shoulder. "I like you, you know."

"I like you, too." Lee felt painfully sober. There was cotton in her mouth and a vice tightening on her neck. She had stopped drinking only a year ago. She couldn't remember being so turned on and so sober at the same time. But Pip's legs, coaxing her closer, were lightening the pressure of her mother's illness. When the music stopped, Pip stood up on her tiptoes and smiled.

Lee kissed her. "Wow," she said dumbly. Had she ever kissed a woman before, ever felt so intimate? Pip's mouth was alive. She *liked* Lee. Lee could feel the liking in the pink neon of Pip's lips. When Lee closed her eyes, colors shouted: purple and red and finally black, the black of the ocean at night, when the big swells roll in and shatter the sand.

Pip was all sinew now, and motion. Miraculously, Lee could follow, pulled by the neon of Pip's hips. Pip was sculpting Lee, letting Lee sculpt her. The music sucked them deeper. Lee remembered something like this once before, in California, on a dance floor with Emily. But that was different; Emily was her lover, and they'd been stoned on cocaine. Pip and Lee were almost strangers.

And yet they had moved now into a dark corner, Pip guiding them to an empty chair. She lifted herself into Lee's lap. The pink neon was pulling Lee's heart down through her chest and into her legs, vibrating, shimmering, back and forth between them. Pip moaned; Lee felt heaven in her legs.

"Did we dance or did we fuck?" Lee asked in the car, driving Pip back to her apartment on Pine Street.

Pip laughed and leaned close to Lee, like Natalie Wood in *Rebel Without A Cause*. Lee felt like James Dean. "Marry me," she said suddenly, on Tenth Street. "Come to California."

Pip sat up; her eyes became solemn. "I'm already married to Marcia." But that was a lie. Lee knew it — from Pip's trembling voice and from her hands, now tightening on Lee's waist, then quickly opening the door.

In her apartment, Pip turned on one small light, made Lee a glass of peppermint tea, poured herself a beer, and lit a cigarette. She sat next to Lee on the sofa, touching Lee's hair with one hand, stroking her small white dog with the other.

"So?" Lee smiled. "What are we going to do?"

"Let's lie down." Pip pointed up to her loft. She showed Lee the bathroom, kissed her little dog, and carried Lee's glass of tea to the loft. Lee clambered up eagerly behind her. They stripped off their clothes in the darkness.

"You've saved my life," Lee whispered, trembling slightly when she felt the smooth length of Pip's naked body beside her. They were dancing again; Pip slid her stomach across Lee's.

"I'm not scared of you anymore," Pip said.

Lee opened her eyes. "Scared?" She touched Pip's cheek with her finger.

"Not *as* scared." Pip sighed; Lee's lips kissed her shoulders. "I'm too turned on to be very scared."

"Why scared?" Lee almost could not talk she was so excited.

"Because you're tall. And sarcastic. And you never noticed me before tonight."

"I *did* notice you."

"Not really. I noticed you two years ago. But Solomon told me you weren't interested." She stopped.

Lee turned her over. "I was in love with Emily."

"And now I'm married to Marcia." Pip's thighs gripped Lee's leg as she rubbed against Lee.

"But you like me," Lee protested.

"No shit," Pip cried as her mons and clit, wet and slippery, rubbed against Lee's knee. Pip's fingernails dug into Lee's back.

"What's wrong?"

"Nothing, you idiot," Pip screamed. "I'm in love with your goddamned knee." And then Pip wrenched and came and held Lee so tightly that Lee felt she might break.

When the light pressed through the gray curtains and Pip's dog barked to be let out, Lee drove home. No one knew that Lee had not slept there. But her mother was close to death. Her head, bald from chemotherapy, lurched back on the pillow; a new red rash, some kind of cancer, covered her arms and breasts. All morning, the mucus rumbled in her lungs, and Lee knew now why this sound was called the death rattle. She lay next to her mother on the bed and held her bony hand. She would not have a mother much longer.

The phone rang. Lee hoped it was Pip. It was her mother's best friend, Lucy. "Lucy would like to come see you," Lee told her mother.

"No," her mother whispered. "I can't. No one today."

"She can't see you," Lee told Lucy. "She's very, very sick."

Lucy was crying. "Call me. Call me if anything..."

"I will. We will."

"Lee," her mother whispered. "Don't hold my arm so tight." Lee blushed, released her grip, and fought her tears. At dusk, her mother's breathing changed. The rasping stopped. Lee and her father stayed by her side, Lee on the bed, her father, ashen, in the chair.

Lee's father took her pulse and looked very, very serious. Lee wished he could cry. For weeks, he had washed her, changed her plastic colostomy bag, given her sips of water and medications, walked her to the toilet, brought her trays of food which she'd pushed away. He was losing his wife of forty-two years.

"I love you, Mom," Lee whispered, over and over again. "Lucy loves you. Dad loves you. You have so many friends. So much love. We're all right here with you."

"We're right here," her father said. "Can you hear us?"
Her mother made no sign that she heard.
At eight, her mother's breathing stopped.
Her father looked at his watch. "She was a remarkable woman. I hope her life will be a model to us all."
Lee did not take her eyes from her mother's face. "Is she dead?"
"Yes," he swallowed.
Her mother's hand was still warm. "I love you, Ma." Lee looked up at the ceiling. She had heard on talk shows that dying people sometimes watch their death from the ceiling. "Hi, Mom," she cried. "I'm right here. I love you. I'll always love you. Don't be scared. I'm right here."
She was shocked to hear her father, in the library across from the bedroom, already making arrangements. He gave the address to the undertaker, requested a hospital autopsy. He was a doctor, after all. He wanted to know about the disease. He called Lucy. "We lost her tonight, at eight p.m." His voice was metallic. A stab of pain cut Lee. It must be true. Her mother was dead. Her father was announcing her death.
Two men arrived; Lee stayed with her mother, watched protectively as they zipped her into a body bag. They carried her down the steps on a gurney and slipped her into the hearse like bakers sliding pizza into an oven. *This is what it is like,* Lee thought, *when your mother dies. Telephone calls are made, and strangers take her away in a hearse. This is actually happening.*

Lee slept in Maggie's office, upstairs, next to the guest room. Maggie had an ancient, furless teddy bear, an antique wooden sled, a black-and-white photo of herself at eight wearing a Saint Louis Cardinals' baseball cap. Lee was born in Saint Louis, although she did not remember anything about the place.
In the morning, Judith and Maggie made a fire in the living room and brought Lee and her father hot chocolate and sandwiches at lunchtime. Her father went upstairs to take a nap. He was getting laryngitis.
"Tell us more about Pip," Maggie said.
Lee sat back. "She is tiny and funny and kind. She has a lover."
"Are you in love with her?" She could feel Judith's eyes studying her.
Lee paused. How could she say it was love, with her mother dead and Pip practically a stranger? "I haven't felt this way in a long time," she said finally.
"Lust," winked Maggie.

"Don't be hard on her, Mags." Judith's blue eyes reached Lee's. "Is it lust? Or is it love?"

Lee could only laugh. "I don't know. She says she loves her lover." When Lee felt how wet she was just talking about Pip, she added, "But I know she likes me a lot. A lot, a lot."

"Of course she does," Judith sighed. "But I wish she didn't have a lover."

Lee fell asleep in front of the fire, dreaming of peppermint tea and Pip's feet on the steps of the loft.

Judith and Maggie drove Lee and her father up to the mountains, to a fork where seven creeks met. It was too cold to fish or even to walk for more than a few hundred feet. They ate at a hunting lodge nearby. Lee's father cleared his throat. "Last March," he said, wiping something from his eye, "not long after the biopsy, my wife and I sailed across the Atlantic, from Bermuda to the Canary Islands, on the Merriweather Post schooner 'Flying Cloud.' The crossing was rough. All the sails blew out. A lot of the passengers were seasick. Vi was a great sport, though. She didn't mind at all. Kept everyone laughing."

They hurried to the car. Her father's laryngitis was getting worse.

For four nights they stayed in the cozy house with Judith and Maggie and the dogs. On the last night, Lee called Pip. Lee's hands shook as she dialed, and her heart raced at the sound of Pip's low, sexy voice, full of pauses. "I'm drunk," Pip said. "I can't stop thinking about you."

"I keep feeling the neon," Lee whispered. "I'm electric."

"Call me," Pip said. "The minute you get home."

The last day, Maggie and Judith fixed the travelers a picnic for their drive home. Lee and her father tried to be cheerful. "How can I thank you?" Lee's father said, giving both women an awkward hug.

"Tell us what happens with Pip," Judith said, holding Lee close. "I love you very much." The words made Lee cry.

On the way out of town, Lee's father suggested they drive home via Ocean City, in New Jersey, in honor of her mother, who had loved the sea. Lee felt happy about that. At the ocean she might see her mother again. But the day was far too cold for a long walk on the beach. The sky was blue and the ocean was hard and immense. Lee tossed stones and forgot things when she closed her eyes and listened to the roar and beat and thud of the waves. They ate crabcakes at a diner and her father lost his voice completely.

She did not call Pip that night. Nor did she call the next day, when she and her father took twenty-two bags of her mother's clothes to the secondhand store. Lee cried when the volunteers at the store told Lee she had assigned her mother's possessions too high a value on the receipt. She called Solomon from a pay phone. "We're at the Goodwill. We can't go home," she whispered. "We're too upset." He invited them for tea; he had spent most of that morning at the hospital, with Ramon, who had pneumocystis.

When her father was using the toilet, Solomon said, "Pip told me about your ... dancing." Lee felt her legs go soft. "She loves Marcia, you know." Lee nodded. "Yes."

"But she likes you very much."

"I know," Lee said.

Pip came over the next night, after dinner. Lee wanted to take her upstairs, but because of her father, they sat in the living room and listened to his mini-lecture on certain types of metastatic cancer. Later, he told Pip about the two women in New York State whom he and Lee had visited. "Judith and Maggie are wonderful girls. Judith was Lee's..." He hesitated.

"Judith was my lover," Lee said.

"Judith was very lucky," Pip said, touching Lee's hand. At ten o'clock, she asked Lee to drive her home.

"You can come in," Pip said.

Inside, Lee played with the dog while Pip opened a beer. Lee put her head in Pip's lap and kissed Pip's fingers, which were cold.

"You know, I'm in love with Marcia," Pip said.

"You keep telling me that." Lee opened her eyes.

"Because it's true."

Lee sighed. "So, what does it mean?"

"It means I'm not free."

Lee swallowed. "Were you free when we went dancing?"

Pip chewed her lip.

"Were you?"

Pip inhaled her cigarette. "You knew about Marcia."

Lee shook her head. "I know what I feel, too. Did you tell her about us? Is that what's happened?"

Pip sipped her beer. "I told her I was attracted to you."

Lee sat up. "And?"

Pip was tired and tense. "She told me I can do whatever I want." Pip's hands shook as she lit another cigarette.

"Don't smoke that." Lee took the cigarette and pounded it into the ash-tray. "She says you can do whatever you want?"

"But I can't." Pip stared at her cigarette.

"What can you do?" Lee said, confused.

"I can hold you like this," Pip said, rubbing her eyes.

Lee didn't understand. Pip loved her. *She* knew that. Why didn't Pip? "Have you taken it back?" Lee said at last.

"Taken what back?"

Lee reddened. "What you gave me before."

"I'm in love with Marcia," Pip said, like a soldier packing her duffel for the front. Pip got up, opened another beer, sat back down. For the first time, her face and body did not look like a child's.

Lee was angry. "So, we can't sleep together again?"

"No." Pip looked away.

"But you can hold me? We can lie on the couch and hold each other?" Lee pushed Pip's hand away and stood up. Then she sat back down and rolled her head back onto Pip's lap. Tears leaked onto Pip's thighs. Pip handed her Kleenex. When the phone rang, they both jumped. Lee was afraid it was Marcia. But it wasn't. It was Lee's father, asking her to come home.

"Night," Lee said. She was wet and horny and her mother was dead.

"Are you angry?" Pip said at the door.

Lee nodded. "Yes, I'm angry. And I'm horny as hell."

At home, her father's bedroom light was on. He was asleep, with a book in his hand — *The Cruel Sea*, by Farley Mowat. He was lying on his side of the bed, the far side, as he always did, leaving room for her mother.

Two and a half years later, on a summer visit to Philadelphia from California, Lee noticed that her father still slept on the far side of the bed. On that same visit, she and her father had an idea. They packed the car and drove to the Catskills to see Maggie and Judith. The trees on the New York State Thruway were lush and endless, beckoning them north. Judith and Maggie were waiting on the porch. After Lee's father went to bed, the women stretched out on the couches in front of the fireplace.

"What do you hear from Pip?" Judith asked, her long-haired dachshund curled against her legs.

Lee felt a shiver of neon. "Didn't I tell you? She moved to Hawaii. To the Big Island, near Volcano."

Judith pushed up on her elbow, her blue eyes wide. "Just like that? What about her lover?"

Lee scratched her head. "Marcia didn't go. Said she couldn't leave her parents' dry cleaning store."

Judith squinted at Lee. "You still have a thing for her, don't you?"

Lee stared into the flames.

"You wouldn't move to Hawaii, would you?" Judith asked suddenly. "That's not..."

Maggie grinned. "I bet you'd move in a flash just to have that lust, or whatever it was, again. If she'd invite you."

Lee paused and looked up at the shelves of books around her. "She *did* invite me."

Judith sat up. "You never told me that."

"Because it wasn't serious."

"But you were crazy about her."

"What'd you tell her?" Maggie asked eagerly. "When she invited you?"

The cat that Judith had put in Lee's lap jumped off. "I told her I would."

Judith was incredulous. "What? You'd move to Hawaii?"

Lee nodded. "I told her I would. I told her if she stopped drinking and smoking, I'd move to Hawaii."

"She had a drinking problem?" Maggie looked puzzled.

"It was okay for an affair," Lee shrugged. "But if we were actually going to live together, it would be a problem."

Judith's sudden movement toward Lee surprised her dog. "You wouldn't really consider it, Lee."

"I did at the time." Lee could feel the neon stir in her knees. "Very seriously."

"What did she say?" Maggie leaned forward. "When you told her your terms? About the drinking."

Lee rubbed her eyes. "I never heard from her again."

"What?" Judith sat down on the couch next to Lee. "How long ago was that?"

"Nine months."

Judith put her arm around Lee's shoulder. "You'll hear from her. One of these days she'll call and say she's ready. She won't be able to resist. But you can't go. California is far enough. I won't let you go."

"You won't have to," Maggie said thoughtfully. "That chapter of Lee's life is closed. I understand it now. Lee's mother was dying, Pip was there,

things happened, there was a moment, and then it passed. Moments pass.
Pip's passed. Am I right?" Maggie asked.

"It's a good theory. Maybe it's even true," Lee said slowly. And then she
closed her eyes and allowed herself to imagine, as she had so many times
since receiving Pip's letter, the feeling of Pip in her arms and the roar of
the Pacific waves pressing up against the long hot shores of Volcano.

# Eating Out at Cafe Z

## by Deborah Abbott

"But, Val," said Judith, her blue eyes wide, looking straight into Val's hazel ones from across the table at Cafe Z, "don't you miss cock?"

Judith certainly hadn't changed, thought Val. Even twenty years after being sophomores in the dorms together, where Val had yet to discover girls and was busy fucking boys, Judith retained her frankness. Val liked that, and though the question itself was hardly original, she had grown to expect it when coming out to friends.

Val took her time to respond, kept her hold on Judith's gaze, let silence hang on Judith's question. Then Val said slowly, letting each word roll off her tongue while raising one hand and curling her fingers into a fist, "I never found a cock ... to fill me ... like this."

Judith choked on her Caesar salad, gulped Chardonnay, choked some more. Val laughed. She watched as Judith struggled to regain her composure, dabbed at her mouth with the linen napkin. It was clear she had been unnerved and hated that it showed.

"I never found one either," Val continued, "to outlast me. Always ended something like this." Val stabbed a leaf of romaine, held it between them, limp and dripping Roquefort. Judith laughed then herself.

"My question for *you* is," said Val, passing the wilted green lettuce over her lips and irreverently grinding it between her teeth, "do you really want to go to your grave never having eaten pussy?"

Judith blushed, put her hands to her face to hide the irrepressible response, but her ten bright red nails only emphasized the color in her cheeks. Judith recovered quicker this time and would not be outdone.

"How do you know I haven't," she said, with only the briefest pause, "eaten pussy?"

A pair of businessmen at the next table turned their heads sharply in

Val and Judith's direction. Val grinned at them and winked.

"Because you wouldn't have asked such a stupid question. About cock," Val answered.

"Oh, no?" Judith said, cheeks flushed again, from the wine or conversation or both. "Maybe I just prefer a big hard-on."

"Well, maybe you've never had a big strap-on," Val shot back. "Choice of colors. Choice of—" Val began to explain, but Judith cut her off.

"It can't be like the real thing," Judith said while she poured more Chardonnay, brought the glass to her lips, and let the shimmery liquid slip inside, leaving lipstick prints at the edges.

"You're right," Val said, grinning again, leaning toward Judith, so close she could pick up the scent of Judith's perfume. "You're right, Judith. It's completely unlike the real thing. It's unnatural. Abnormal as hell. Really, really fucking sick."

Val was feeling good, like she'd regained her ground, until she suddenly noticed lace peeking from the V of Judith's blouse, creamy lace set against Judith's lovely brown skin. In spite of herself, Val felt her cunt give a powerful squeeze.

"Anyway," Val continued, "don't knock it if you haven't tried it." Val was disgusted with herself for resorting to that old tired line, but she was desperate for words to cover up what had just happened between her legs.

"Okay," said Judith, her turn to look Val full in the eyes.

"Okay?" Val asked, one eyebrow raised, confused at Judith's meaning.

"Okay, I'll try it," Judith answered.

Val felt her heart fall and land somewhere under the table, along with the fork she had dropped a moment ago. *Oh shit*, she thought, *Judith has gone off and trumped me. If I don't take her up on her dare, she'll have me for sure. On the other hand, here I am, a femme, admittedly a broad-shouldered butchy kind of femme, sitting across the table from one very, very femmy kind of femme.* Val had always proclaimed loudly that polished nails and shaved legs were her two major turn-offs, yet here was Judith, with ten fire-engine-red claws, wearing heels and Hanes. Here was Judith, her old dormie, straight as the asparagus spear lying untouched on her plate, propositioning Val. Val had always been sure that it took at least a femmy butch to get her off. But the damp spot spreading across her panties was throwing that theory all to hell.

Pride was pride, Val conceded, and said to Judith, "I believe you should excuse yourself to the ladies' room. With all that wine ... you must need ... to relieve yourself."

Judith didn't miss a beat. She stood, set her napkin down on the table, and started to the rest room. Judith was a little tipsy; Val was stone sober. To keep herself from chickening out, Val concentrated on the image of Judith's brown breasts framed by the lace. She had to confess she'd had no experience whatsoever with slips, only with tank tops, which tore off with one good yank. She followed Judith through the maze of tables, half hoping Judith would have a change of heart now that Val had accepted the challenge. Val tried to think of a way to salvage Judith's ego, but came up empty. Walking behind her, Val remembered Judith from swim team. Judith had just told her she was still swimming. The thought of a woman's brown muscled back with pale, crisscrossing strap lines never failed to turn her on.

Judith reached the door marked Ladies, held it open for Val. The bathroom was  bigger than Val's studio, and certainly cleaner. Val took one look and smiled over their good fortune. Thank god — a handicap stall. Plenty of room for two, and bars to hold on to. No one tended to bang on the doors, figuring people with disabilities took hours to pee. Besides, Val could always stick the brace she wore on her right leg under the stall for proof. See, I qualify. Now leave me to my fucking, thank you very much. Val enjoyed this one little perk and cashed in on it as often as she had the chance.

Val pushed Judith into the stall, then latched the door behind them. She didn't let Judith turn around, wasn't sure she wanted Judith to kiss her. Though Val sometimes wore lipstick herself, she preferred to leave smudges, not have them left on her. And Judith was wearing deep crimson, only slightly dampened by her lunch.

"You're not gonna miss cock," Val whispered into Judith's ear, reminding Judith, preparing her.

"I'm not so sure," Judith whispered back, pulling her breath in sharply. "You guarantee it?"

"Guaranteed," Val said, "over my ... lesbian body." Judith sounded hot already, and Val had second thoughts about Judith's lesbian virgin status. *In fact,* Val thought, *Judith sounds hotter than me.* Suddenly Val felt her dyke credentials on the line. This motivated her like a slap to the jaw. *I'll be damned if I let some straight girl beat me to it,* Val told herself, feeling pure energy flood her body like adrenaline after a mile-long swim.

Val pinned Judith against the cool tile wall and pressed Judith's cheek to it. She unfurled her own tongue against Judith's exposed throat, crawled into the hole of Judith's ear, retreated as quickly as she'd entered, then sucked the lobe and the pearl earring at its tip, pretending it was the hard ball of Judith's clit. As Judith gasped, Val's own clit stood up.

"I'm gonna show you," Val whispered, plunging back into Judith's ear. She could tell this was one of Judith's hot spots by the way Judith started making low sounds deep in her throat, sounds that stirred something in Val, too, making her shudder. "You won't regret it. Won't forget it. Won't look back, not even once. You won't even remember how to spell *cock* when I get through with you."

Val could tell Judith liked this, liked being talked to, liked being turned on by Val's tongue thrusting into her ear hole in this public place. Getting it on in girls' bathrooms was not something straight girls had usually done with boys.

Just as Val started to loosen her hold on Judith, to turn her around and work her tongue in the direction of Judith's warm brown breasts, the bathroom door slowly heaved open.

Judith stopped breathing, stared down at their four feet, then looked up at Val with unmistakable panic. Val took Judith by her waist, soundlessly lifting her until her feet straddled the toilet seat. Val held her finger to her lips, then took advantage of the moment to unbutton Judith's blouse. Val was eye level with Judith's breasts, which were full under layers of her silky slip and bra. Val began rubbing her face in slow motion all over that smooth laciness that smelled sweet like powder, like the inside of a lingerie drawer. *Oh, god,* she thought, a moan inadvertently escaping. Val liked this more than she could have guessed, could ever have admitted to anyone, almost to herself.

The woman who had entered the bathroom went into the stall next door. Val listened to her unbuckling her belt. Good idea, Val thought, and, synchronized with the stranger, unzipped Judith. Val pictured the stranger pulling her slacks down, down over a full round ass, saw panties slipping, too, pictured the stranger letting herself down onto the seat, her legs spread, pussy exposed. Val's lips began throbbing at the thought.

Then Val heard the stranger's piss come splashing into the basin. Val had an incredible urge to stick her face under Judith's cunt and have her pee, too. But she wasn't sure how to convey this to Judith and suspected this was too much indecency to ask of a straight girl who had no doubt never ventured far from the missionary position. Besides, Val wasn't keen on going back to the dining room with an earful of piss.

Judith was squatting on the seat, steadying herself with a hand on each of the metal bars. While the stranger flushed, Val got Judith's panties all the way down, till they were draped, sheer white, over her ankles. Without any warning, Val pulled Judith's lips apart, found her clit, nearly forgot the sheet of plastic wrap she always carried, paused to get it out and over the spot, and then, with the stiff tip of her tongue, went down on Judith. Judith let out a cry that was only half covered by the stranger's flush. It was the kind of cry that told Val that no one, no man, had ever eaten Judith with any finesse at all. The kind of cry that told Val she would soon have Judith, quite literally, in the palm of her hand.

The stranger was at the sink now. The hygienic type. Val heard the soap dispenser bang twice, pictured liquid squirting over the stranger's upturned palms, the stranger wringing her broad hands under the warm spray. Suddenly, Val pictured one of those big bony hands plunging into her cunt, and at the mere suggestion of it, her pussy clenched, shooting wetness clear through her jeans.

Val's tongue kept playing with Judith's clit, and Judith kept making those deep, half-muffled cries. Val knew she was good at this, had been told so more than once, and had had a couple of decades to refine the technique. Not that it felt like technique with Judith. It was more like instinct. She was drawn to Judith like a wild dog keening to scent. She felt like she had known this woman's cunt before. She recognized the distinctness of its groove, recognized its hot, pungent odor. Which was crazy, Val knew, impossible.

Judith, who was hanging by her hands from the upper edges of the stall, shifted. In pausing to look up at Judith's face, Val could see Judith struggle to keep from shaking the stall walls, struggle to hold back her cries, struggle to keep herself from arching away from Val's mouth. It was clear Judith was deep in struggle, but deeper still in bliss.

Val knew Judith couldn't hold on much longer. In more ways than one. Val herself was soaked, from her mouth on Judith and the thought of the stranger's slick hand up her. Judith was slick, Val could feel that. Val brought out latex, took four fingers, way more than a cock's worth, and slid them into Judith. *Easy,* Val told herself, *easy girl.* Judith's pussy strained against such a handful, but clutched at the same time, like a lost child finally finding her mother. Val began fucking Judith, slow and steady. She looked up. Judith's eyes were closed, and she was breathing as quickly and as quietly as she could through those crimson lips, which were shaped like the letter *o* and were as swollen as her cunt.

*Oh, yes, oh, yes,* Judith mouthed, lower than a whisper. Val could read her lips. Val kept working her up and down, with a rhythm that increased incrementally with each thrust, that went as deep as Val could go at this weird angle. Val took her eyes off Judith's face, and put her mouth back on Judith's clit, which was now as hard as that pearl on her lobe. Even beneath the wrap, Val could feel Judith's clit throbbing like the heart of a pearl oyster, pumping, straining, ready to burst.

The stranger was rinsing, rinsing for the longest time. *Some compulsive hand washer,* Val thought. No doubt she was listening to Judith's panting, Val's thrusting, Judith's juices sloshing. Val considered the possibility that the hand washer had taken her hands out from under the spigot, put one down her slacks, and was now lobbing away at her own cunt. *A kind of ménage à trois,* Val thought, liking the idea.

Judith came then, her cunt nearly breaking Val's four fingers as it spasmed. Her cunt held on to Val for dear life, squeezing and only slightly releasing, over and over, as if it had never come so powerfully before and might never come like this again and so had to keep this rapture going forever. The stall walls shuddered violently under Judith's grip, until she let go and collapsed over Val.

Val let Judith's orgasm wind its way down. When the pulse in Judith's cunt was faint and the muscles loosened their hold, Val finally pulled out, wiped a dripping, gloved hand on Judith's ass, found the nipple that was poking through the lace against her cheek, latched on, and sucked for a long, quiet minute.

The stranger was still involved in her hand washing ritual, but had progressed to drying, using the little drying machine. Judith had only half recovered, but Val was so hot and ready for sex herself that she seized the opportunity by grabbing Judith's hand and shoving it down her jeans.

Judith rose to the occasion, had no trouble finding Val's clit. Val was drenched, wet as any butch had ever made her. Val sat down on the floor, carrying Judith's hand with her, Judith's nipple still between her teeth. Val leaned back against the wall. She didn't give a damn what the stranger saw anymore and knew Judith herself was beyond caring. It was Val's turn to surrender; she was hoping Judith could pull it off, could carry her, because Val was longing to let go.

Val buried her face deeper in the silk and rubbed her cheeks back and forth over the cool cloth, losing herself in the sensation. Judith reached up with her free hand, brought one of her breasts up and out of the lace, and offered it to Val. Val accepted, her throat aching so badly she could barely swallow, the roof of her mouth pounding painfully with wanting Judith's uncovered tit. Val played with the firm, warm mound, licked at the puckered areola, then couldn't help herself any longer. She attached herself to Judith's stiff nipple like something helpless and half-starved, and sucked, hard, knowing Judith would have bruises for days after. But Judith seemed to understand Val's need, and didn't protest. While Val sucked, Judith's finger rounded Val's clit, circled like she no doubt circled herself when there wasn't some cock nearby.

Then Judith took her breast away, brought her mouth to Val's, and gave Val a long kiss, her bold tongue pushing through the last of Val's resistance. It was hard to believe Judith hadn't been kissing girls all of her life. But the thought of being first, of being Judith's very first lesbian kiss, made Val groan. She fleetingly remembered Judith's lipstick, which she knew was now smeared all over her own mouth. But Val didn't give a damn about the lipstick. Or about the stranger who was still drying her hands — or fucking herself with her hands, or frozen in a state of horrified arousal, just listening to Judith and Val fuck. Judith kissed her so long, so deep, yet so tenderly, Val thought she would explode from excitement or lack of air. Judith's finger never stopped teasing her the whole time. Val realized she was just dying under this straight girl's hand, realized that this complete novice, total femme, cock-sucking straight girl was taking her to some place no butch had ever taken her. It killed her to admit it, but it was true.

There was only one thing missing. Val grabbed a handful of Judith's hair and twisted her head so Judith's ear was next to her mouth. "Inside," Val whispered against Judith's lobe, taking one of her own hands and pressing at Judith's. But Judith hesitated, only circled lower, her fingers cautious, as though she were approaching the mouth of a cave, afraid to enter, afraid to find out what wild beast lived there.

"I need you," Val insisted, wrenching away from Judith's kiss, "inside." Val needed Judith up her cunt so badly she could scream. She did scream, and pounded her hand once, hard, against the stall wall.

"Don't you know how," she gasped, her voice hoarse, "to fuck ... a woman?"

As soon as she said it, Val realized that Judith *didn't* know how. And Judith said then, softly, almost like an apology, "No, Val, I don't. But show me. Will you show me? I want to ... to fuck you."

Val believed her. Val took her own right hand, which trembled between them, and brought her fingers together like she was going to pray. And she was praying. Praying this straight girl was a fast learner, because she was so close to coming, and yet, without Judith inside her, so far away.

"Like this," Val demonstrated, "all of this. See?" Val slowly curled her fingers into a fist. "Just ball me. *Ball* me. You understand?" Val used that old term, *balling*, one they had used twenty years ago in the dorms. Val hoped Judith would remember, would relate to this. And, as Judith made a fist, her nails curling into themselves, her hand *was* like a ball.

That's all the instruction Judith required. Val was so open, so wet, Judith could have dived, like she used to dive back on swim team, head first into Val. After a minute, Judith found a good rhythm, and Val urged her further, sinking her teeth into Judith's shoulder as a way of letting her know. Val's jeans were at her ankles and she was pulling back on her thighs as Judith's forearm disappeared into her cunt.

Val could tell that Judith was getting into fisting her. Getting fucked by a woman was one thing, but fucking one was quite another. Judith, on her knees, picked up the pace, sweating and grunting from the effort, getting slick and hot again herself.

Val let go of her thighs, brought one hand to her rear, and plunged a finger up her asshole. The rush about tore her in two. Then she took her free hand, spit on her forefinger, reached down and touched it to her clit with just the right pressure, just the way she liked it, and just like that she came. It was a massive orgasm. It seemed to take all of Judith's strength to hold on to Val and keep her from seizing all over the floor.

Judith kept working Val the whole time she came. As Val's head arched, the fluorescent globe on the ceiling, full as the moon, pierced her closed eyelids with a strong, white light. As Val came, she howled like a dog leaning back on her haunches at the mouth of her own cave. With cum pouring out of her onto the tile floor, she howled into Judith's ear and the stranger's ear and maybe into all of Cafe Z. But Val didn't care. She knew nothing beyond her cunt pounding and Judith's fist pounding, beyond sound and the penetrating light. And then Val knew, too, with dead sureness in her wild-dog gut, that Judith wasn't now, wasn't ever, wasn't for a minute, missing cock.

# The Dance

## by Kiriyo Spooner

I t was Saturday night in a smoke-filled room. Wall-to-wall women were dancing, laughing, talking, hanging out.

Ruby's was an old-fashioned place, a single open room with a bar that ran the length of the room and dark scarred tables with wobbly chairs. A collage of photographs of singers — Tina Turner, Anne Murray, Meg Christian, k.d. lang — decorated one wall; another corner of the place was reserved for the occasional live band. In summer the rear door was propped open so you could cool off in the scrubby backyard after dancing.

Ruby's was the place women came to see and be seen, and to lose themselves and their troubles in dancing. So naturally it was the place to go if you wanted to watch women dance. Which I did.

I was feeling kinda sorry for myself, alone again.

Then I saw her. Dressed in a short black leather skirt and a low-cut blue silk blouse, she damn well knew that the eye of every butch in the place was on her. She walked slowly and casually across the room, her hips swinging, her long black hair flicking across her back, and settled herself on a stool by the bar. I noticed she didn't carry any cigarettes. Good. And she ordered before anyone could buy her a round. Even better. I like strong femmes.

Of course, I was not the only one pretending to casually ease over to where she sat. I got edged out by a tough number in a pinstripe suit. I shrugged and took a seat at the bar and watched them dance.

The tough danced okay, but *she* was fabulous. Kinda languid and slow, but sure of herself, moving her hips in a slow and sensuous roll. I found myself wondering what else she could do with those hips.

They returned to the bar after the song, but the tough didn't last very long. I watched, combing my hair. Another woman came up and offered her a cigarette; she lost out fast. That's when I went over. I stood there, not too close, and looked her up and down, real slow. She met my challenge and looked me over, too, from my black jacket down to my jeans and boots. "You like?" she asked, but it wasn't really a question. "Yeah," I said, cool, like I didn't really care. "Wanna dance?"

The music was good and fast; it gave me a chance to show off a bit. I threw in a few fancy moves. She had more than a few moves of her own. I particularly liked how her breasts swayed beneath her sleek blouse, and the way she swung that long hair around. She circled around me on the floor, brushing me with her hips as she passed. When the song ended I felt kinda warm. We stayed on the floor through another couple of songs and started really getting into it, dancing and flirting, moving close and apart, dancing the slow stalk of sexual pursuit.

A slow song came on, and it was natural for us to stay. She moved closer and flowed into my arms. Her head came up to my nose, and the aroma of her perfume filled my nostrils. I held her close, feeling the heat of her body as it pressed against mine, brushing my lips against her ear as we slowly fondled each other. God, could she move! Her hips started grinding against me, and I slipped my right leg in between her thighs. She wasn't shy: she started moving slowly up and down my leg, clenching it with her thighs, and making a noise in her throat that sounded almost like a purr. I swayed with her, swiveling my hips in a figure eight and drawing her tightly to me, one arm around her waist, the other at my side. Her head fell back, and I drank in the view of her beautiful breasts.

My hand traveled to her ass and started kneading her soft flesh. She moaned softly and kept her body close on my leg. Her arms drew tighter around my neck. I heard her breathing more heavily, and I felt us both getting more and more turned on. As the music changed and sped up again, our rhythm increased, but her position didn't. The music throbbed and we did too, moving up and down on each other, her head against my chest. Both my hands were busy on her ass, holding her to me. She threw her head back, and I held her eyes with mine so she could see my intensity as we burned together on the dance floor. By now my body was on fire. We pounded against each other, stronger and faster. Her hair was flying around me. Then she grabbed my arms, hard, cried out, and pressed solidly against my thigh. I knew she had come. She took a couple of deep shuddering breaths as we slowed to a stop, then brushed her hair back off her face, kissed me hard, and walked off the dance floor.

I took more than a couple of deep breaths myself as my eyes followed her across the bar to the bathroom. I was so hot I hardly knew what to do. I gulped a drink as I tried to regain my composure, wondering if she'd ever emerge from the bathroom again and what I would do if she did.

Then after a few minutes I saw her coming back across the floor, walking cool and slow and sultry, and, oh, God, up to me again.

"I liked that. I want more," she said, and took me by the hand to the corner where the empty bandstand waited in the dark. Behind the old upright piano, she reached up and put her arms around my neck and turned her mouth to mine. Our tongues danced around each other as our bodies melded together, and I felt my own wetness spreading. She put her hands inside my jacket and brushed them over my t-shirt, feeling my hard nipples. I returned the caress, pinching and rolling her nipples between my fingers through the sleek fabric of her blouse. I probed her mouth with my tongue as we kissed, and ran my hands down the firm muscles of her back to cup her soft ass in my hands.

I realized then that she had taken off her underwear while in the bathroom.

Oh, honey, I knew what she wanted. And I was so willing to give it to her.

I slowly sank to my knees in front of her and pushed up her skirt. Running my hands up the back of her legs, I licked up the insides of her thighs to where her clit waited, hard, hot, inviting. I grabbed it with my lips. She pressed against me and moaned deeply. I thrust my tongue in her cunt, sucking on her outer lips, running my tongue through her labia. I drank her in. Then I went to work on her clit. As I nuzzled and lapped, swirled and twirled it in my mouth, her clit grew under my tongue. I purred.

Holding her writhing body to me with one hand, I unzipped my jeans with the other. My own clit was throbbing and my cunt was open and hungry, and I started stroking my clit in rhythm with my tongue's pattern on hers.

She thrust her hips against my mouth, smearing her juices on my face. She tasted sharp and bitter and sweet. I put a couple of fingers into her cunt and held her clit tight against my mouth. She jerked in rhythm as I fucked her, and growled a long, low sound in her throat as her passion increased.

I felt her orgasm coming on. Her lips were swollen and hard. Her clit drew back under the hood, then flared out again as she moaned and heaved against me. I almost drowned in the sea of her as she came over my face. I stroked myself harder and felt my own orgasm wash over me as well.

We slowly moved back to the lighted part of the bar, where the crowds danced, oblivious. She kissed me once more, slow and gentle, as we swayed together in time to the music. She smiled with her twinkling eyes, and then, as I watched, walked away from me and out of Ruby's front door.

She turned and winked at me as she left.

# Renaissance

## by Wendy Caster

A s soon as I see Dorothy and Anita, I know they've become lovers.
They're across the backyard at Tony's finally-got-a-decent-job
party, listening to Tony's boyfriend Ethan, and there's something
in the way their shoulders turn toward each other, just a little bit, that tells
me their relationship has changed. I've suspected for a while that they're
interested in each other, but Fay keeps telling me I'm wrong.

Ethan is doing his version of *Phantom of the Opera,* complete with falling
chandelier and dramatic removal of the mask, but Dorothy and Anita
keep looking at each other rather than at him. Once, they forget to turn
back toward Ethan, who finally waves his hand between them as if he's
trying to trip an electric eye. All three laugh, and Dorothy and Anita once
again focus on Ethan. Soon, though, Anita reaches over and brushes
something off of Dorothy's light blue t-shirt. Dorothy blushes. Anita
whispers something into Dorothy's ear, and her blush deepens. Ethan
flaps his hands at them, as if to say, "I've had it with you two," and walks
away smiling and shaking his head. They don't notice him leaving.

Dorothy turns to Anita carefully, as though her body feels new to her,
and both women smile shyly, or perhaps slyly. Dorothy turns and points
to a hibiscus bush, and Anita shadows her movement like a sea flower
swaying in a gentle current. Dorothy is still blushing.

It's been a long twenty years since Fay and I were like that, aglow with
new love, absolutely conscious of each other's bodies, but I remember
every detail, every sensation. How I would love to feel that way again!

Anita runs her hands through her long black mane, holding it out like
a fan and then letting the hair fall through her fingers. Dorothy's blush
deepens from pink to red. I'm surprised they aren't ripping off each other's
clothing. Maybe they don't want to shock Tony's new co-workers. Or
maybe they want to keep their new intimacy private. But I *know* they're

lovers. Ethan knows they're lovers.

I flash on what they must look like in bed, Dorothy's white skin, wide shoulders, and big breasts contrasting with Anita's olive complexion, lithe frame, and long neck. Now I'm blushing.

Fay sits next to me on the blanket under the camphor tree, puts her arm through mine, and says, "Watcha up to?"

"Watching those two," I say, in what I hope is a casual voice. "What do you think now?"

Fay replies, "Oh, please, there's no way they'll ever be lovers. I've told you twenty times: they don't get along." Dorothy and Anita laugh, then lock eyes. The air between them ripples. Fay looks at me, eyes wide, and we both giggle nervously, like junior high school kids reading their first sex scene in a cheap novel.

Fay leans her chin on my shoulder, still looking at Dorothy and Anita, and says, "I can't believe it." Her breath brushes pleasantly across my ear. Pleasantly! I imagine the thrill Dorothy felt when Anita whispered in *her* ear — the thrill I felt years ago when Fay and I were new.

Tony brings us club sodas, then takes Fay's hand, pulls her to her feet, and leads her away. "This very wealthy young man is looking for an excellent carpenter to build a deck for his house," Tony explains to Fay. "I told him you're the best, since you are." Looking over his shoulder, he yells back at me, "I know *you'll* be okay on your own, Ms. Butch!"

Will people ever learn that I also get scared and shy? Yes, I'm big and loud — I guess I seem like a lioness outside — but inside I feel like a little pussycat. Am I really butch? Am I really a lioness? I wonder. Compared with Dorothy and Anita, I feel kind of, well, tame.

I sip my drink, and watch Dorothy and Anita. Most of the yard is in late-afternoon shade now, but they find a patch of sun. As they sit, they constantly touch each other. Dorothy holds Anita's elbow. Anita hangs on Dorothy's shoulder. They are oh-so-casual, but I imagine that their insides are connected by some sort of invisible red silk sash.

Across the yard, Fay listens to a tall man whose gaunt face and pot-belly seem to belong to separate people. I can tell from the look on Fay's face that she's bored; she has on this dead-looking smile where her mouth curves upward but her eyes stay bland. The guy yapping at Fay doesn't notice — or perhaps he doesn't care. I'm annoyed at Fay for letting him dominate her, but I decide to rescue her anyway. I know I'm playing the butch lioness — again — but I guess I *am* more assertive than Fay.

I walk over and say to the monologist, "Sorry, we have something private to discuss." Then I put my arm through Fay's and pull her to the other side of the yard.

"Thank you, Chris, bless you," Fay says. "What an asshole that guy is! He was telling me about pig futures. Pig futures! Can you imagine!" We stand under the camphor tree. The setting sun glows through the light green leaves.

I smile at my socialist, vegetarian lover and shake my head. "I don't know why you're so polite to people," I say, sounding a little more cranky than I intend. Fay doesn't seem to notice my annoyance.

Fay leans against the tree trunk, twirling a twig she found on the ground. "Well, he's a potential customer. Anyway, if I told him he's a selfish twit, he'd tell me how sensitive he is!" Fay laughs, that loud snorting laugh she sometimes has that's just one step short of fingernails on a blackboard. I cringe inside. "Actually," Fay continues, "I ignored him and watched Dorothy and Anita. They make me feel like singing 'Hello Young Lovers.' " She strokes my arm. "You know what?" she says. "They remind me of us, a million years ago."

I'm ridiculously grateful that Fay remembers how we sizzled when we met. We're the grand old couple of our friends now, and our relationship is sweet and comfortable, but sometimes I miss the intensity we had. What we have now is wonderful. It is. But watching Dorothy and Anita has got me slavering for early-in-a-relationship, mess-up-the-sheets, lose-your-mind, sticky, sweaty animal sex.

Tony puts on the overture to some Broadway show really loud, and Tony and Ethan dance out of the house, holding trays of sandwiches and salads and fruits and bread and twirling in circles. "Imagine high kicks," says Ethan, as he does one last twirl. They place the food on a long table covered with an art deco tablecloth.

"I'll get us some food," Fay says. She goes straight to the trays of fruit, while Dorothy and Anita join the line that has already formed by the bar-becue. I sit and lean against the camphor tree and watch Dorothy and Anita. Mr. Pig Futures steps between them and starts talking. I guess he thinks he's talking to two single women. The jerk doesn't notice that they're oozing lust for each other.

I, on the other hand, can't stop noticing. I'm turning into a middle-aged voyeur! I want so badly to feel as rapt and special and intense as Dorothy and Anita.

I remind myself that I'm satisfied with the friendly, cuddly sex that Fay and I have. With our lives. With Fay herself. Sure, I wish she would be more assertive. Sure, I wish she wouldn't snort when she laughed. Sure, I wish she'd seduce me more often, instead of always waiting for me to start.

But I love Fay. She's the sweetest woman on earth. And I *am* satisfied with sex with Fay. I really am. Really.

Dorothy and Anita reach for the barbecue sauce, and their hands brush. My insides jolt as though someone has touched *me*. It's embarrassing to experience other people's sexuality, but it also feels good. Frighteningly good.

I glance over at Fay, sweet Fay, who's cutting a piece of watermelon. She chews on her lower lip, and a strand of her long curly gray hair pulls out of her ponytail and grazes her cheek. My heart melts as I watch her, and I love that familiar sunny sensation. But what must Dorothy and Anita be feeling!

Dorothy reaches past Anita to get the ketchup. She seems to be teasing Anita, not quite touching her but getting very, very close. *Touch her,* I think. *Go for it!*

I look around me, frightened that someone has somehow overheard what's going on in my head. What am I going to do with myself?

Fay walks over to me, balancing two plates piled high with watermelon, honeydew, and grapes. She hands me one and I mumble, "Thanks."

Fay sits, looks closely at me, and says, "Chris, what's the matter?"

"Nothing." I take a bite of watermelon. Across the yard, Anita plops a grape into Dorothy's mouth.

Fay and I eat in silence, then Fay says, "Please don't be offended, but I am so jealous of those two I can't stand it." I look at her and she's smiling at me, but she has tears in her eyes. "Look at them!" she says. "When they leave this party, they'll be in bed within minutes, tearing off each other's clothes." We both try to remember the last time we tore off each other's clothes. It's a long time ago.

Fay touches my knee. "I'm sorry, but just watching them is turning me on!"

"You too?"

Fay looks at me, and a smile spreads slowly across her face. She reaches out her hand. "Let's go home," she says. "Let's go home and be new lovers."

"Excuse me?"

Fay stands, bends one arm across the front of her waist, one behind her back, and bows. "My name is Katharine," she says, with a bad French accent. "Pleased to meet you."

I stand and hold my hand in the air. She takes it and kisses it. "And I'm Annabel," I say. I curtsy.

Fay raises one eyebrow, slightly sucks in her cheeks, and says, "How vould you like to come to my place and see my etchings?"

We sneak along the side of Tony and Ethan's house, saying good-bye to no one. Katharine/Fay stops me, pushes me against a trellis lush with jasmine, leans her whole body against mine, puts her hands on my hips, and kisses me deeply. I'm astonished.

I'm thrilled.

We get into the car quickly, and Katharine/Fay drives home, stroking my thigh when she's not shifting gears. She's humming "Hello, Young Lovers."

*Who is this Katharine?* I wonder. *What does she look like undressed? What does she taste like? What noises does she make when she comes?*

I'm thirty instead of fifty, and I'm squirming with excitement.

When we get home, we grab each other. We are Katharine and Annabel, new to each other and ecstatic. But we suddenly become shy, because we are alone for the first time. Katharine/Fay strokes my cheek, then leads me to the cat-scratched couch, lies down, and pulls me on top of her. Rozie, our oldest cat, immediately jumps on me and starts kneading my back. She settles on the back of my thighs and curls there, purring. Our old selves giggle, then Katharine and Annabel take over.

We kiss, tentatively at first, tasting each other for the first time. I like this Katharine's mouth, her full lips and amazingly agile tongue. In short minutes, we grow frenzied, frantic, all lips and tongues and sweet wetness, as though we have been waiting for years to reach this moment. Katharine/Fay reaches between us and unbuttons my shirt, then strokes my sides and back. She slides her hands into my pants and under my Jockeys for Her to the small of my back, carefully avoiding tickling my ribs. For a second I'm grateful that she *is* Fay, my longtime lover, who knows how jumpy I get if I'm touched in certain ways. But I like the fantasy, so I remind myself that this is Katharine, someone I barely know. She rubs her cheek against mine like one of our cats, then nips at my earlobe. We're breathing quietly but heavily, and her breath on my neck sends chills down my spine. Soon we are rocking together on the couch, and Rozie jumps off my back, mewling her protest.

Fay's hands are rough from years of carpentry work, and I love the way they lightly scratch me. Again I remind myself that she isn't Fay, but a new lover, as she nibbles along my shoulder, pulling my bra strap down with her teeth. She kisses my breast, and I feel a molten heat in my nipple that I haven't felt in years. Suddenly I realize that I am dripping wet between my legs, wetter than I've been in years.

Katharine/Fay whispers to me, "Let's go to bed," and I slide off of her, kissing her shoulders and arms and hands as I move. She leads me out of the living room. To maintain the fantasy, I try to look at our familiar beat-up furniture and haphazard decorating as new, but I don't really care where I am. I just want to touch Katharine/Fay some more.

In the bedroom, Fay lights one candle, then starts unbuttoning her white frilly blouse. I sigh happily. She's often shy about taking her clothes off, and I know I am being given a gift. I lean back on the bed to watch her disrobe, and soon she is totally nude. After all these years, her one breast no longer looks lopsided to me, and her scar has faded into an intriguing snake shape on her chest. I look at her round belly, her gray pubic hair, her skinny legs, and her beautiful half smile. Her arms are at her sides, her palms facing me, as she stands there and calmly offers herself. She smiles slightly. My eyes fill with tears. She is so beautiful.

"What was I thinking!?" I say. "Why would I want it to be anyone but you?" I put my arms around her and hold her tight yet tenderly, as one might hold a newborn kitten. "I love you, Fay."

"I love you, Chris." We kiss a gentle kiss of sweet emotion.

"I want to feel you," Fay says. "I want to feel all of you." She removes my bra, then unbuttons my 501s. I strip off the tight jeans, along with my underwear and socks, and we fall into each other's arms again. Our bodies fit in the old familiar way, her head against my left shoulder, my cheek in her hair, her arms around my waist, mine around her shoulders. But there's something different. We are new lovers; somehow, we have recreated ourselves.

We kiss, and we stroke each other's backs and sides. Every inch of our bodies is completely alive. Each tiny downy hair on my spine is an erogenous zone. We are both panting now, both laughing a little too, because we are frightened of this new place. Can we really get closer?

We can. We drift onto the bed, and we stroke each other's breasts and bellies and thighs, again and again and again, gaining in speed and intensity until we are electric. Fay takes my nipple in her mouth, rolling it around with her tongue. My whole body tingles in response. My thighs rub compulsively. I am so swollen between my legs that it hurts, but it's a wonderful hurt, a throbbing, living hurt. I am so full of sensation that I am almost scared, but, I remind myself, this is Fay. Sweet Fay.

Still licking my nipple, Fay reaches down and puts her hand between my legs. When she reaches my hot wetness, we both moan. She slips fingers into me quickly. Although I usually prefer — and need — her to start slowly, she knows this is a special night and fucks me hard and quick. Each thrust causes a flower to bloom in me, until my body is a glorious bouquet of roses. As the sensations build, I know I must explode, flower petals everywhere, yet instead, I stop Fay and pull her on top of me. I want to be holding her when I come.

Fay climbs on top of me, and we hold each other tight. She kisses me deeply, slides a hand between us, and reaches down between my legs — where I am waiting for her. Although only minutes ago I was like an animal, she senses that now I need her to touch me gently. We hold each other tight, kissing deeply, as she moves her finger on me, gently yet firmly, with twenty years of assurance. We are imploding with all the energy we have created tonight, and we meld together, floating through space with all the light of all the stars trained on us.

When I come, my love for Fay spreads from my center through my muscles and tendons and flows through my veins until I feel I must be glowing. We hold onto each other, lost and found, survivors of living, murmuring in each other's ears, hanging on for dear, dear life.

We stay that way for minutes, and I think that we will never move again, but soon my hunger for Fay overtakes me. I roll her onto her back and start kissing and biting her belly. There is nothing in the universe but her shiny wet skin. Fay moans with each nibble.

For years, Fay has been shy with her remaining breast, but tonight I dare to kiss it. She gets quiet and still but doesn't stop me. When I reach her nipple, she pushes up into my mouth and holds my head against her, letting me know that she wants me to lick her hard. As I do, I realize that she is crying softly. I reach up and cup her cheek with my hand, while continuing to play with her nipple. Her hips rock back and forth and her muscles grow tense, then tenser. I lick her nipple hard and fast, and she cries out, then her hips stop and her muscles relax, and she releases my head.

I'm still hungry for her, and I slide down between her legs. She is so wet and swollen that just looking at her makes me gasp. I start licking her and soon my cheeks and chin are dripping. I lick her with long ravenous licks, and I think briefly that I am the luckiest woman alive. Then I stop thinking and dive in, licking and sucking and feeling sacred and raunchy at the same time.

Fay can come very easily, but I want to lick her forever, so I tease her. I bring her close to orgasm then dart my tongue inside her, deep and strong. I suck on her labia, then draw circles around the opening of her vagina. I place my tongue flat up against her vulva and move it slowly, subtly toward her clit. When I flick her clit with the tip of my tongue, she gasps and pulls my head closer to her. I lick her with quick even strokes, and she comes with a roar. I gently suck her clit, and she comes again. And again. I lay my head against her thigh and stroke her, then move up to hold her in my arms.

We collapse entwined together in a puddle of sweat and fulfilled desire, sticking together and gently panting. I silently thank the universe for this magical night.

We fall asleep in each other's arms.

The next morning the room smells lightly of jasmine and women and there is still magic in the air. We decide that we will cuddle forever. But biology wins out, and soon we get up to eat. We put on our bathrobes, then follow a trail of yesterday's clothing out of the bedroom. As we have done for years, Fay grinds the coffee while I put in the toast. She hums "Hello, Young Lovers." Everything is familiar, but brand new, too.

While we eat breakfast, the phone rings. We let the machine answer. Fay's sister asks her to call; we can hear Fay's teenage nieces arguing in the background. The phone rings again. Mr. Pig Futures from yesterday (was it only yesterday?) wants to know if Home Depot has good lumber prices.

We chat about Dorothy and Anita, safe now to enjoy their pulsing sexuality. "I'll tell you one thing," Fay says in an "old-lady" voice, "I bet those two young whippersnappers don't have sex like we did last night!" We both giggle, then Fay starts snorting really loudly. The hairs begin to stand up on the back of my neck, but I laugh — at me and Fay and the universe.

I roll my eyes and hug Fay. She sips her coffee while keeping one arm around my waist. This is my lover. This is my life.

# Tattoo

## by Nisa Donnelly

It was dark but still early when Phoenix Bay stepped into the gloom and glitter of the West Hollywood bar. She'd long since shed her stockings — too hot — and had her shoes dangling in her left hand. "Put your shoes on, doll," the sleek blond bodybuilder at the door whispered. "The health department." She winked, extending her forearm to Phoenix for balance. "Nice," she observed; her eyes were focused on Phoenix's breasts. And Phoenix, giddy from the drive and promises of the night, winked back. *Later,* her look promised, *if nothing better turns up.* Something about being in a strange city made Phoenix feel reckless, bad, and beautiful; no familiar eyes to answer to.

You can tell a lot about a woman by the way she stands when her back is to you, when she isn't aware she's being watched. At the end of the bar, alone because it was still early or because she was a stranger or both, stood a woman. Hard and sure and easy. The woman turned, for no reason, really, and looked back over her shoulder toward the spot where Phoenix was standing. The words *grimly beautiful* flashed across Phoenix's mind. And that is how she would always think of Jinx. A dozen feet away, Phoenix willed her to turn, to look again, to step into her life. She had never considered herself brazen, but she was that night, slipping into the space between the grimly beautiful stranger and the bar. When the woman finally looked up, Phoenix was waiting. But she misjudged, and fell into a pair of pleading eyes.

"Jinx?" she would ask later on the dance floor. "Is that a name or a character reference?" The grimly beautiful woman smiled, leaning close, whispering against Phoenix's neck, "I guess, it's whatever you want it to be." In heels, Phoenix was a good three inches taller than Jinx, so she'd shed the shoes early, never mind the bodybuilder at the door, and buried herself in the arms of this woman, who smelled of peppermint soap and beer, cigarette smoke and sweat. Content to memorize the little creases in her neck, the taste of salt, Phoenix felt the tight muscles that moved under her hands. Patterns of blue and green trembled beneath the woman's white shirt that glowed against the permanent dusk.

At a tiny table, Jinx leaned close, listening to Phoenix talk, rolling up her sleeves absently, exposing forearms, the right one colored in dark patterns. Where a watch might have been on another woman, the tail of something wrapped around her wrist and ended in a point just below the knuckle of her right middle finger. Phoenix stared, then pushed Jinx's shirtsleeve up a little higher, struck by how her fingers looked against this woman's skin, trailing them across her shirt, careful to avoid the gentle rise of breasts. Jinx was watching her closely, still smiling the way she had earlier. She curled her hand into a fist, then flexed her fingers, the skin on her forearm rippled like the hide of a strange and exotic animal. Phoenix took her hand back a little too slowly.

"What do you think, Chicago?" There it was again, that loose, worldly, and just-left-of-arrogant grin.

"Phoenix," she corrected, almost automatically. "I'm from Chicago."

"I know," Jinx said, still smiling. She locked her hands behind her head and stretched her legs on either side of Phoenix's chair. And Phoenix had the sudden impulse to slide up this woman's leg like a snake, licking against the soft leather, tearing at it with her teeth. Shuddering, Phoenix leaned forward instead, tucking her feet back into the shoes.

The bar was only slightly more full than when Phoenix had first arrived. Obviously the Hollywood angels were all somewhere else that night. Not that it mattered; Phoenix had found what she wanted.

"What do you think?"

Pushing the chair back and standing, Phoenix listed a little. "I think it's time to go home." But home was two thousand miles away and nothing more than a couple of cats and a roommate, an MTV junkie who spent her evenings sprawled on the couch. Phoenix would find a hotel, then decide what to do in the morning; in the morning she would regret not having made love to a grimly beautiful woman with a lizard crawling up her arm.

Jinx, taking Phoenix's statement as an invitation, shrugged and hauled herself upright. "Have you ever been to Disneyland?" Phoenix shook her head. Intense as only a drunk can be, Jinx brought her face close. "You should go. You want to do that tomorrow?"

"Why not now?" Phoenix said, catching the hand with the lizard's tail in her own and stepping into the night.

"It's a long drive from here."

"I'm in no hurry."

The motel Jinx picked was pink and in the shadow of Disneyland. Years later, Phoenix would remember that, but not the name. Something about candy. A small, graying man, his eyes rimmed in red, looked at Phoenix suspiciously through a Plexiglas plate in the office door as she dropped her credit card into the security drawer, the kind gas stations use.

"We're going to Fantasyland," Phoenix offered, although he hadn't asked.

The man in the booth smiled. "Well, then, you'll want to get there early, lines are hell this time of year." A key with a large pink plastic room number clattered into the drawer. Room 316 was a gritty pink, trimmed in red, like candy canes. Over the years, Phoenix would forget the name of the song Jinx hummed that night, all night it seemed at the time, but she could never forget that missing tile, the three patches of glue against the gray of the ceiling. Just as she could never forget Jinx, the way she looked as the neon changed outside their window, blue and red streaking across her chest where a wild, winged lizard dipped its tongue around her left nipple.

It wasn't the first time Phoenix had opened herself to the arms and tongue and hands of a stranger. But that night she was brazen and wanton and selfish, and nothing in the world mattered except that room and the woman beside her, the flash of heat rising through her belly, the prickle of cold air against bare flesh, the salt of her skin. Jinx was clean, the way morning is clean, without traces of the past. Jinx called her beautiful, and Phoenix believed it was true. So much seemed true with Jinx, who could raise sparks from her very touch. And when Jinx pulled Phoenix to her feet, stripped away the dress, the scraps of nylon and lace, Phoenix had the feeling she was at last free. Jinx was perfect, with magnificent breasts and a snake that slithered from her navel toward a brown and curling jungle, then out again and down her thigh.

Phoenix swallowed the snake, felt the lizard grow hard and angry under her tongue, its head in her mouth. Its tail disappeared between her own legs, pushed the breath out of her, until the room twirled and tilted, until Phoenix Bay was no longer able to tell where she ended and this grimly beautiful woman began. The lizard moaned when Phoenix sunk her teeth into its flank, and Jinx tightened against her, the lizard smooth and slick, not like a real lizard at all. Inside Jinx was warm and slick, too; Phoenix's fingers explored the strange and beautiful terrain. So much flesh to command, a mountain, sweet and slick, and all at Phoenix Bay's command, all brought down to that one burning core. They fell through the night that way, into a place where flying lizards beat their tails in deep pools.

They lost most of the next day to that small room and didn't make it across the street to Disneyland until late one night, just before closing. In an orange sky tram that rocked slowly, high above the flying elephants and the twirling teacups, Jinx taught her that maybe they truly were in the happiest place on earth, like the sign says. Maybe so, maybe so. They were happy then. Giddy with freedom and new love and possibilities. The next day, Phoenix turned her dead father's Jeep Cherokee north to San Francisco, instead of east where her old life waited in Chicago. And with Jinx beside her, she stepped into a world as beautiful and as dangerous as any she would ever know.

The first time Phoenix Bay saw San Francisco, the streets seemed to open like a promise. Jinx's studio was in a loft in a mostly nameless area where warehouses clustered and a few straggling flowers planted in front of small clapboard houses fought for sun. In the three weeks she was there, Phoenix never saw any neighbors, never saw anyone come and go from the houses with the struggling geraniums. For all she knew, it might have been a movie set.

Over the years, various inhabitants of the loft had added thin walls and dividers, until it was a crazy quilt of strange angles and spaces. A large door opened onto a fire escape that looked down on a patch of broken concrete and asphalt, where a half dozen cats played in the moonlight. Every morning Jinx fed the cats, talking with them in a guttural monotone she must have imagined to be feline. The most brazen of the cats would stretch up around her, their front paws on her thighs; the others would wait for her to come to them. Once, when Phoenix was left alone, she ventured into the back lot, her hand outstretched. "Here, kitty kitty." But the half-wild creatures eyed her with distrust; finally Phoenix slunk back into the building, feeling curiously betrayed.

Jinx's studio was all creaking plank floors and thick glass windows embedded with chicken wire, so that the sun was always a little filtered. Nothing like the lofts in the movies or the ones that now dot San Francisco. Trucks came and went from the first floor, huge and rumbling, so the whole place shook every morning at four o'clock and again when they returned at eight or nine or ten at night. Jinx had settled into one of the strange small rooms, a futon on the floor, the walls hung with her maps and threadbare tapestries. Tiny blue Christmas-tree lights were strung across the ceiling, so it always looked as if the sky had suddenly given birth to blue stars. That was where they fell in love — or what they called love.

"Why do you teach English?" Jinx asked one night, when the blue lights finally had settled back and the trucks were quiet. Phoenix could hear the cats calling to each other, plaintive sounds. What could she say? The truth hurt. English was safe, safer than the girls she'd taught years before, girls who came to her with broken spirits and battered lives. She was supposed to lead them back, but she was too weak. She couldn't save them, couldn't even save herself. So she'd quit. Walked away like the coward she'd always known herself to be. Phoenix had seen herself in them, and the reflection had terrified her. But she told Jinx none of that. Instead, she took Jinx's nipple into her mouth, teasing back and forth through her teeth until the question was forgotten, or until they pretended it was. She would rather Jinx think her noble, trying to save young minds or at least to open them. She answered with a question: "What's with the neon? I thought you did tattoos." On the workbench across the room, Jinx was making a large pair of flashing red neon lips that puckered then smiled. Already on the north wall of the studio was a green and blue neon that winked out the message *No Moleste* followed by *Art Zone.* The neon delighted Phoenix, lights glowing like promises.

"I do everything." Jinx seemed so strong and sure, the kind of woman Phoenix could lose herself in for a long time. Phoenix breathed deeply, inhaling Jinx's essence the way animals must, locking her arms around this woman she knew so intimately and so little. Already, she was slipping away from herself, and she had no regrets, not one.

Later, when the warehouse was dark and silent, the night slow and heavy, she felt Jinx watching her. Turning toward her, Phoenix opened her arms automatically. Jinx smiled and kissed Phoenix lightly, smoothed her hair, kissed her eyes. And Phoenix moved under her, pulling Jinx down for a long moment, before she leaned back on her knees, balancing herself on Phoenix's thighs. The neon outside the room shone blue and red and green across skin. The lizard watched as Jinx's right hand moved lightly across Phoenix's breasts, down her ribs, then on to the fine down of her belly. Raising her eyes to Jinx, Phoenix expected to see her new lover smile. But Jinx's eyes were on the pale skin of Phoenix's belly, looking at her the way an artist looks at a blank canvas. "What?" Phoenix asked, sure she'd disappointed this woman.

Jinx smiled — a look Phoenix would remember years later. "I was just thinking." Her fingers were tracing small circles on Phoenix's belly, making Phoenix's back arch and her eyes close. She relaxed under Jinx's fingers concentrating on that one spot. *This is the way a cat must feel*, she thought, trembling a little. "You are like a cat," Jinx said, reading Phoenix's thoughts. "A tigress." Yes, Phoenix would like being a tigress, strong and sure, determined, beautiful, deadly. "Here." Jinx placed her hand at an angle against Phoenix's waist, so that the fingers pointed toward the tangle of light brown hair. "A green-eyed tigress stalks." Jinx's eyes were green. And slowly, Phoenix realized she was talking about a tattoo.

"Yes." The answer came sure and without hesitation. "There." Jinx pulled herself off Phoenix; her feet made little shuffling sounds against the raw boards as she padded out into her studio. The night prickled against Phoenix's flesh, but they hadn't bothered with blankets or sheets. Rising on her elbow, Phoenix stretched to watch and was more than a little disappointed when Jinx pulled on jeans and a t-shirt — black, with the sleeves ripped out, with the lizard peeking through a tear in the shirt. When Jinx came back to the bed, she wrapped Phoenix in a frayed blue silk kimono, the fabric colder against her skin than the night. Jinx kissed her lightly, then led Phoenix into the studio to a futon under a pair of lights.

"I've been working on this for days." Jinx unrolled a drawing of a tiger prowling through a magical jungle. She'd only begun coloring it in, and then only a pink amaryllis. The drawing was intricate but not delicate, like the woman who had made it. Jinx's eyes were suddenly shy. The tiger's shoulder gleamed under the light. "It's beautiful," Phoenix whispered. She had never seen any of Jinx's drawings before, except for the quick sketches she sometimes made at breakfast or after dinner, when she was explaining an idea or trying to remember one. But those were nothing like this. Perhaps Jinx would finish it, color it in, send it away with her. Phoenix would frame it and keep it over her bed in Chicago. When Jinx came to visit, she would see it and smile. Phoenix watched their reflections in the chrome light reflectors. Floating. *This is what passion is,* she thought, as Jinx opened Phoenix's kimono and kissed the skin there. Phoenix held Jinx's head against her belly, her cheek warm like her breath against the skin that already was cooling from the night. Phoenix could no longer remember what her skin felt like without Jinx's touch.

"How much do you trust me?" An odd question, Phoenix would think later, much later. She knew this woman so little, they were hardly more than intimate strangers. Yet, in those first weeks, Jinx already had made all the other women of Phoenix Bay's life seem like nothing more than a dress rehearsal for this moment, for this woman. Phoenix nodded and Jinx smiled.

Phoenix Bay had never connected the idea of pain, hot and insistent, with tattoos. No one mentions that. Or the blood. Only how they were drunk or foolish or both, or worse; or how the final result is worth any pain. Prickling, one woman called it. That night, when the needle first pierced her skin, Phoenix trembled until she was sure she would vomit. Pride was all that kept her from it, from running, pride and then Jinx's voice, "You're doing fine. It's always worse at first. You're fine." Those words became a lullaby. In the window, their reflections watched, and she watched shadows, until tears washed away even those, until she was somehow above the pain, no longer part of it. *Make me feel,* she remembers thinking, before floating away from it all. And when Phoenix returned, there were the beginnings of a pink amaryllis on her belly.

Jinx worked relentlessly: first on the picture and then the tattoo. By August, the flower was pink and perfect, the jungle was growing, and a shadowy tiger was beginning to prowl. Over the years, the jungle would bloom across Phoenix's belly, vines trailed down her thighs. As Jinx worked on the tattoo, Phoenix would become accustomed to the pain, sometimes anticipating it, other times understanding it, but never, ever slighting it. Or Jinx. Or what they would become together.

(This story is an excerpt from the novel *The Love Songs of Phoenix Bay,* published by St. Martin's Press, 1994.)

# Underneath

## by Linnea Due

I'd already passed where the Wall used to be — where most of it still was — except now people were chipping away at its pitted concrete surface with mallets and chisels, trying to gouge out a piece decorated with red or blue graffiti. The people who weren't hacking at the Wall were stamping their feet with cold, or trying to chat with the Poles who were renting the chisels from makeshift portable tables.

Only a block further east, six or seven Russian soldiers were huddling over a bonfire of broken-up chairs, beating their woolen-shirted arms against their chests. Two lucky ones still had their coats to sell, or their watches, or their souls, because they came drifting toward me like wraiths out of the warmth of their fire, muttering, *"Entschuldigung, mein Herr,"* in what even I recognized were bad German accents. I shook my head hard, and they jumped back as if I'd struck them. What could I say — they'd scared me worse than I'd scared them? I kept my mouth shut and moved on into the darkening evening, toward what someone in the blinking neon, in the bright lights of the West, had told me was the only dyke bar in East Berlin.

I kept trying to picture what this district had been like during the war. Linden trees. Banners. Black cars running to and fro like voracious animals that snatch people up, devour them, and then spit out the bones as they cruise through an intersection. No one watches the picked-clean skulls crazily rolling across the pavement until they fetch up with a faint clack against the gutter.

Not liking my imagination, I wandered near some workmen who were demolishing a building, wanting to be jolted by their jackhammers back to January 1990. I looked on as they removed sections of foundation to uncover piles of debris. Under the debris was more rubble — crumbled stone, brick, broken crockery, glass, even pieces of a child's doll: a leg, an arm.

It took me a moment before I figured it out. Bombs and shells had leveled this whole section of the city, so nothing had been left *but* rubble. What could they do but build on top? Every structure around me had its feet in despair.

Standing here forty-five years afterwards, atop acres of broken cement, seeing this battered gray building being destroyed so it could be replaced by another gray behemoth, the new one leading the way to capitalism with as much hope and trepidation as the other had ushered in communism, made me blink back tears so hot they scalded my cheeks. One of the workers looked at me in surprise. Then he leaned over gracefully, as if he were a ballet dancer, scooped the doll's leg off the ground, and held it out to me. I had to take it, though it made me nauseated. I dropped it in my coat pocket and nodded at him gravely. Then, mutually embarrassed at being caught showing emotion, we dropped eyes and went back to no-feel/no-see, the art of avoiding connection that equals caution in the late twentieth century.

I continued on my way, wondering how people can live with what they know is underneath. I'm an expert at underneath. I passed my hand over my smooth cheeks, scratched my upper lip to assure myself I was now me. Me didn't happen often, and hardly ever on these trips abroad, when I must chair international conferences. It's probably why I'd come to these gray streets where even the birds knew enough to stay away. The finest scientific minds of our generation would not be cavorting in a dumpy little lesbian bar in the Eastern sector.

The heavy wooden door was unmarked, but I could hear women laughing inside. I pushed it open and stood revealed by a naked bulb that swung merrily in a gust of wind. I swung the door shut, but the bulb continued to dance, casting wild shadows into every corner, revealing women here, there, all of them silent and looking at me. I pictured what they saw: too tall, too thin, a face both hard-edged and sleek, gray eyes, dark brows, a topcoat that was too fine. As the bulb ground down, they turned away, but I could feel them mark the place so they could return later. Why? Because I didn't look like them? As if I'd eaten cabbage all my life and smoked cigarettes when I had not even a cabbage?

Only one woman continued to stare, and she too was different. I stepped to the bar, ordered a beer, and then nodded at her. The bartender sent a drink her way. She sipped it, watching me. I put my foot on the rail. Someone whispered something to her. She didn't respond. She kept looking.

She was blond and solid, the kind of woman who seems ordinary until you catch her eyes and realize how magical she is. She glanced down at the floor when I moved my foot from the rail. I liked that. When I smiled slightly, she didn't, and I appreciated that too. She was wearing a cashmere coat, and her hair was professionally trimmed. She'd never eaten cabbage in her life.

After a very long half hour, she wrapped her scarf around her neck, opened her purse, and applied lipstick the exact color of her lips. I didn't move. The bartender, a big woman with a soup bowl haircut, flashed me a sign that meant, Beautiful people belong together. I ignored her, ignored the blonde, even when she stopped by my table to softly murmur, *"Danke,"* in a low, quiet voice that sent an earthquake through me.

The bartender shook her head as the blonde moved toward the door, as she hefted it open with difficulty and slipped out. The light did its erratic dance. I drank off my beer, shrugged on my coat, donned my cap. Then I winked at the bartender and made for the door.

She was half a block away, walking west fast. I stuck two fingers in my mouth and whistled. She stopped, then swiveled around on one heel as if she couldn't believe what she'd heard. When she saw it was me, she kept her foot poised for a beat while we both stared at each other. Then I crooked my finger and made her walk all the way back. When she stood in front of me, I caught the ends of her scarf and pulled her toward me. If she didn't want it rough, I didn't want it, and we might as well know the score now.

*"Nicht hier,"* she muttered, but she kept her hands at her sides, and her pale eyes suffused with something deep that tore at me as well, until I was almost gasping. To hide how she'd gotten to me, I bit her neck, and she shut up with the objections, instead beginning to swoon until I was afraid I'd have to scrape her off the pavement. "English?" I asked.

She shook her head regretfully. No more regretfully than I, who'd been told to take German by my advisors in undergraduate and graduate school. Nobody would dare to tell me to take it anymore — nobody would tell the great Dr. Brewer a damned thing — but I wished they'd told me why I might *really* want to learn German. *Someday you'll meet a woman...* But she was touching my elbow gently, coaxing me, begging me with her eyes to follow. I did.

She lived in a walk-up on the east side, in a building that no one else seemed to live in, or even near. Maybe she didn't live there either, because she had trouble fitting the key in the lock, and she studied the numbered apartments we passed as if she'd never seen them before. Finally she stopped before a door and used the same key. That worried me. Could anybody get into every room? It was pitch-black inside, and I didn't like that either. She sensed my anxiety and put her hand on my wrist, kissing it quickly, as if I were a colt she needed to gentle. Then she leaned over and lit a candle. She removed my cap with a quick apology, placed it almost reverently on a chair, then returned to smooth back a shock of my hair. My heart stopped thudding, or more precisely, it started thudding more pleasantly. I wanted her, and here would do as well as anywhere. At least it was warm. A radiator hissed somewhere in the shadows.

I could make out a mattress on the floor, covered with one of those big goose down comforters Northern Europeans use as bedcovers. I made a twirling motion with my index finger, and she got the message, taking off her cashmere coat, placing it with my cap on the chair, and moving in a slow circle, her arms upraised, so I could see her. She kept her eyes on me as long as she could, then whipped her head around so she wouldn't miss anything. "Bitte," she murmured. "Bitte, komm her." But I didn't. I made her come to me, I made her kneel down, I made her take off her blouse button by button, and then her bra. Her breasts were as large as cantaloupes, and as weighty, and it was all I could do to keep my hands off them. But I stayed back. I made her undress all the way, on her knees, and enjoyed her struggle to stay upright as she pulled at her hose and her shoes. Then she wanted to touch me, but I wouldn't let her do that either.

I got down on my knees too, yanked her hands to her sides, and began kissing her, licking her closed eyes, which made her shudder, and plunging my tongue into her ear, which made her gasp. Then I kissed her very gently, slowing it down, letting her pick up the pace until she was heaving against me, rubbing like she was in heat, her heavy, firm breasts pressing into me like glory, like when you fall in the freshest smelling, softest pile of grass or the coolest, silkiest pond on a very hot day. I thought that I'd waited all my life to feel those breasts against my chest and then I told myself I was being a fool.

Because I was getting confused with all these bests and mosts, I wanted to do something I knew how to do, so I began touching her with my hands. It was quicker than I would have liked, but I couldn't bear this mushy feeling that kept welling up like hot candy that burns even as you gobble more and more of it. But touching her didn't help.

Instead, there was a strange instant when I felt shocked and delighted all at once, as if a bird I hadn't seen had trilled right next to my ear. The world turned on its head, and I never wanted to leave. That's what happened just because I touched the skin on the inside of her arm.

I spent a worthless period wondering what it meant. Worthless because I already knew, I just wasn't ready to admit it yet. Suddenly I knew a lot of stuff all on top of each other, like why I couldn't put off touching her, why I hardly touched anyone, why I lived the reclusive way I did. And I understood that this woman whose name I didn't know, whose language I didn't speak, would never leave me again, at least not in her soul.

I don't like to act crazy, even with myself. Maybe *especially* with myself, because my life is so very circumspect and controlled. So I stared at my hand, where it was still pressed against the pores of her skin that felt like salvation, and I wanted to shout with joy but I also wanted to gnaw the goddamn thing off, like a fox will when it's caught in a trap, sacrifice that traitorous limb to save *me*. Yes, me. The remarkable Dr. Brewer, ice-cold and razor sharp. Right now I needed both those qualities.

Why this woman, I asked myself. But I had no explanations, only certainties. For a scientist, that's a very uncomfortable place to be. So just as I'd thought touching her would get me past the mushy stuff, I bowed my head to go after her nipples. I wanted the familiar. I wanted to dominate her, to overpower her, to control her. Not that it would help, I already knew that. But I had to try something.

She began moaning, and I really hoped we were the only ones in this strange building. Unlike the hot candy that backed up in my throat, her nipples were like jujubes that never get sucked away. I gnawed at the jutting head, where it's hard and rubbery, while my tongue worked over the sweet spot in the middle. She whimpered when I bit her, started panting when I tweaked her hard. Then I pulled off my shirt and made her suck me, twisting her hair whenever she got too rough, while I continued to torment her nipples with my nails and the tips of my fingers. I could feel the whimpering come right out of my tit, hear the gasp when she couldn't keep sucking through the pain. I was so wet by the time I pulled her off that I was leaking all over my shorts. I passed a hand between her legs. She flooded the finger I trailed between her lips.

I pushed her on her butt. She managed to fall gracefully, and sat with her legs apart, the way she'd landed. She was smiling at me. She knew too, knew I couldn't cut off my mouth like I could my hand, knew I couldn't

cut out my cunt. I was lost. "Slut," I told her. She looked expectant,
searching my face for clues to the meaning of this new word. "You'd go
home with anybody who whistles at you. Spread your legs for strangers,
wouldn't you?" We were long past being strangers, but not knowing
English, she didn't get the joke.

I pulled my knife out of my boot and smiled, holding it up for her to
see. Then I caught the nub of her nipple on its tip. She stopped breathing. I left it there until she took a very careful breath, and then I pulled it
forward and up a hair. She stopped breathing again. I took away the
blade, careful not to tear her skin. She was whimpering and grabbing at
the hand that wasn't holding the knife, wanting me to fuck her. I shook
my head. "You're getting too greedy," I said. "Entirely too greedy."

I unbuckled my belt and made her pull it out with her teeth. She was
good at that; maybe she did it all the time. She offered it to me in her
mouth, her eyes soft and sweet. I turned her over my knee and started out
slow. She liked pain; she began plunging her hips up and down in rhythm
with the strapping, and soon she was sighing in pleasure even as she was
yelping from the blows. I kept bringing down the belt until she was hot
all over her butt, until she started jerking away and crying out louder than
I thought was wise. I stopped, grasped her hips, and wrestled her up on
her knees with me behind her. It was when I was unbuttoning my jeans,
about to put my prick into place, that I saw the woman in the corner.

I hadn't seen her before because my eyes hadn't adjusted to the dim
light, and after they had, I'd been too busy and blown away to do anything but fend off the inevitable. Besides, she looked more like a fantasy
than anything. Dressed entirely in black, her head encased in a discipline
hood, she stood absolutely motionless, her arms invisible, breasts jutting
forward. Her hands must have been tied behind her back, and her elbows
as well, judging by the way her tits were presented, as if she were thrusting them at us.

I had been staring at her, but there was no reaction in those eyes I
could, in any case, barely see. And because of the hood, I had no other
clue to her state of mind. I glanced at my blonde, who was looking at me,
the corner of her mouth slightly uplifted. So my blonde was a top, I sur-
mised, switching in front of her girlfriend, and forcing her to watch. What
else could this kinky little scene be?

I looked at the blonde, then at the hand I'd strapped her with. Did I still
need to gnaw it off, or had I been freed from the trap by the presence of

the hooded woman? But nothing had changed; I knew that just as I'd known everything all at once. The only difference was that now I was angry, realizing I was a mere design element in the blonde's minor masterpiece. She'd shown up at the bar hoping to lure me. No, not me. Any top. Anyone who'd follow her to this spider's lair.

Except I didn't believe that. She had wanted me, Dr. Brewer, but that made no sense either. And what now? I wasn't sure I cared for my walk-on role as the heavy; it made me feel used. When I feel used, I get nasty, but that would feed right in to Ms. Top's script. I rocked on my heels, thinking about it. I could walk out of here, but what would that get me but a case of blue clit?

Then my blonde leaned forward and stroked my cheek with the backs of her fingers. She brought her fingers to her lips, kissed them, and touched my cheek again, saying, "Shave?" in a tentative voice as she stroked down to my jaw. Then she traced a line across the slight rash on my upper lip. The woman in the corner never moved a muscle. And I decided, like I had about the dark room and the keys and the trap and even the certainties, that I didn't give a damn. I pulled her against me and we kissed. And wondered whether she'd said "slave" instead of "shave." It seemed like a funny word for her to know.

She rolled the condom down my prick with her mouth, and then she took the bulbous tip between her lips. I kept my hand on the back of her neck but I hardly needed it. The girl was the original deep throat, and it took me only a couple minutes to come, then come again. The nice thing about being a dyke is I can shoot all I want and still have a load in my rifle. And right then I wanted to be inside her in the worst way. So I pulled her around and settled her down on the floor with her hips in the air. She laid her head on her scissored arms and got ready. I knelt behind her, shoved her hips down a trifle, and guided in my prick. She took it easy, and I whomped her butt, still hot from the strapping, back so it was jammed against me and her juice was dripping all over my thighs. As I pumped her, she started making weeping noises that got progressively lower and more guttural.

I looked up at the woman in black and saw those eyes had come alive. They were piercing me like arrows, but they were neither murderous nor excited, and they sure weren't resigned. As I kept watching her watching me, I started to get frightened. This was no slave forced to witness her owner twisting and screaming under the pounding of somebody else. And twist the blonde did, like a snake trying to keep down a rabbit who refuses to die. She wanted to stay impaled on my rod, but she also wanted to move and she wanted me to move. I obliged her even as I kept my eyes on the woman in the hood. I didn't know who she was, and I wanted to keep it that way.

But that didn't stop me from plowing her girlfriend. In fact, the fear made me exultant, like I'd just walked off a cliff and discovered that in death I was saved. Nothing else mattered, not at that moment. I was free and flying. I kept ramming my prick into her from behind, and she kept grunting like a miner carrying a heavy load up a long ladder until she suddenly shrieked and spread her arms, splaying out her fingers. I came too, and collapsed over her back, slick with sweat. We rested there, exhausted, until I realized the woman in the corner was no longer in the corner, that she was, in fact, coming closer, and that the arms I'd assumed were tied behind her back were rising from her sides. She was wearing a cape, so those arms resembled bat wings, no doubt to match her mask, which had not been a hood at all, but was more a hard leather shell, with flaring sides and a raptor's beak.

I didn't lose it, but I did pull out pretty fast, causing my blonde, whose orations had plunged into baritone, to revert to soprano. I stuffed my prick unceremoniously into my pants, then got to my feet and backed off a step as the woman in black came another two steps closer. The blonde was watching both of us like we were a fascinating TV show; I wanted to sock her and save her at the same time. As I was backing up, I tripped over my shirt, and it just took an instant to pull it on. Nothing left but my coat. I'd leave the belt and the cap.

By now those bat wings were parallel with the floor and the woman had begun to make a hissing noise that sounded so much like the radiator that I began to wonder if I'd fantasized the heat, too. I wanted this to be a nightmare, and even more, I wanted to wake up. That's when I found my coat and the door and scrambled out into the hall. And walked very quickly down the dark, dingy staircase to stand outside and stare up at the building. To see nothing, no lights, no bats, no blondes. Most of the windows were broken or boarded up. The boards wouldn't last, I thought as a few Russian soldiers scuttled by; they glanced at me speculatively. I threw a few cigarettes on the pavement to distract them and then walked toward Kurfurstendamm, where lights still blazed and people talked and drank liquor and steaming hot coffee and no Russians crouched over burning chairs.

I woke in the night screaming, on my knees in the bed, grabbing at my shoulders as if I could tear them off. A giant hawk was digging its talons into my flesh, its wings beating at my sides, its triumphant cry shrieking in my ears. I lay back down, sweating like a pig in the freezing room, trying to ignore the discreet knock on the door: "Dr. Brewer? Are you all right?" Finally I had to drag myself up to murmur something reassuring when all I wanted to do was sob with terror. But when I woke again, my head was fuzzy and heavy, and I wondered if I'd made up the woman in the corner. And made up my certainty too. I'd never felt more uncertain in my life.

An hour later, I was at the conference, among my colleagues and too many fawning acolytes. Today I liked the attention, and that bothered me. If I needed adulation, I was in worse shape than I'd realized. I had turned toward the men's room to try to pull myself together when I noticed the blonde. I stood mesmerized as she swept past me. She wore a blue badge, which meant she was a presenter, and as I spotted her name, I saw she was the author of the paper I had planned to hear next. So intent was she upon reaching her session, scheduled to begin in two or three minutes, that she didn't notice me. But her partner did.

"Dr. Brewer," the woman said, nodding slightly. "I do hope Lisette and I did not frighten you last night." She had a faint accent, Latvian, I decided. Trying to place it calmed me slightly. I glanced at her badge and was not surprised to see that she was from the Soviet delegation.

The woman reached out as Lisette had, touching my cheek with a single nail. I don't know why I didn't jump away, but I seemed paralyzed, my arms hanging uselessly at my sides. "Lisette was so fascinated that you shaved, but I told her those soft cheek hairs are a giveaway. I suggest you eliminate the mustache, though. You hardly need to establish your 'credentials' any longer, and that rash is not becoming."

It was absurd to ask who Lisette was, or who the Latvian was. I knew perfectly well who they were, scientists like myself, and with less to hide than me.

"Exactly, Dr. Brewer," said my companion, as if I'd spoken. "The wonderful thing about Lisette is that she is like a very beautiful, crystal-clear lake in which you can see all the lovely little fish and the sparkling pebbles. Whereas you and me are like old muddy farm ponds, with so much muck in our souls that we are choking on it. Wouldn't you really like to find out what's underneath the brilliant Dr. Brewer, who never could have achieved such fame had it been known that Nicholas is really Nicola?"

She smiled and I remembered the talons in my shoulders, the claws digging into my flesh, going right for the bone, where they'd find purchase, find something to hang onto...

"I'm sure you'll be going to Tokyo in April, Dr. Brewer. Lisette and I shall be expecting you. Now good day." She started down the hall, but then she halted and whirled on her high heels. "Oh, Nick, I nearly forgot. Lisette thought it was so charming that you fancied she didn't know English. She asks that you come prepared with an array of humiliating names she can pretend not to understand." She laughed lightly, like an antique glass shattering, and I wished again that I had never seen those eyes.

"Lisette is like a child sometimes," she said with an indulgent smile. "And you, I suspect, may not like being her plaything. But you look so cute when you're angry." She planted her nail against my eyebrow this time, and I heard conversations behind me stop as people turned to look. "But don't worry. After Lisette has had her fun, the two of us shall have plenty of time for a tryst. We'll see whose mud we can sling, isn't that the expression?" Her shoulders were shaking in amusement as she clicked off across the gray marble tiles. My face beet red, I plunged my hands into my coat pocket only to pull out that terrible doll's leg, and I knew nothing would ever be right again.

# Vision of the Enchanted Forest

## by Juana Maria Paz

We are standing in a small clearing in the forest, a space the trees seem about to swallow up. The earth floor is brown with pine needles and the branches hang low. They catch in my hair if I am not careful. It is cool, and the brief chill reminds us that winter has come. We are standing near the tepee that is also in the clearing. The circular shadow of the canvas protects us, surrounds us in its folds. You are standing very still and near. You are holding my hands.

"Can you let go of me now?" I ask softly. "I need some time. I'll come back when I'm ready."

"Ready for what?" you ask, with quiet, steady deliberation.

"For tonight," I say. "I thought it's what we both wanted."

"Yes, it's what we've wanted," you say, and a great burden falls away from us. Your face is clear. I turn and descend the path that will take me to the water. It is very close and I reach the gently running stream in a few moments. I bend down with my feet in the wet earth, on the bank of the stream, and place my hands in the icy coldness of the water. It is cold and harsh against my skin, but it is good and real and fills me with warmth.

I begin the ritual. I anoint my body with drops of water, first my breast where the folds of my dress fall open at the neck, then my wrists and ... I hear a noise on the path behind me, just above in the trees. The rustle of leaves against the forest floor and the sound of branches swaying against your body tell me that you have come.

I rise and turn to meet you. The water is dripping, cold, from my hands. The stream is just behind, rippling softly and lending music to our words. The branch above is gently touching my hair.

"You are sooner than I expected," I say.

"I know you said you needed time—" you begin.

"I'm ready now," I answer.

A swift breeze, the rapid flutter of fallen leaves, and the branches swaying about our heads remind us again that winter has come. My dress falls
long and white against the path. Two strings hold it together at the neck
and waist. I reach up and loosen the first string. You begin to move, then
stop. The old apprehension returns.

"Will it be too cold?" you question.

"No," I answer.

Your hesitation blows away with the wind. The sun filters through the
ceiling of branches overhead. We are standing still in the enchanted forest and as the rest of the strings of my dress give way beneath my fingers,
my dress falls to the forest floor. The dress is very light against the brown
of the earth. As I descend to meet the earth and you prepare to join me,
you speak only once.

"At last..."

# Illegal Alien

## by Diana Thompson

I met her at a lesbian dance. It was after the gay and lesbian parade and I was looking too good for words. Sort of urban-third-world-Afrocentric chic. I was unattached and looking to latch on to a good thang — not so easy to do in the '90s, girlfriend. I stood at the doorway to the dance hall for a little bit and let everyone have a good look at me. Then I made my slow way around to the back of the room.

They have gambling in the back of the hall, two tended bars, and free nibbles. Headin' toward the bar I see her. From the back. She's sitting at a tall table by herself. She has straight gray hair down to her shoulders, hair with that Asian look and swing. *Oh,* I think, *it's nice to see more older dykes out,* and then I forget her.

I dance a little, drink a little. I am exotic in my silks, East Indian pants and long emerald-green mandarin jacket. My copper-colored skin is smooth and soft, and my eyes are the color of milk chocolate. My black dreadlocks are long and fall gently around my face. From one hole in my right ear hangs a bronze shooting star; from another, a jade stud earring glitters. For Portland, I am a rare bird of paradise. It's fun and nice to be so popular, but the faces coming at me are all pale. I'm hungering for my sisters, my lesbians of color.

Later, I walk the perimeter of the crowded dance floor, a little tired. I stop at a tall table to rest, watching the wimmin's bodies move as they dance in the half-light.

"Hello."

I look to my right. I see dark skin surrounded by pale hair. Strong, high cheekbones jut like cliff edges, a long strong nose stands sharp and chiseled. Her lips are thin and smiling; her eyes dark and small with Asian-like eye folds. I smile.

"Hello," I say, recognizing the older dyke I spotted earlier. I hadn't seen her dancing. She looks alone. "Are you enjoying the dance?" Great

Goddess, I sound like I'm talking to my ancient Aunt Sophie!

"I like it more when I see you come in."

Whoa! I take a closer look at this womon. She doesn't look old. In fact, she doesn't have any wrinkles at all. Her skin has that taut fit of youth. And she's coming on to me! Goddess, thank you!

"My name is Diana, Goddess of the hunt. What's your name?" I say with a big grin, moving in a little closer to hear her over the music and the sound of wimmin's laughter.

"I am Toak." At least that's what her name sounds like. She has some kinda accent. And a nice voice. Throaty. Pleasant. She's young. Prematurely gray. "You dance very good." Definitely foreign.

"Would you like to dance?" I ask. Yes, let me get my arms around this womon. She shrugs and smiles.

"I do not know how."

I look at her hands. They're large and strong looking with short nails and longish fingers. Nice hands. They rest on each other as she leans a little closer to me across that table. She smells like an orange grove on a summer day, when acres and acres of orange trees are in bloom and the spicy-sweet aroma floats on the warm wind and you suck it down into your lungs like manna from the Goddess.

I stand in front of her and let my energy pour into her. "Let me show you how."

She returns my soul-deep stare and smiles. "I would not be good. It is different where I come from."

"Where are you from?" I ask.

"Far away. Very far away. It is very hot in here."

I look at what she's wearing. Blue jeans, a denim jacket, partially buttoned up. Some kinda dark material shows underneath. Kinda reminds me of Lycra, but it isn't shiny. She has on dark, flat-heeled boots. It's a nice July night, warm but not hot or humid. I wonder why she's so buttoned up if she feels hot.

"Would you like something cold to drink?" I ask, butchlike. She shakes her head, no. "Hungry? Can I get you some food?" No again. Great Goddess! She doesn't want to dance, she doesn't want food or drink. Where's my opening here? Of course, she is foreign. She probably doesn't know the American rules of dyke cruising. I rack my brains.

"We go out for a smoke?" she says suddenly in that throaty voice of hers.

"Oh, sure! I don't smoke, but I'll join you."

She stands up. And up. And up.

I'm a good height, not too tall, not too short. Kinda medium. But this womon! My head falls back as I look up into her face. I'm about eye level with her boobs. She smiles down at me and I grin back.

"You're a big one, ain't cha?" I say, cause she's big. Really big for an Asian womon. "What are ya? Six two? Six five?" She shrugs, still smiling, and heads for the door. I follow her, watching the dykes' heads turn her way as she passes, and I get a good look at her from the back.

Her jeans are skintight. She has super-long legs and a nice butt. Her hair flutters behind her and she moves with a strange floating grace.

I catch up with her in the brightly lit corridor and get another surprise. Her eyes. They're not dark as I had thought, but gray. A thundercloud gray. And they look funny. Not really Asian, but not round either. Her skin is definitely yellow though. Actually it's very yellow.

Biracial, I think, maybe Japanese and something else. That's cool. Everyone watches us as we pass, and we walk down the marble staircase of the Masonic temple in silence.

Outside are the usual diverse dyke types smoking cigs and squintin' at the passing cars, jivin' and laughing with each other. I know a couple and we nod. They look at Toak with interest. I look at her, too. She breathes in a deep breath of air, and it seems to take at least thirty seconds of steady inhalation for her to fill her lungs. I watch her chest expansion with great interest.

She looks down at me, still smiling. "We walk?"

"Walk? Sure!" I say, and we take off for a stroll around the block.

I can tell she's walking slow just for me; those long legs could cover a lot of ground. She sticks her hands into the pockets of her jean jacket, looking very comfortable in her skin.

"Hey, aren't you going to smoke?" I ask.

"Smoke, yes." She breathes in another metric ton of Portland summer air and lets it out.

I get it. She didn't want to smoke a cigarette; she wanted a breath of fresh air. "So," I say, "have you been in America long?"

"Not long."

"You know anybody here in town?" She shrugs. What the hell does that mean? She doesn't know anyone or she doesn't have the English to tell the story? We turn the corner and continue.

"How do you like Portland so far?"

"I like. It is very different from where I come."

"Are you from Japan?"

She looks down at me. "I do not know that word."

Oh, hell! I'd forgotten how hard it is to talk to someone who doesn't know English very well. A truck passes us and a pale male face hoots and squeals at us. I sneer at him and flip him the bird. "Bitch!" he yells as the truck turns the corner. Toak looks at me, a puzzled frown on her face.

"Rednecks," I tell her with a shrug. "Assholes."

We turn the corner and I see the pickup truck double parked next to a jeep. The headlights are on and two guys are standing by the hood.

I get an instant adrenaline jolt and automatically slow down as I look around me. Quiet street of office buildings. No people except for us. I briefly think about running, but I'm feeling my ovaries tonight, so I don't. They probably just want to run their mouths, anyway. Still, I wish I had on my stomping-dyke boots instead of these light "cute" black flats. I let my arms hang loose and ready at my sides and try to project a "don't fuck with me" vibe. We get closer and I see two more boys get out of the other side of the truck. Bad news. This don't look good.

"Hey, bitch, did you flip me off?" one says, real evil-like. I give him a hard stare, but say nothing and keep walking. I don't have time to look at Toak. I hope she knows enough to keep walking. Then the boy says the N word. "N——, I'm talking to you!" he says and starts coming toward us. My heart starts to pound. Run or brazen it out? If it were one boy, I'd take him, but four? Then Toak stops.

I want to tell her to keep moving, but it's too late. The four boys are surrounding us in a half circle, cuttin' off any escape routes. Goddess, are you watching over me?

"A n—— and a chink," one says. He's wearing a baseball cap over greasy looking short hair, and he's young. They're all young — in their twenties or so. "What're you, dykes? You from that dyke thing around the corner?"

Oh, so that's it. Gay-bashing. My first time.

"Fuckin' dykes! Fuckin' queers!"

"I hate queers!"

"Yeah, man, they should all be killed!"

I'm trying to memorize their faces, but I'm distracted by the prospect of getting my head stomped. If one of them says all I need is a good fuck--!

"Stop," Toak says to them. Surprise. I look up at her. She's staring at the boy directly in front of her. She's taller than him. She's taller than all of

them and her voice is rock steady. Not scared sounding at all. Goddess,
let the stereotype be true just this once and let this big dyke kung fu
stomp their asses!

"The chink's talking to me! You talking to me, chink? What're you —
the man?"

"You will stop and go away," Toak says in the same steady, cool voice.

"What, you gonna make me, lezbo?"

Out of the corner of my eye I see one boy start toward Toak's back.
Typical boy shit! I turn toward him, ready to yell a warning at Toak, but
something happens.

Toak turns around quick. I mean *real* quick, like a blur, and when the
boy's fist smacks up against her palm, she closes her hand around it. The
boy yelps and goes to his knees. Then the other boys jump her.

What happens next happens fast. Toak lets the whimpering boy loose
and pushes me behind her, out of the way. I stumble backward against the
building and I see the other three boys cover her like jackals on a deer.
She grabs one by the collar of his Forty-Niner jacket and tosses him, I
mean really tosses him, about five feet away. He sails through the air like
a frisbee and hits the street with a thud and a groan. One boy is workin'
on her stomach like Muhammad Ali workin' on a punching bag, and the
other is on her back, riding her, with an arm around her neck, choke-hold
style.

She lifts one leg and kicks at the boxer boy and he goes tumbling like
an empty trash can in a high wind. The last boy is cussing, his face red
and his legs clamped around her waist. She takes hold of his wrist and
pulls it from around her neck like it's nothing, but I can tell by the strained
look on his face he's trying to resist. With her other hand, she flicks a finger at his right kneecap. He howls like he's been shot and his legs go limp.
She then pulls him off her and holds him up in the air by his arm, dangling him about five inches off the ground. She's studying him like a bug
she's never seen before.

Then the boy she tossed into the street is up and coming toward her.
He's got something in his hand. Shit! A knife! One of them buck things
with a big nasty blade.

"Toak!" I shout. She glances at me, looking very unworried, then looks
at the charging boy. I see her frown, and when her hand tightens around
the dangling boy's wrist, I hear something crunch in his arm. He yelps
again and she throws him at knife boy. He hits and they both go down.

Then there's a short whoop — the kind a cop car gives off when the cop wants you to pull over. She and I both look around and see a cop car heading toward us. Toak comes to me, grabs me up in her arms like I'm a baby (and I'm a good 150 pounds of muscle and bone) and runs.

Runs? Hell, she takes off like a fuckin' deer, with me pressed against her chest, and we are moving! She ducks around the corner and runs alongside the freeway and she's not even breathing hard. She turns a few more corners and I wonder if she knows where she's going. She zips across the street overpass, and suddenly we're on the local urban college campus, about fifteen or so blocks away from the dance. She stops then and puts me down, looking all around her at the same time.

Me, I'm kinda shocked. I stand there looking at her. I think my mouth's hanging open. She looks at me.

"Are you all right?" she asks. I nod. That's all I can do. She looks around again and seems to be listening. I recognize where we are. Next to the science building on the far end of the campus. "We should walk," she says. She takes a step forward. I just stand there, staring at her. She stops and looks back at me. "Maybe we should sit down," she says, nodding at a nearby bench. She sits down, her hands in her pockets, and I just stand there staring at her. She gazes back, her head tilted to one side.

"Okay," I say, "what happened back there?"

"They meant to harm you. I protected you."

I frown at her. "Who are you? How can you just pick me up and run like that?" The light from a nearby streetlamp illuminates her slight frown.

"Do not be afraid. I will not hurt you."

Well, I hadn't been afraid until she said that. Not that I'm really afraid, just very, very wary. Maybe she's some foreign athlete on steroids or something. Those types can snap at any moment. I keep out of her arm's reach and think that this might be a good time to leave.

"I am sorry. I did not mean to frighten you. I only wanted to protect you," she says, and it dawns on me that she's speaking English better. A lot better.

"You're speaking English a lot better," I tell her. She nods.

"Yes. I feel I can trust you now."

Things start to add up and curiosity gets the better of me. "You're not supposed to be in this country, are you? I mean legally?"

She nods. "I cannot let anyone in authority know I am here."

I relax. Illegal dyke alien. I let out a sigh and go over to sit down next to her. "That's why you ran from the cops, but why take me along?"

"I did not want them to question you. Did you want to stay?"

"Hell, no! I would've been right behind you! You're pretty strong." She shrugs. "So now that you trust me, are you going to tell me who you are and stuff?"

"I am Toak."

"You're a dyke, right?"

"Dyke?"

Oh, geez! "Dyke. Lesbian. Bulldagger. Queer. Gay. Womon-identified. Homosexual. Sapphist. Tribade. Womon-loving womon—"

"Yes, womon-lover."

Finally! "You got a girlfriend? A womon you love?" She shrugs. I take that as a no. "You got a place to stay?"

"No."

I sit there looking at her. Part of me says leave it alone, and another part of me says sisters take care of sisters. She *is* cute and she did save me from being bashed...

"Look, I got an extra room. You can stay there until you get something together — if you want." She smiles at me and I feel something inside me melt.

"I want. Thank you."

I smile back and stand up. "We've got to go back to the dance so we can pick up my car."

"No, not back there. It is dangerous for me to go back."

"Okay, you wait here and I'll go and bring back the car for you."

"No. Dangerous there for you, too."

I pause. Maybe she's right. Those boys might be blabbing to the police and pointing out the dyke dance. Cullid peoples can't afford to mess around with no po-lice.

"We can walk?" Toak says.

I frown. "It's a long walk. I live on the other side of the river. Besides, I don't want to be seen walking around downtown. Cops." I scratch my head. "I guess we could call a cab."

"Cab?" she says, puzzled.

I grin at her. "Come on, I'll explain it on the way to the phone booth."

We get home all right and I find out that Toak is *really* big. She has to duck under the doorway to enter my old Victorian rental, and the doors are six feet six inches tall. This girl is *big!*

Inside, I run around (you know how it is when you bring somebody home unexpectedly) turning on lights and doing the hostess thang, though she doesn't want food or drink. She looks hot and sweaty as she sits down on my sofa, her long legs stretched out in front. Not that it is hot. I think it's kinda coolish. Sixty or so degrees, maybe. But I open the windows and the front and back doors, and get a good stiff wind whipping through. Well! I button up my jacket and sit down on the opposite side of the sofa from her.

"Is this more comfortable?" I ask her.

"A little better..." she says, which means no.

"Maybe you'd be a little cooler if you took off that denim jacket," I point out in my urban black-girl drawl, half sarcasm, half attitude. She hesitates for a few heartbeats, then unbuttons the last two or three buttons of her jean jacket with her nice-looking hands. Her *hands?* I squint a little in the forty-watt glow of my table lamp. Did this girl have an extra finger on each hand? Then she leans forward to pull the jacket off her arms and back and the moment is over. I take a good look at her.

First thing I notice are her arms. She's probably got what — two, three percent body fat? Nice muscular arms — not the bulging kind, or the stringy-knotty kind, but nicely defined wimmin's muscles. Yep, she must be an athlete of some sort. She's wearing a sleeveless, space-age-looking black top that seems to continue under her jeans like a bodysuit and looks as though it were painted on her. She has very nice boobs, not too big, not too small.

"Well!" I say, looking at her and smiling. "You got a steady squeeze?" She looks blank and I shake my head. "Just kidding." I look at the clock. Twelve forty-five a.m.

"Tell me about yourself," Toak says suddenly. "Do you have a 'steady squeeze'?" She catches me by surprise. I'm supposed to be the one questioning her!

"No, not right now," I say, suddenly shy for some damn dumb reason, and I feel my desire for this womon waft back to me. She looks good. She smells good. I want her.

"Your eyes are very beautiful. They speak to me," she says, her voice going throatier, and those eyes of hers seem to be more silver than gray. If she really knew what my eyes were saying, she'd be over here instead of way over there.

"I thank you for bringing me here and giving me shelter. Where I come from such a thing is a gift of life."

"So where are you from? Is it really hot there?"

She shakes her head, her silver hair swaying gently with the motion. "No. Where I am from it is very cold."

Cold? Maybe she's from Mongolia? That's kinda an Asian country, isn't it? And those steppes do get pretty cold. And her height could be from her European side...

"What's the name of your country?"

"You would not know it," she says, her voice soft.

"Try me," I say, and she looks at me real searchingly and then says some foreign word. I raise both eyebrows high. "Excuse me?" She says it again. Ka-lid? Ca-leel? I give up. "You can show me where it is on the map tomorrow," I tell her, letting it drop. She nods.

"You're probably tired and I've got a brunch to go to early tomorrow, so I'll show you where your room is and you can go to bed whenever you're ready."

It's not really a spare room; it's my study, where I write. The bed I'm offering is the twin-bed futon I use for long writing sessions. The room is tiny, about twelve square feet, a cubicle saved only by the high Victorian ceiling. Inside is the futon, two desks, books and bookshelves, posters and plants. Toak makes the room seem tinier still.

As I start laying out the futon and spreading the sheets and blankets, Toak stands next to my writing desk looking at a *National Geographic* poster of "The Known Universe: A Journey through Time and Space." It's a great poster and it helps me a lot when I write. She stares at it the entire time I make up the futon.

"Nice poster, huh?" I say to help conversation along. This girl doesn't talk much. She points to the Milky Way section of the poster where our galaxy looks like an egg sunny-side up.

"There," she says, smiling at me like she's made a big discovery.

"Yeah, home sweet home," I say, smiling back. Then she notices my air conditioner in the window.

"What is that?"

This girl's never seen an air conditioner before? I start picturing dusty little villages with no electricity or running water and people who look like her hovering around cowshit fires as savage winter blizzards roll off the barren steppes of Russia. Poor kid.

"That's a machine that makes the air cold," I explain.

"Cold? Will you turn it on?"

"Okay, but it'll get pretty cold in here. You'll need another blanket," I say and switch it on. A rush of air hums from the machine and Toak squats her long legs down and sticks her face right in the air current coming from the main blower. Her hair flies back from her face, her thick bangs drying as she closes her eyes. She plainly enjoys it. I watch for a while as she drinks up the cool air, then I turn to go.

"Well, I'll see you in the morning—"

"Do not go," she says suddenly, turning to look at me. She's still squatting on the floor, and for the first time since we met, I'm taller than she is. Her eyes look dark again in the dimmer light and they reach out to me. "I would like you to stay..."

"Stay?" I repeat, feeling nervous again. She takes my hand in hers and I can't help noticing how hot it is. As though she has a high fever.

"Yes, stay here with me."

I look down at her hands, the one holding mine and the one that's flat on the carpet, supporting her. She does have six fingers! An extra pinkie on each hand. No big deal — I have a cousin who has six toes on each foot. I sit down on the closest thing, the futon, and we're eye level again. Something grabs me and I lean forward to kiss her.

Her lips are soft and hot and she kisses me back with just enough pressure to tell me she wants me. Nothing sloppy, no tongue or anything like that — a nice kiss. I really appreciate a good kisser. Just when I'm thinking about getting up to fetch the dental dam and rubber gloves, she stops the kiss and stands up to close the study door.

"Do you trust me?" she asks me, real serious-like.

"Sure I trust you, or I wouldn't have brought you to my house," I tell her, looking up at her tall height as I sit perched on the end of the futon.

"You will not be afraid?"

"Afraid of what?"

"Me."

"Nooo, I don't think so," I say slowly, wondering what's coming.

"I am not like you. I am — different."

She unbuttons her 501 Levi's and I see she *is* wearing a bodysuit. She shimmies the jeans down her long, long legs and kicks them off with her boots. I take a good look at her outfit.

On her upper right torso, just above her breast, is some kinda foreign writing in gold, all curlicues and swirly looking. There's a thin gold pin-stripe running down the outsides of her legs. It looks kinda militaryish. The bodysuit covers her feet, too, like footsie pajamas. She has a nice body, a bit more slender in the hips than I like (I think lush, curvy hips are so sexy!) and she hasn't much of a waistline, but that's okay. After I finish looking at her body, I look up at her face.

"So far I'm not scared," I say, kinda joking, lightening the moment. She seems so serious! Then she reaches up to her neckline, and suddenly a seam appears, and as she runs her finger down to her waist the seam opens.

Her skin is blue.

I stare. I can feel my mouth drop open and I watch as she pulls the garment farther apart, showing blue breasts with lavender-tipped nipples and a blue stomach. She pulls the garment off her shoulders and arms and lets it hang down at her waist. *She's blue!*

I freeze. Everything becomes really quiet as the pieces start to fall into place. Her English. Her height. Her running speed. Her running from the cops. Her six fingers. Her eyes that, now as I stare into them, look definitely rectangular shaped. Like coin slots. And her sky blue skin.

"You're not from around here, are you?" I say, kinda joking but also kinda scared.

"No. I am from another world. Are you frightened?"

"Well, you're not here to capture me or do any strange experiments on me, are you?"

"No! I would never hurt you! Please believe me."

My heart stops pounding so hard. She seems really sincere. After all, she didn't *have* to tell me anything.

"Yeah, call me crazy, but I believe you. I've always thought we earthers aren't the only life in the universe. Why are you here?"

"You sent out a thing, I do not know the word in your language, but it showed us who you were and where to find you. There were words and music. It was called Vo-gau-ger—"

"Voyager," I correct her, feeling kinda numb. "Yeah, we did invite you to drop by. So you're not here to conquer the earth and make us all your slaves?" She looks puzzled and I realize she probably didn't understand half of what I said. "Where you come from, wimmin love wimmin?"

"On my world there are only wimmin. Not the ones you call men."

Great Goddess! Extraterrestrial lesbians! Hot damn; my dream come true! I relax completely now and smile at her as I pat the futon next to me. "Come sit down," I say. And she does. I touch her arm, and it's as hot as a cat's asshole, but satiny soft with the hardness of muscle underneath.

"On your world, you wimmin have babies together?" I ask.

"Of course," she says, looking amused at my ignorance.

Paradise! I wonder if I can arrange a visit. I touch her face. Her skin is soft and hot and she smells great with that orange blossom scent. She smiles at me, her gray eyes kind.

"How did you get your face that color?" I ask her.

"It is something that rubs on, so I could be with your people. We saw that there is no one on your world with skin my color."

Extraterrestrial lesbians of color! Aw right! "No one on my world knows you're here?"

"No," she says, and I'm fast falling in lust with her.

I kiss her again, my hand reaching for her perfect left breast. I feel the nipple harden under my stroking fingers. I keep on kissing her and she keeps kissing me back. The next thing I know we're both naked. I'm shivering a little in the chill of the air-conditioned room, but her body is so nice! We lie together breasts to breasts, my dreadlocks falling against her cheek and her silky hair against mine.

We roll around on the narrow futon, our legs and tongues tangling, our hands touching and feeling each other. I reach between her legs. She has a soft fuzz of downy hair covering her vulva, and I slip one finger inside her very human outer labia. She has thin inner labia that cover her vagina opening kinda like shutters, and when I tickle them with my finger, they seem to draw back. Her vaginal opening feels different in some way, more open, and I wonder if she's had a bunch of kids. I stick my finger inside her and she's hot and slippery with juices, her vaginal walls smooth instead of corrugated. She seems to like my finger. Her vagina closes on it and her whole body trembles. I lay her flat on her back and sit next to her. She opens her eyes and looks at me. In the incandescent light of my desk lamp, her eyes are definitely silver, and they look incredibly sexy.

"I like your hair," she whispers, fingering my dreads with her six-fingered hand, her other hand hot on my thigh.

"I like you," I tell her in a husky voice. "Can I give you pleasure?" *Goddess, do aliens climax?* I wonder. She smiles a sweet smile and nods.

I sit between her open legs. She bends them flat against the bed as though she's double-jointed, and I look at her sex. The fleshy outer lips are stretched back to reveal the inner labia, now flushed lavender with blood, quivering around the distinctly star-shaped opening of her vagina.

I bend forward to blow gently on her genital star and she gasps, shivering her hips against the bed in response. I think she's ready. I curl up between her thighs, stick out my tongue, and paint a wet diagonal swath across the purple-centered star.

Her hips snap off the bed in electric response and she makes soft mewling sounds, her voice echoing pleasure. I curl my arms around her thighs and pull her back to my waiting lips, savoring her juices. As I seal my lips to her star, it opens large enough for my tongue to enter. Her peach-tasting juices trickle down around my lips as my tongue slithers around and around and in and out. For long minutes I work on her with my eyes closed, lost in her body.

I glance up at her and see her consumed by arousal: her head flails from side to side, her long hair arcs around her face like flashes of light, her lithe body quakes with passion.

Goddess, she tastes so good! I gulp and slurp at her as though I were dying of thirst and she were the eternal spring of life. Time passes, lost to me. I am entranced. Enthralled. In ecstasy. Then something unexpected happens. Her inner vaginal lips, the ones I had felt quivering against my cheeks, suddenly reach out and pat me, plastering peach-scented juices on my face. Wha--? I think, and then there's no time for thinking as she comes.

Her hips arch high off the bed, carrying me along, and she goes stiff and still, her cries hissing from between her clenched teeth in a sizzle of release. Liquid fills my mouth, sweet and mellow, and I gulp it down. It slides down my gullet like honey, like ambrosia. Her labia shivers against my face and I am lost, lost in a whirl of desire unlike any I've ever known before. Then her hips collapse back onto the bed, her sweet pussy breaking away from my mouth and bringing me back to the ordinary world. I look down at her.

She lies with her head on the pillow, her eyes closed and her high cheekbones flushed. Her silver bangs cling wetly to her forehead and her hard lavender nipples point straight up at the ceiling, rising and falling with her rapid breath. She's lying in a puddle of ripe peach wetness, but she doesn't seem to mind.

By now my own pussy is drenched and throbbing and swollen; my clit engorged with blood and lust. I crawl up over her and lie against her warm, soft and hard body, causing her to open her eyes and look at me. "Was that all right?" I ask. Silver light sparkles in her eyes. She smiles.

She wraps her arms around my hips, lifts her head, and kisses me — a deep endless tongue kiss that makes me shiver with desire. I grab her shoulders to hold onto her and kiss her back for all I'm worth. Her hands slide slowly over my butt, then settle their hot caressing warmth between my thighs. Very gently, she opens my legs wider, shifting me higher up on her body until we are hip to hip and pussy to pussy. I feel her hot fingers gliding over my hairy vulva, parting the swollen outer lips. She skates her fingers around in my thick, slippery pre-cum juices, tickling my pussy hole and driving me crazy with wanting her. Then she holds open my inner labia with the thumb and index finger of each hand, and I feel something slick itself over my freshly bared sex, making my hips jerk and me moan. I don't know what it is, but it sure isn't her fingers. This is softer. Slippery. Almost like a little tongue. No, two little tongues. I pull away from her kiss.

"What—? What are you doing?"

"Pleasuring you as we do on my world. With these—" she says, gently fluttering my inner labia. "But mine can move on their own. I can make them do what I want. Do you want me to do this?"

"Hell, yes!" I say, and kiss her again, my tongue exploring her sweet mouth as I let myself drop into a deep well of passion.

"You must try not to move," she whispers between kisses. I feel her inner labia sliding around and across my clit in an erotic dance of arousal.

The feel of her dewy labia skimming over my wide-open pussy and teasingly probing the spasming opening of my dripping vagina makes me feel as though the top of my head is going to explode in sensation. I break the kiss to breathe and cry and moan, trying not to move while she nibbles my neck and shoulders and mumbles words in a language I don't understand.

Her labia dance lasts for years ... centuries ... bringing me to the edge of orgasm. I teeter there, hot with passion, waiting. Then I feel her enter me. Not one by one but together, in a thick spiral of hot wet flesh, slowly easing through the tight ring of muscle that guards my pussy opening. Slowly. Centimeter by centimeter. I moan and whimper with each steady, tiny advance, my pussy relaxing and opening wider and wider to accommodate her creeping progress. It takes forever. I want it to take forever.

Then she stops. I gasp as I feel her hotness deep inside me. My pussy walls open and close around her buried labia; my closed eyes roll up into my head. As my body spasms in convulsions of almost unbearable delight, my pussy responds by bearing down and squeezing her labia, and she gives out a sharp moan of unmistakable pleasure.

Her labia are soft and flexible inside me, like two big tongues, and they spend the next ten minutes sliding over my vaginal walls and cervix in hot wet swipes that leave me sobbing with pleasure. One labia slips out and I feel it curl itself around my bulging clit while the other one curls around my womb tip, covering it like a cap. Then they both start to vibrate.

I want to move now. Have to move now. But she clamps her hands tight on my butt and holds my hips against hers as my climax speeds forward. I bury my face in her damp, soft neck, moaning and babbling with pleasure, my legs flailing as release nips at the heels of desire.

"Diana..." I hear her whisper, and I slowly raise my head to look into her face.

Her gray eyes are shot silver. They burn as light in her face and hold me mesmerized. Suddenly, my consciousness shifts to another place. A place I've visited only under the auspices of acid.

It is a place of total contact. A contact so profound and authentic I feel as though we've exchanged places. I am in her body looking out of her eyes and she is in my body doing the same. I can feel what she feels: now it is *my* genital labia vibrating *her* clit and womb and I can feel the pressure of *her* sex pressing back in rhythmic, agonizing waves of pleasure.

Then it's gone and I'm back looking into her luminous eyes. But a whisper remains as I stare into her moon-bright gaze. I can feel our energy or love or sex or whatever it is passing back and forth between us with every movement, every quiver. It crackles like electricity, uniting us, and a dynamo-like hum fills my ears. I find I can't honestly tell where I end and she begins. We are one body. One voice. One orgasm.

She cries out and her hips leap upward as she comes, taking me up with her. Then release explodes inside me and I rear back in electric climax, arching my back into something like a C curve. She holds me locked into place from the waist downward as pleasure ripples over us in ever-widening circles. I scream with coming: it is the best, the greatest, the most encompassing orgasm I've ever felt. She screams too, her ecstatic cries joining mine, and our voices soar together in an unrehearsed song of passion whose last note hangs quivering in the sudden, panting silence.

I wake up dripping with sweat, my t-shirt and panties soaked, and the familiar feeling of having just climaxed. I blink and look around me. My computer is on; yellow words dot the monitor. My current novel.

I look at the clock. It's four a.m. At around two, I had lain down on my folded-out futon to rest my aching back and butt after several hours of steady writing. Now, dreamily, I run my fingers through my damp pussy hairs, eyes half-closed as I smile to myself.

Wait until I tell my steady squeeze, Aiko, I dreamed she was an alien amazon dyke from outer space and that we did the wild-girl thang together! Talk about wet dreams...!

# After the Bath

## by Jenifer Levin

With her dress, tight fit and dark leather straps, and heels high enough for drama but not too high to dance on, she looked nice standing on the sidelines in shadows and moving bodies, her mostly finished drink, wine I guess, held perfectly between fingers. We caught eyes and nodded.

"You don't dance, do you?" She got a cigarette and looked for matches, but I plucked some out of my own pocket sooner. Years ago some woman had stumbled up in a bar somewhere, eyelids heavy with booze, and asked for a light. Oh, I said, I don't smoke. She laughed. But honey, she replied, someone like you should *always* carry matches.

It had been sweet of her, really, to say that.

I'd carried them ever since, in various parts of the world. Hopefully.

Now, I lit one. Cassie touched my hand to steady it.

"Thanks."

I wanted to ask how she knew that — that I didn't dance — we recognized each other only vaguely, through parties, large dinners, friends of friends. The match did its job and I tossed it, then she was talking.

"Dell says some French girl broke your heart."

I didn't respond.

She shrugged. The dark smoke-filled place was kind to her. There were blurred old acne scars on each cheek, must be deep, she'd used a lot of makeup. But she was pretty anyway, nice lips, bright eyes. Now the lashes fluttered, sparking mischief.

"What's the story with Dell?"

"She thinks you're cute."

"Yucch! Damn me with faint whatchamacallit, why don't you? Anyway, she's got someone — right? Right. Of course."

"Would you like to dance?"

She thought about it. Then said yes, yes actually, that would be very nice. So we did. Two minutes into music you could bounce around to old sixties style, manic, not touching, things segued into something slow. That's when fear stabbed, and I got even clumsier. But she was smooth, Cassie was, and managed somehow to balance quietly without even the appearance of precariousness, patient, seeming to enjoy herself while I fought hesitation, adjusted my stance and all, and finally pressured the small of her back to lead. It was nice, a long, long song. After some of it I realized she'd laid her head against my shoulder. Her hands had found their way under the flaps of jacket, pressed lightly on silk shirt and each rib cage and, underneath things, I was sweating.

"What do butches want?"

"Is that what I am?"

She pulled her head back a moment, eyes rolled mockingly.

"Oh God, honey, come *on.*" But she laughed.

"Well, what do you think?"

"I don't know — I'm curious. I mean, I like to *watch* you, all of you, everywhere, even when you're just standing still. I'd like to see what's going on in your head — I *know* it's different from what's going on in mine."

Oh, I told her, don't be so sure.

Well, but then again, maybe.

What do we want? I thought.

You.

But said nothing.

Just before the song ended I caressed that part of her, right on top of the place where buttocks meet thighs, very lightly, barely touching at all, and could tell that she felt it. We stood around talking then. I bought her more wine, lit her more cigarettes.

Dell came by, looking irritated in new silks and leather and linen, and a pair of fur shoes colored black and white. She said hi to Cassie, pulled me aside. "Can you lend me twenty? I met someone, I want to buy her a drink. I think she might go to bed with me tonight."

"Congratulations."

"This place is really getting on my nerves. Maybe I ought to leave. Maybe I ought to take a Xanax. You think I should? Or a Valium? But then I might fall asleep. On her, I mean. I might not be able to come. Or to make *her* come. Then the whole thing would be a disaster."

"Well, Cassie likes you."

"Oh, she's cute, but she's not my type. Anyway, she lives right in my neighborhood. It might spoil things with Karen. Then Karen would get pissed and move out, and I'd be a nervous wreck again like I was after Tess left. Come to think of it, maybe I'll just go back *alone*. I feel like I'm getting too old to keep engaging in this search for ecstasy. It's always so futile and so incredibly disappointing."

I gave her two tens and told her it looked like a skunk had died on her feet. She urged me to go to hell, as quickly as possible. That was okay. We were old friends and loved each other. Dell was the epitome of a bottom: she'd fight to be the one on her back. It was all fine and dandy with me — there was nothing like sex between us, anyway; but I couldn't figure out what she and Cassie would ever possibly do with each other in bed, assuming they made it that far, except lie side by side, full of wishes and unfulfilled desire. When she wandered off another slow song started — obviously the deejay was thinking about winding things down. I didn't ask this time but gestured, in a courtly way that made Cassie giggle: bending slightly at the waist, sweeping one arm grandly toward the dance floor. Around us, couples clutched in the beginnings of loss or passion, energy ebbing, fatigue settling softly like extra weight in the shadows and smoke. She cupped a hand to my ear.

"Want to fuck?"

"Yeah, Cassie. But I like to say when, okay?"

As I said it, I realized it was true. And, as I realized that, I gained all kinds of power. Moving her in slow effortless circles and steps, dancing felt easy for the first time ever. I sensed her melting in against me, and held both of us up, moving, while my insides began to ache and burn.

At her place, later, after the first time, she showed me all about bubble baths. I'd rarely bothered with stuff like that before — I was strictly a shower jock, stepping out of and into towels and steady hot modulated streams; and, I told her, the gypsies had a saying about baths, which they deemed an untrustworthy and inferior way to get clean: *Why should I soak like an old tea bag?* But Cassie's tub was different. Deep, aged, worn but clean, sunk like unmovable stone in the tiniest room of her tiny apartment, something about it felt seductive. Sinking into bubbles there was like sinking into a cloud, a pillow, a woman. She sat primly on the polished wood toilet seat, frayed satiny robe clutched protectively over both breasts, as if we hadn't just spent the past several hours making love — first shyly, then unrestrained raw fucking, then sweating close up against each other, and then again shy.

She was great, though, and made a big fuss about everything: the mixture of bubbles and lotions had to be just right, the washcloth her best, expensive skin creams were arrayed on shelves, waiting. I was touched by all this delicate consideration. It wasn't love — at least, not yet — but pleasing her had been exciting, and, now, I couldn't keep my hands off. When I stepped out dripping fragrant foams, she toweled different parts of me gently.

"I like your body."

"Yeah?"

"I like how strong you are."

I wanted to tell her that physical strength wasn't the same as a big grown strength inside. But it occurred to me that maybe it *was* — a corresponding strength, anyway, at least to the extent that it tangibly represented the fruits of work and a kind of courage — and, considering this silently, I reconsidered myself. That I even liked what I saw; not just tolerated it, but got some pleasure out of it as well — this image of her and me together in an age-speckled mirror — was wonderful. Something in me started to want, then, in a different, deeper way. I wondered if I'd let her make love to me some time. Not just as a tender femme service, the after-dinner drink on our sexual menu, but in a way that was scary, penetrative, requiring real trust and release. That — that was what *she* wanted, from the start: to be gotten deep inside of, to give up all control. I was glad of it; at the same time, could barely imagine submitting or surrendering myself that way and calling it pleasure.

We *were* very different.

I dried my hands to light another cigarette and gave it over to her. She blew smoke in the direction of the mirror. In that moment she seemed very far away, exotic, her otherness electrifying. We started to kiss and touch again. Then she was lying on her open robe, on the bed, with me full on top of her. Bubble bath soaked into sheets. She had all the right playthings, Cassie did, and plenty of latex and lube — tricks of the trade, she said, smiling in a half hard, half sad way, old massage parlor girls never show up unprepared — but then again, so did I. If I shut my eyes against her hair, touched yielding flesh, it seemed as if the bed spun round and round.

I started to fall hard then, and wanted to move all the way inside her where the world's sharp edges were muted and soft. Wanted to push in rhythm with a deep, dark strapped-on weight that would strain her and please her, invade on invitation, a burden we both could feel, then let go of, until it brought us to some unforsaken place of home and finality and love.

What happened: we became lovers, Cassie and I. A home, lace curtains, white picket fence, apple pie in the oven on Sundays — we had all that eventually, yes, but we had it in city rooms and clubs and streets, within ourselves and each other; and, inside, there was lots more too. Dyke stuff, tough and sweet. Things that cannot be described.

No one would let us adopt kids, so we took in homeless cats and dogs and, when everyone around us started dying, we cared for them in their illness, took in *their* cats and dogs after death, wept at many funerals. Another vomit-soaked sponge. Another kiss good-bye. Ceremonial washing of the hands. Bouquets of roses, incense, memorial speeches, listening over and over again to the favorite poems of dead young men. Afterwards, I'd walk her home in the dark. Protective. As if her electric femme-ness was a fragile thing, instead of the sure gut-deep strength it was, too good for the hard straight world around us. As if I were more than a woman myself, a fiercely muscular giant, stronger than most men.

There is a darkness inside us, and also a light. These qualities are neither bad nor good; they merely exist deep down with all the other barely tangible reflexes of life. So that sometimes we hurt, and sometimes nurture. And sometimes, both are wicked; and, sometimes, both are love. What Cassie taught me, after the bath, was that pain is not the same as suffering. We can have our sorrows and use them well, not just gyrate desperately to get rid of them. We can reach in and give and take. Reach in, or out, and be taken.

Reaching in is what I did with Cassie, my woman, on many many nights. As time went by I let her reach deep inside of me, too — oh, not often, mind you, maybe once or twice a year, like I was giving her a gift she knew to treat carefully — and she'd touch something suffering then, a darkness, a womb-tip or star. Later we'd lie glued with sweating skin. Different bodies. Different fears. And, in this age of plague, we got over each drop of our shame. We learned to use our pain. We forbade nothing and accepted all. Until straight people everywhere began to imitate us. Then they grew to full human stature, and together we saved the world.

# About the contributors

**Deborah Abbott** likes to get wet as often as possible; thus, she is apt to be found on or in wet places such as rivers, lakes, oceans, swimming pools, bathtubs, and lesbians. She is a rafter, kayaker, swimmer, counselor, mother, lover, and writer. Her poems, stories, and essays have been widely anthologized, most recently in *Sportsdykes* (St. Martin's Press), *Another Wilderness: New Outdoor Writing by Women* (Seal), and *Lovers* (The Crossing Press). She is coeditor of *From Wedded Wife to Lesbian Life: Stories of Formerly Married Lesbians* (The Crossing Press).

**Carmela F. Alfonso** is a native New Yorker currently living single in our nation's capital. She is active in the gay community's live music and theater scenes. Although she has been writing all her life and has published reviews, "Briefly" is her first fiction publication. She has recently completed a novel set on Broadway in New York City and is actively seeking a publisher. The author of "Briefly" is particularly fond of black leather and young blonds with a propensity for black hose and high heels.

**Katya Andreevna** is the pseudonym of a New York-based writer and editor. When she's not writing, she spends much of her time shopping. She has yet to find the perfect pair of pumps.

**Lucy Jane Bledsoe** is the author of *Sweat: Stories and a Novella* (Seal Press, 1995). She is the editor of *Goddesses We Ain't* (Freedom Voices Press), an anthology of writings by women in San Francisco's tenderloin district, and coeditor of *Let the Spirit Flow: Writings on Communication and Freedom* (Berkeley Reads), an anthology of work by newly literate adults.

**Paula K. Bodenstein** is a former psychotherapist who has lived on both coasts and traveled a lot between them. She's now settled in the foothills of the White Mountains with her lover of ten years and their understanding dog. She was startled, even shocked, by her first erotic writings, which evolved from a writing exercise. She finds writing erotica a process of continual self-discovery as well as a delightful occupation.

**Wendy Caster** wrote *The Lesbian Sex Book*. Her short stories have appeared in *Bushfire, Lesbian Bedtime Stories 2, Cats (and Their Dykes)*, and *Silver-Tongued Sapphistry*. She has had over three hundred opinion columns published in lesbian and gay newspapers, and she and Jayne Relaford Brown are currently coediting *A Lesbian Feast*, an anthology celebrating lesbians and food. "Renaissance" is dedicated to Sarah and Heather — and, of course, to Liz.

**Delane Daugherty** has been writing lesbian fiction and erotica for six years and has recently completed her first novel. At present, she teaches and lives in the great Northwest, loved and supported by her daughter and cat.

**Nisa Donnelly** is best known as the author of *The Bar Stories: A Novel After All*, which won the Lambda Award for Lesbian Fiction, and *The Love Songs of Phoenix Bay*. Her short fiction has appeared in *Women on Women 2*, *Erotic Interludes*, *Brother and Sister: Lesbians and Gay Men Write About Their Lives Together*, and in various magazines.

**Linnea Due** is a writer and editor at the *Express*, an alternative newspaper in Berkeley, California. She is the author of three novels, *High and Outside*, *Give Me Time*, and *Life Savings*; *Joining the Tribe: Growing Up Gay and Lesbian in the '90s*; and co-editor of *Dagger: On Butch Women*. Her feature articles have covered the gamut, from sex clubs in San Francisco to feral cats in Berkeley, from Queer Nation to the Jewish Film Festival.

**Jane Futcher** lives in Novato, California with her lover, Erin Carney, a home-birth midwife. She is the author of the novels *Crush* and *Promise Not to Tell*. Her erotic writing has appeared in the anthologies *Bushfire*, *Afterglow*, *Lesbian Adventure Stories*, and *The Poetry of Sex*. She teaches English as a Second Language and has recently become an editorial writer for the *Marin Independent Journal*.

**Carolyn L. King** lives in San Francisco with her girlfriend, Carol, and her dog, Madeleine, and is one-third of the African-American lesbian comedy group, 4 Big Girls. She works for the AIDS Legal Referral Panel. She makes jewelry and writes erotica about Black lesbians to keep her sanity. She would like to thank her sweet Creole honey-colored lover, Carol, for her support, inspiration, and hours of perspiration. "Shoe Stop" is her first published story.

**Etelka Lehoczky** writes on feminist and queer issues for numerous small publications around the country. She lives in Chicago and is considering getting a cat.

**Jenifer Levin** is the author of four novels: *Water Dancer*, *Snow*, *Shimoni's Lover*, and *The Sea of Light*. Her short stories have been widely anthologized. Her nonfiction work has appeared in the *New York Times*, the *Washington Post*, *Rolling Stone*, *Ms.*, *Mademoiselle*, the *Advocate*, and many other publications. She has worked, studied, and traveled in Europe, the Middle East, South America, and Southeast Asia, and currently lives in New York City.

**Anita Loomis** began writing erotic tales at age twelve, but "Bridging the Gap" is the first to be published. Loomis is a performance artist and writer whose work has been funded by the National Fund for Lesbian and Gay Artists. She is a member of the Chicago performance collective MatchGirlStrike, with whom she makes art out of "obscenity," women's magazines, and airborne sex toys. She hopes some day to be sensei. She dedicates this story to Barbara DeGenevieve for "changing my mind."

**Ronna Magy** is a writer of short fiction living in Los Angeles, California. She wrote "The Arroyo" dreaming of earth and water, women and Mexico.

**michon** is an African-American woman discovering "the real world" as a recent college graduate. She is simultaneously gasping for air in the quest for a resurrection from the daily routine of life: finding fantasy in words. "Hot Wheels" is her first story.

Joan Nestle is a 55-year-old woman who likes to write about lesbian sex. Her most recent work is *Sister and Brother: Lesbians and Gay Men Write About Their Lives Together*, which she coedited with fellow pornographer John Preston. She is working on a new collection of writings called *A Fragile Union*.

Lesléa Newman is the author of fifteen books and the editor of four anthologies. Her titles include *The Femme Mystique*, *Heather Has Two Mommies*, *Sweet Dark Places*, and *Writing From the Heart*. Her story "Me and My Appetite" is taken from her newest short story collection, *Every Woman's Dream*, which contains several other erotic short stories.

Teresa Palomar lives in Baltimore with her life partner, Janet Goldstein, several computers, and a television in front of which she spends entirely too much time. When not relaxing at home, she spends her days teaching middle school math and social studies, thus successfully wasting a perfectly good English degree. She aspires to continue in the blissful comfort of her current life as long as she can, though she suspects an eventual return to the rigors of academia.

Juana Maria Paz is a New-York-born Puerto Rican lesbian and former welfare mother, presently living on a commune while her daughter attends college nearby. Her story is not fiction, but wishful thinking. It was written to a womyn named Onita from the lesbian-of-color land called La Luz de la Lucha. She never saw her again and would welcome contact. Juana c/o Twin Oaks, Rt. 4 Box 169, Louisa, VA 23093.

Susan Fox Rogers is the editor of *Another Wilderness: New Outdoor Writing by Women* (Seal Press, 1994) and *Sportsdykes: Stories From On and Off the Field* (St. Martin's Press, 1994).

Maria Santiago is the pen name of Miriam Laskin, who lives in New York City, where she is an adjunct assistant professor of English, a freelance journalist, fiction writer, rock sax player, and kinky-girl dyke. She has published nasty (but somehow romantic!) sex stories in *Venus Infers* and *Bad Attitude* magazines; she will also be represented in the forthcoming Alyson anthology, *The Second Coming*, edited by Pat Califia and Robin Sweeney.

Kiriyo Spooner is a 41-year-old womon, originally from the Midwest, who recently ended the long-distance aspect of her relationship by moving from Connecticut to Oakland, California. That distance was, in part, the inspiration for her erotic writing. She's worked in bookselling and publishing for the last twenty years, although this is her first publication as a writer. She's currently working on a travel guide to women's history sites in the U.S.

Judith P. Stelboum is a writer of fiction, poetry and essays. She has published in *Common Lives/Lesbian Lives*, *Sinister Wisdom*, and in the anthologies *Sister and Brother*, *Resist: Essays Against a Homophobic Culture*, *Dyke Life*, and *Not the Only One*. She is a reviewer for the *Lesbian Review of Books*.

Tristan Taormino is a New-York-based writer whose work has appeared in *Venus Infers*, *Blue Blood*, *Girljock*, and *The Femme Mystique*, edited by Lesléa Newman. She is working on a collection of her erotic fiction and is coeditor of the forthcoming anthology *Ritual Sex* (a collection of essays on sex and spirituality). She is also editrix of *Pucker Up*, "the zine with a mouth that's not afraid to use it."

**Lindsay Taylor** is a native of New England. She admires women and words for their strength.

**Diana Thompson** lives in the Great Pacific Northwest, where she enjoys the rain, the company of her cat, and a damn good cup of coffee. She is currently completing her erotic science fiction-adventure novel, *The Undoing*, and has had a short story published in *Gathering Ground: Northwest Women of Color Anthology* (Seal Press).

**Kitty Tsui**, the author of *The Word of a Woman Who Breathes Fire*, is at work on a historical novel, *Bai She, White Snake*. She hopes that "Special Delivery" passes your "wet test."

**Karen X. Tulchinsky** is a Jewish lesbian writer who lives in Vancouver, Canada. Her stories have appeared in numerous anthologies including *Afterglow, Sister and Brother,* and *The Femme Mystique*. She also writes for *Deneuve* magazine and is coeditor of *Tangled Sheets*, an anthology of lesbian erotica.

*Alyson Publications publishes a wide variety of books
with gay and lesbian themes. For a free catalog or
to be placed on our mailing list, please write to:*
Alyson Publications
P.O. Box 4371
Los Angeles, CA 90078
*Indicate whether you are interested in
books for gay men, lesbians, or both.*